Chinese Ghost Stories

This edition is first published in 2024 by Flame Tree 451

FLAME TREE 451
6 Melbray Mews,
Fulham, London SW3 3NS
United Kingdom
www.flametree451.com

Flame Tree 451 is an imprint of Flame Tree Publishing Ltd
www.flametreepublishing.com

A CIP record for this book is available from the British Library

Print ISBN 978-1-80417-798-3
ebook ISBN: 978-1-80417-930-7

24 26 28 27 25
1 3 5 7 8 6 4 2

Cover image was created by Flame Tree Studio, based on elements courtesy Shutterstock.com/Joel Askey/ The7Dew/Celiafoto/showcake.

Printed and bound in Great Britain by Clays Ltd, Elcograf S.p.A.

Chinese Ghost Stories

With an introduction by
Xueting C. Ni

451
FLAME TREE

Contents

A Taste for the Fantastic

From mystery to crime, supernatural to horror, fantasy to utopian, dystopian and the foundations of modern speculative fiction, the terrific range of paperbacks and ebooks from Flame Tree 451 offers a healthy diet of werewolves and mechanical men, bloodlusty vampires, dastardly villains, mad scientists, secret worlds, lost civilizations and escapist fantasies. Discover a storehouse of tales gathered specifically for the reader of the fantastic.

Great works by H.G. Wells and Bram Stoker stand shoulder to shoulder with gripping reads by titans of the gothic novel (Algernon Blackwood, Charles Brockden Brown, Arthur Machen), and individual novels by literary giants (Jane Austen, Gustave Flaubert, Charles Dickens, Emily Brontë) mingle with the intensity of H.P. Lovecraft and the pure psychological magic of Edgar Allan Poe.

Of course there are classic Conan Doyle adventures, Wilkie Collins mysteries and the outlandish fantasies of Robert E. Howard, Edgar Rice Burroughs and Mary Shelley, but there are so many other tales to tell: *The White Worm, Black Magic, The Murder Monster, The Awakening, Darkwater* and more.

Check our website for regular updates and new additions to our incredible, curated range of speculative fiction at flametreepublishing.com

Introduction

From as far back as the shamanist beginnings of its civilization, the supernatural has been an ever-present part of life in China. Whilst the Confucian school of thought, which rose to prominence during the Warring States, decreed the supernatural as 'zi buyu' (something not to be talked about by scholars and gentlemen), it never fully dispelled China's fascination with ghosts and spirits.

As China developed, territories and states uniting and dividing, there was a great deal of collapse, and change in the political and social landscapes. It was during one of these times when China split into multiple kingdoms, of Han and non-Han cultures, that vibrant popular beliefs flourished, enhanced by the competition between Buddhism, introduced from India; and Daoism, China's indigenous beliefs. All these different elements found a messy compromise of cohabitation in the minds of the Chinese, each coming with their own ideas, not only of virtue and modes of behaviour, but of ghosts, demons and the monstrous. A tradition of supernatural literature emerged around the Wei, Jin and Northern and Southern Dynasties. Whilst later Neo-Confucian secularism dismissed these stories, there were foresighted arguments that these tales should be preserved for posterity. This, combined with the demand for leisurely entertainment from well-to-do urbanites, led to the infusing of popular literature in the centuries to come, with elements of the fantastic.

The most unique and influential kind of supernatural tales from China are the *zhiguai* (志怪), or 'Tales of the Strange', account-style narratives that combine legends, hearsay and fiction. One of the pinnacles of this form was the seventeenth-century collection *Strange Tales from the Lodge of Leisure* (*Liaozhai Zhiyi*), a selection from which makes up a significant part of this volume. Its author, the scholar Pu Songling, famously set up a tea stall by his cottage, where he would spend the day conversing with travellers from across the land, exchanging refreshments for stories, before spending his nights recording these fantastic tales. This timeless compilation of nearly 500 stories offers an unparalleled insight into Chinese attitudes to, and beliefs in, ghosts and spirits.

In many traditions around the world, ghosts are beings that induce fear, and whilst Chinese culture has been no stranger to ghosts, not all of them are dangerous or malevolent. Some of the earliest venerative rites, found during the Shang era, were group worship of familial ghosts (often referred to now as ancestors). In the aligned Chinese belief systems, ghosts and spirits constantly surround us, just going about their business, on a different plane, sharing our world. A lot of them are friendly and mean us no harm, such as those featured in 'Spirit of the River' and 'Miss Lien-Hsiang'. In the more spirit-attuned times of the seventeenth century, these amicable ghosts appear to mortals openly, without the fearful theatrics that usually accompany them. The Chinese word for ghost, *gui* (鬼), does carry many negative connotations, though not always related to the undead, as in *guizi* (a wartime term for invaders), *neigui* (a spy) and *jiugui*, (a drunkard). In other words, it can just refer to something separate and distanced, such as *guilao*, which means foreigner.

Throughout Chinese storytelling, there is the idea however, of people returning as ghosts, or being turned into metaphorical ghosts, either following unjust deaths, or after being cast out from society. Zhongkui, China's well-loved demon slayer, was a thwarted scholar in life who returned as a ghost-devouring ghost himself. Tales such as 'River of Sorrows' and 'The Marble Arch' explore this aspect of Chinese ghosts. Often ghosts are manifestations of guilt and wrongdoings hidden from the living. The *yuangui*, wronged ghosts, or *ligui*, vengeful ghosts, are the ones that lurk in dark corners and leap out at unsuspecting mortals. These are the types that most commonly appear in modern ghost stories, in which they haunt characters to distraction. The intense sense of fright that accompanies this form of visitation may be puzzling to someone outside of the culture. The Chinese have great reverence for the spirits of the dead, want them to be happy in their realm, but do not want them back. There is something terrifying about a being that has broken the taboo, traversed the forbidden boundaries and made themselves visible to the living. It is a sign that something is deeply wrong. The Chinese psyche still has a vivid sense of *baoying*, or a sense of comeuppance, stemming from the Buddhist ideas of Karma. Often these ghosts are stuck in the spaces where their mortal remains are interred, hence the hauntings. These tales, in which wrongs are righted, reflect the common wish to see justice served, one way or another. Other times, we see fully vicious ghosts, in tales designed to make skin creep and the blood run cold.

Through its complicated historical encounters with the West, to many here, China has seemed a mysterious yet fascinating land, especially during the Victorian period, when studies of ancient civilizations and the paranormal developed hand in hand with imperialist ventures and evangelical missions. This led to a great deal of the traditional stories of the supernatural being collected by scholars and missionaries, whose writings are still well known to Anglophone readers today, such as the ones that open this collection. It also includes two of the most famous tales from *Liaozhai*, 'The Magic Sword', immortalized by the 1987 Hong Kong film released under the name *A Chinese Ghost Story*, and 'The Painted Skin', which has been adapted countless times in China on stage and screen, and famously in the influential 2008 film, staring Donnie Yen and Zhou Xun.

The *zhiguai* hold an inimitable place in the supernatural narrative traditions of China, moulding the ways in which people perceive and represent the paranormal, permeating and integrating themselves with modern ghost stories, where strange mountains, wandering women and urban legends still hark back to those ancient stories. With a modern resurgence of horror writing in China coming through translation to an Anglophone audience, these classic tales are a very valid way to familiarize yourself with the relationship that the Chinese culturally hold with the spirits of the dead and the world around them, help you gain a good grounding to understand modern ghostly narratives. I hope you will pass some very enjoyable hours with this collection, perhaps remembering Pu SongLing, by reading over a few cups of tea.

Xueting C. Ni

FANTASTIC TALES

Chinese Ghost Stories

The Soul of the Great Bell

Lafcadio Hearn

The water-clock marks the hour in the Ta-chung sz', – in the Tower of the Great Bell: now the mallet is lifted to smite the lips of the metal monster, – the vast lips inscribed with Buddhist texts from the sacred *Fa-hwa-King*, from the chapters of the holy *Ling-yen-King*! Hear the great bell responding! – how mighty her voice, though tongueless! – KO-NGAI! All the little dragons on the high-tilted eaves of the green roofs shiver to the tips of their gilded tails under that deep wave of sound; all the porcelain gargoyles tremble on their carven perches; all the hundred little bells of the pagodas quiver with desire to speak. KO-NGAI! – all the green-and-gold tiles of the temple are vibrating; the wooden goldfish above them are writhing against the sky; the uplifted finger of Fo shakes high over the heads of the worshippers through the blue fog of incense! KO-NGAI! – What a thunder tone was that! All the lacquered goblins on the palace cornices wriggle their fire-colored tongues! And after each huge shock, how wondrous the multiple echo and the great golden moan and, at last, the sudden sibilant sobbing in the ears when the immense tone faints away in broken whispers of silver, – as though a woman should whisper, "Hiai!" Even so the great bell hath sounded every day for well-nigh five hundred years,

– Ko-Ngai: first with stupendous clang, then with immeasurable moan of gold, then with silver murmuring of "Hiai!" And there is not a child in all the many-colored ways of the old Chinese city who does not know the story of the great bell, – who cannot tell you why the great bell says Ko-Ngai and Hiai!

Now, this is the story of the great bell in the Ta-chung sz', as the same is related in the *Pe-Hiao-Tou-Choue*, written by the learned Yu-Pao-Tchen, of the City of Kwang-tchau-fu.

Nearly five hundred years ago the Celestially August, the Son of Heaven, Yong-Lo, of the "Illustrious," or Ming, dynasty, commanded the worthy official Kouan-Yu that he should have a bell made of such size that the sound thereof might be heard for one hundred li. And he further ordained that the voice of the bell should be strengthened with brass, and deepened with gold, and sweetened with silver; and that the face and the great lips of it should be graven with blessed sayings from the sacred books, and that it should be suspended in the centre of the imperial capital, to sound through all the many-colored ways of the City of Pe-king.

Therefore the worthy mandarin Kouan-Yu assembled the master-moulders and the renowned bellsmiths of the empire, and all men of great repute and cunning in foundry work; and they measured the materials for the alloy, and treated them skilfully, and prepared the moulds, the fires, the instruments, and the monstrous melting-pot for fusing the metal. And they labored exceedingly, like giants, – neglecting only rest and sleep and the comforts of life; toiling both night and day in obedience to Kouan-Yu, and striving in all things to do the behest of the Son of Heaven.

But when the metal had been cast, and the earthen mould separated from the glowing casting, it was discovered that, despite their great labor and ceaseless care, the result was void of worth; for the metals had rebelled one against the other, – the gold had scorned alliance with the brass, the silver would not mingle with the molten iron. Therefore the moulds had to be once more prepared, and the fires rekindled, and the metal remelted, and all the work tediously and toilsomely repeated. The Son of Heaven heard, and was angry, but spake nothing.

A second time the bell was cast, and the result was even worse. Still the metals obstinately refused to blend one with the other; and there was no uniformity in the bell, and the sides of it were cracked and fissured, and the lips of it were slagged and split asunder; so that all the labor had to be repeated even a third time, to the great dismay of Kouan-Yu. And when the Son of Heaven heard these things, he was angrier than before; and sent his messenger to Kouan-Yu with a letter, written upon lemon-colored silk, and sealed with the seal of the Dragon, containing these words: –

"From the Mighty Yong-Lo, the Sublime Tait-Sung, the Celestial and August, – whose reign is called 'Ming,' – to Kouan-Yu the Fuh-yin: Twice thou hast betrayed the trust we have deigned graciously to place in thee; if thou fail a third time in fulfilling our command, thy head shall be severed from thy neck. Tremble, and obey!"

Now, Kouan-Yu had a daughter of dazzling loveliness, whose name – Ko-Ngai – was ever in the mouths of poets, and whose heart was even more beautiful than her face. Ko-Ngai loved her father with such love that she had refused a hundred worthy suitors rather than make his home desolate by her absence; and when she had seen the awful yellow missive, sealed with the Dragon-Seal, she fainted away with fear for her father's sake. And when her senses and her strength returned to her, she could not rest or sleep for thinking of her parent's danger, until she had secretly sold some of her jewels, and with the money so obtained had hastened to an astrologer, and paid him a great price to advise her by what means her father might be saved from the peril impending over him. So the astrologer made observations of the heavens, and marked the aspect of the Silver Stream (which we call the Milky Way), and examined the signs of the Zodiac, – the Hwang-tao, or Yellow Road, – and consulted the table of the Five Hin, or Principles of the Universe, and the mystical books of the alchemists. And after a long silence, he made answer to her, saying: "Gold and brass will never meet in wedlock, silver and iron never will embrace, until the flesh of a maiden be melted in the crucible; until the blood of a virgin be mixed with the metals in their fusion." So Ko-Ngai returned home sorrowful at heart; but she kept secret all that she had heard, and told no one what she had done.

At last came the awful day when the third and last effort to cast the great bell was to be made; and Ko-Ngai, together with her waiting-woman, accompanied her father to the foundry, and they took their places upon a platform overlooking the toiling of the moulders and the lava of liquefied metal. All the workmen wrought their tasks in silence; there was no sound heard but the muttering of the fires. And the muttering deepened into a roar like the roar of typhoons approaching, and the blood-red lake of metal slowly brightened like the vermilion of a sunrise, and the vermilion was transmuted into a radiant glow of gold, and the gold whitened blindingly, like the silver face of a full moon. Then the workers ceased to feed the raving flame, and all fixed their eyes upon the eyes of Kouan-Yu; and Kouan-Yu prepared to give the signal to cast.

But ere ever he lifted his finger, a cry caused him to turn his head; and all heard the voice of Ko-Ngai sounding sharply sweet as a bird's song above the great thunder of the fires, – "For thy sake, O my Father!" And even as she cried, she leaped into the white flood of metal; and the lava of the furnace roared to receive her, and spattered monstrous flakes of flame to the roof, and burst over the verge of the earthen crater, and cast up a whirling fountain of many-colored fires, and subsided quakingly, with lightnings and with thunders and with mutterings.

Then the father of Ko-Ngai, wild with his grief, would have leaped in after her, but that strong men held him back and kept firm grasp upon him until he had fainted away and they could bear him like one dead to his home. And the serving-woman of Ko-Ngai, dizzy and speechless for pain, stood before the furnace, still holding in her hands a shoe, a tiny, dainty shoe, with embroidery of pearls and flowers, – the shoe of her beautiful mistress that was. For she had sought to grasp Ko-Ngai by the foot as she leaped, but had only been able to clutch the shoe, and the pretty shoe came off in her hand; and she continued to stare at it like one gone mad.

But in spite of all these things, the command of the Celestial and August had to be obeyed, and the work of the moulders to be finished, hopeless as the result might be. Yet the glow of the metal seemed purer and whiter than before; and there was no sign of the beautiful body that had been entombed therein. So the ponderous casting was made; and lo! when the metal had become cool, it was found that the bell was beautiful to look upon, and perfect in form, and wonderful in color above all other bells. Nor was there any trace found of the body of Ko-Ngai; for it had been totally absorbed by the precious alloy, and blended with the well-blended brass and gold, with the intermingling of the silver and the iron. And when they sounded the bell, its tones were found to be deeper and mellower and mightier than the tones of any other bell, – reaching even beyond the distance of one hundred li, like a pealing of summer thunder; and yet also like some vast voice uttering a name, a woman's name, – the name of Ko-Ngai!

And still, between each mighty stroke there is a long low moaning heard; and ever the moaning ends with a sound of sobbing and of complaining, as though a weeping woman should murmur, "Hiai!" And still, when the people hear that great golden moan they keep silence; but when the sharp, sweet shuddering comes in the air, and the sobbing of "Hiai!" then, indeed, all the Chinese mothers in all the many-colored ways of Pe-king whisper to their little ones: "Listen! that is Ko-Ngai crying for her shoe! That is Ko-Ngai calling for her shoe!"

The Legend Of Tchi-Niu

Lafcadio Hearn

In the quaint commentary accompanying the text of that holy book of Lao-tseu called *Kan-ing-p'ien* may be found a little story so old that the name of the one who first told it has been forgotten for a thousand years, yet so beautiful that it lives still in the memory of four hundred millions of people, like a prayer that, once learned, is forever remembered. The Chinese writer makes no mention of any city nor of any province, although even in the relation of the most ancient traditions such an omission is rare; we are only told that the name of the hero of the legend was Tong-yong, and that he lived in the years of the great dynasty of Han, some twenty centuries ago.

Tong-Yong's mother had died while he was yet an infant; and when he became a youth of nineteen years his father also passed away, leaving him utterly alone in the world, and without resources of any sort; for, being a very poor man, Tong's father had put himself to great straits to educate the lad, and had not been able to lay by even one copper coin of his earnings. And Tong lamented greatly to find himself so destitute that he could not honor the memory of that good father by having the customary rites of burial performed, and a carven tomb erected upon a propitious site. The poor only are friends of the poor; and among all those whom Tong knew; there was no one able to assist him in defraying the expenses of the funeral. In one way only could the youth obtain money, – by selling himself as a slave to some rich cultivator; and this he at last decided to do. In vain his friends did their utmost to dissuade him; and to no purpose did they attempt to delay the accomplishment of his sacrifice by beguiling promises of future aid. Tong only replied that he would sell his freedom a hundred times, if it were possible, rather than suffer his father's memory to remain unhonored even for a brief season. And furthermore, confiding in his youth and strength, he determined to put a high price upon his servitude, – a price which would enable him to build a handsome tomb, but which it would be well-nigh impossible for him ever to repay.

Accordingly he repaired to the broad public place where slaves and debtors were exposed for sale, and seated himself upon a bench of stone, having affixed to his shoulders a placard inscribed with the terms of his servitude and the list of his qualifications as a laborer. Many who read the characters upon the placard smiled disdainfully at the price asked, and passed on without a word; others lingered only to question him out of simple curiosity; some commended him with hollow praise; some openly mocked his unselfishness, and laughed at his childish piety. Thus many hours wearily passed, and Tong had almost despaired of finding a master, when there rode up a high official of the province, – a grave and handsome man, lord of a thousand slaves, and owner of vast estates. Reining in his Tartar horse, the official halted to read the placard and to consider the value of the slave. He did not smile, or advise, or ask any questions; but having observed the price asked, and the fine strong limbs of the youth, purchased him without further ado, merely ordering his attendant to pay the sum and to see that the necessary papers were made out.

Thus Tong found himself enabled to fulfil the wish of his heart, and to have a monument built which, although of small size, was destined to delight the eyes of all who beheld it, being designed by cunning artists and executed by skilful sculptors. And while it was yet designed only, the pious rites were performed, the silver coin was placed in the mouth of the dead, the white lanterns were hung at the door, the holy prayers were recited, and paper shapes of all things the departed might need in the land of the Genii were consumed in consecrated fire. And after the geomancers and the necromancers had chosen a burial-spot which no unlucky star could shine upon, a place of rest which no demon or dragon might ever disturb, the beautiful chih was built. Then was the phantom money strewn along the way; the funeral procession departed from the dwelling of the dead, and with prayers and lamentation the mortal remains of Tong's good father were borne to the tomb.

Then Tong entered as a slave into the service of his purchaser, who allotted him a little hut to dwell in; and thither Tong carried with him those wooden tablets, bearing the ancestral names, before which filial piety must daily burn the incense of prayer, and perform the tender duties of family worship.

Thrice had spring perfumed the breast of the land with flowers, and thrice had been celebrated that festival of the dead which is called Siu-fan-ti, and thrice had Tong swept and garnished his father's tomb and presented his fivefold offering of fruits and meats. The period of mourning had passed, yet he had not ceased to mourn for his parent. The years revolved with their moons, bringing him no hour of joy, no day of happy rest; yet he never lamented his servitude, or failed to perform the rites of ancestral worship, – until at last the fever of the rice-fields laid strong hold upon him, and he could not arise from his couch; and his fellow-laborers thought him destined to die. There was no one to wait upon him, no one to care for his needs, inasmuch as slaves and servants were wholly busied with the duties of the household or the labor of the fields, – all departing to toil at sunrise and returning weary only after the sundown.

Now, while the sick youth slumbered the fitful slumber of exhaustion one sultry noon, he dreamed that a strange and beautiful woman stood by him, and bent above him and touched his forehead with the long, fine fingers of her shapely hand. And at her cool touch a weird sweet shock passed through him, and all his veins tingled as if thrilled by new life. Opening his eyes in wonder, he saw verily bending over him the charming being of whom he had dreamed, and he knew that her lithe hand really caressed his throbbing forehead. But the flame of the fever was gone, a delicious coolness now penetrated every fibre of his body, and the thrill of which he had dreamed still tingled in his blood like a great joy. Even at the same moment the eyes of the gentle visitor met his own, and he saw they were singularly beautiful, and shone like splendid black jewels under brows curved like the wings of the swallow. Yet their calm gaze seemed to pass through him as light through crystal; and a vague awe came upon him, so that the question which had risen to his lips found no utterance. Then she, still caressing him, smiled and said: "I have come to restore thy strength and to be thy wife. Arise and worship with me."

Her clear voice had tones melodious as a bird's song; but in her gaze there was an imperious power which Tong felt he dare not resist.

Rising from his couch, he was astounded to find his strength wholly restored; but the cool, slender hand which held his own led him away so swiftly that he had little time for amazement. He would have given years of existence for courage to speak of his misery, to declare his utter inability to maintain a wife; but something irresistible in the long dark eyes of his companion forbade him to speak; and as though his inmost thought had been discerned by that wondrous gaze, she said to him, in the same clear voice, "I will provide." Then shame made him blush at the thought of his wretched aspect and tattered apparel; but he observed that she also was poorly attired, like a woman of the people, – wearing no ornament of any sort, nor even shoes upon her feet. And before he had yet spoken to her, they came before the ancestral tablets; and there she knelt with him and prayed, and pledged him in a cup of wine, – brought he knew not from whence, – and together they worshipped Heaven and Earth. Thus she became his wife.

A mysterious marriage it seemed, for neither on that day nor at any future time could Tong venture to ask his wife the name of her family, or of the place whence she came, and he could not answer any of the curious questions which his fellow-laborers put to him concerning her; and she, moreover, never uttered a word about herself, except to say that her name was Tchi. But although Tong had such awe of her that while her eyes were upon him he was as one having no will of his own, he loved her unspeakably; and the thought of his serfdom ceased to weigh upon him from the hour of his marriage. As through magic the little dwelling had become transformed: its misery was masked with charming paper devices, – with dainty decorations created out of nothing by that pretty jugglery of which woman only knows the secret.

Each morning at dawn the young husband found a well-prepared and ample repast awaiting him, and each evening also upon his return; but the wife all day sat at her loom, weaving silk after a fashion unlike anything which had ever been seen before in that province. For as she wove, the silk flowed from the loom like a slow current of glossy gold, bearing upon its undulations strange forms of violet and crimson and jewel-green: shapes of ghostly horsemen riding upon horses, and of phantom chariots dragon-drawn, and of standards of trailing cloud. In every dragon's beard glimmered the mystic pearl; in every rider's helmet sparkled the gem of rank. And each day Tchi would weave a great piece of such figured silk; and the fame of her weaving spread abroad. From far and near people thronged to see the marvellous work; and the silk-merchants of great cities heard of it, and they sent messengers to Tchi, asking her that she should weave for them and teach them her secret. Then she wove for them, as they desired, in return for the silver cubes which they brought her; but when they prayed her to teach them, she laughed and said, "Assuredly I could never teach you, for no one among you has fingers like mine." And indeed no man could discern her fingers when she wove, any more than he might behold the wings of a bee vibrating in swift flight.

The seasons passed, and Tong never knew want, so well did his beautiful wife fulfil her promise, – "I will provide"; and the cubes of bright silver brought by the silk-merchants were piled up higher and higher in the great carven chest which Tchi had bought for the storage of the household goods.

One morning, at last, when Tong, having finished his repast, was about to depart to the fields, Tchi unexpectedly bade him remain; and opening the great chest, she took out of it and gave him a document written in the official characters called li-shu. And Tong, looking at it, cried out and leaped in his joy, for it was the certificate of his manumission. Tchi had secretly purchased her husband's freedom with the price of her wondrous silks!

"Thou shalt labor no more for any master," she said, "but for thine own sake only. And I have also bought this dwelling, with all which is therein, and the tea-fields to the south, and the mulberry groves hard by, – all of which are thine."

Then Tong, beside himself for gratefulness, would have prostrated himself in worship before her, but that she would not suffer it.

Thus he was made free; and prosperity came to him with his freedom; and whatsoever he gave to the sacred earth was returned to him centupled; and his servants loved him and blessed the beautiful Tchi, so silent and yet so kindly to all about her. But the silk-loom soon remained untouched, for Tchi gave birth to a son, – a boy so beautiful that Tong wept with delight when he looked upon him. And thereafter the wife devoted herself wholly to the care of the child.

Now it soon became manifest that the boy was not less wonderful than his wonderful mother. In the third month of his age he could speak; in the seventh month he could repeat by heart the proverbs of the sages, and recite the holy prayers; before the eleventh month he could use the writing-brush with skill, and copy in shapely characters the precepts of Lao-tseu. And the priests of the temples came to behold him and to converse with him, and they marvelled at the charm of the child and the wisdom of what he said; and they blessed Tong, saying: "Surely this son of thine is a gift from the Master of Heaven, a sign that the immortals love thee. May thine eyes behold a hundred happy summers!"

It was in the Period of the Eleventh Moon: the flowers had passed away, the perfume of the summer had flown, the winds were growing chill, and in Tong's home the evening fires were lighted. Long the husband and wife sat in the mellow glow, – he speaking much of his hopes and joys, and of his son that was to be so grand a man, and of many paternal projects; while she, speaking little, listened to his words, and often turned her wonderful eyes upon him with an answering smile. Never had she seemed so beautiful before; and Tong, watching her face, marked not how the night waned, nor how the fire sank low, nor how the wind sang in the leafless trees without.

All suddenly Tchi arose without speaking, and took his hand in hers and led him, gently as on that strange wedding-morning, to the cradle where their boy slumbered, faintly smiling in his dreams. And in that moment there came upon Tong the same strange fear that he knew when Tchi's eyes had first met his own, – the vague fear that love and trust had calmed, but never wholly cast out, like unto the fear of the gods. And all unknowingly, like one yielding to the pressure of mighty invisible hands, he bowed himself low before her, kneeling as to a divinity. Now, when he lifted his eyes again to her face, he closed them forthwith in awe; for she towered before him taller than any mortal woman, and there was a glow about her as of sunbeams, and the light of her limbs shone through her garments. But her sweet voice came to him with all the tenderness of other hours, saying: "Lo! my beloved, the moment has come in which I must forsake thee; for I was never of mortal born, and the Invisible may incarnate themselves for a time only. Yet I leave with thee the pledge of our love, – this fair son, who shall ever be to thee as faithful and as fond as thou thyself hast been. Know, my beloved, that I was sent to thee even by the Master of Heaven, in reward of thy filial piety, and that I must now return to the glory of His house: I am the Goddess Tchi-Niu."

Even as she ceased to speak, the great glow faded; and Tong, re-opening his eyes, knew that she had passed away forever, – mysteriously as pass the winds of heaven, irrevocably as the light of a flame blown out. Yet all the doors were barred, all the windows unopened. Still the child slept, smiling in his sleep. Outside, the darkness was breaking; the sky was brightening swiftly; the night was past. With splendid majesty the East threw open high gates of gold for the coming of the sun; and, illuminated by the glory of his coming, the vapors of morning wrought themselves into marvellous shapes of shifting color, – into forms weirdly beautiful as the silken dreams woven in the loom of Tchi-Niu.

The Tale of the Porcelain-God

Lafcadio Hearn

Who first of men discovered the secret of the *Kao-ling*, of the *Pe-tun-tse*, – the bones and the flesh, the skeleton and the skin, of the beauteous Vase? Who first discovered the virtue of the curd-white clay? Who first prepared the ice-pure bricks of *tun*: the gathered-hoariness of mountains that have died for age; blanched dust of the rocky bones and the stony flesh of sun-seeking Giants that have ceased to be? Unto whom was it first given to discover the divine art of porcelain?

Unto Pu, once a man, now a god, before whose snowy statues bow the myriad populations enrolled in the guilds of the potteries. But the place of his birth we know not; perhaps the tradition of it may have been effaced from remembrance by that awful war which in our own day consumed the lives of twenty millions of the Black-haired Race, and obliterated from the face of the world even the wonderful City of Porcelain itself, – the City of King-te-chin, that of old shone like a jewel of fire in the blue mountain-girdle of Feou-liang.

Before his time indeed the Spirit of the Furnace had being; had issued from the Infinite Vitality; had become manifest as an emanation of the Supreme Tao. For Hoang-ti, nearly five thousand years ago, taught men to make good vessels of baked clay; and in his time all potters had learned to know the God of Oven-fires, and turned their wheels to the murmuring of prayer. But Hoang-ti had been gathered unto his fathers for thrice ten hundred years before that man was born destined by the Master of Heaven to become the Porcelain-God.

And his divine ghost, ever hovering above the smoking and the toiling of the potteries, still gives power to the thought of the shaper, grace to the genius of the designer, luminosity to the touch of the enamellist. For by his heaven-taught wisdom was the art of porcelain created; by his inspiration were accomplished all the miracles of Thao-yu, maker of the *Kia-yu-ki*, and all the marvels made by those who followed after him; –

All the azure porcelains called *You-kouo-thien-tsing*; brilliant as a mirror, thin as paper of rice, sonorous as the melodious stone *Khing*, and colored, in obedience to the mandate of the Emperor Chi-tsong, "blue as the sky is after rain, when viewed through the rifts of the clouds." These were, indeed, the first of all porcelains, likewise called *Tchai-yao*, which no man, howsoever wicked, could find courage to break, for they charmed the eye like jewels of price; –

And the *Jou-yao*, second in rank among all porcelains, sometimes mocking the aspect and the sonority of bronze, sometimes blue as summer waters, and deluding the sight with mucid appearance of thickly floating spawn of fish; –

And the *Kouan-yao*, which are the Porcelains of Magistrates, and third in rank of merit among all wondrous porcelains, colored with colors of the morning, – skyey blueness, with the rose of a great dawn blushing and bursting through it, and long-limbed marsh-birds flying against the glow;

Also the *Ko-yao*, – fourth in rank among perfect porcelains, – of fair, faint, changing colors, like the body of a living fish, or made in the likeness of opal substance, milk mixed with fire; the work of Sing-I, elder of the immortal brothers Tchang;

Also the *Ting-yao*, – fifth in rank among all perfect porcelains, – white as the mourning garments of a spouse bereaved, and beautiful with a trickling as of tears, – the porcelains sung of by the poet Son-tong-po;

Also the porcelains called *Pi-se-yao*, whose colors are called "hidden," being alternately invisible and visible, like the tints of ice beneath the sun, – the porcelains celebrated by the far-famed singer Sin-in;

Also the wondrous *Chu-yao*, – the pallid porcelains that utter a mournful cry when smitten, – the porcelains chanted of by the mighty chanter, Thou-chao-ling;

Also the porcelains called *Thsin-yao*, white or blue, surface-wrinkled as the face of water by the fluttering of many fins.... And ye can see the fish!

Also the vases called *Tsi-hong-khi*, red as sunset after a rain; and the *T'o-t'ai-khi*, fragile as the wings of the silkworm-moth, lighter than the shell of an egg;

Also the *Kia-tsing*, – fair cups pearl-white when empty, yet, by some incomprehensible witchcraft of construction, seeming to swarm with purple fish the moment they are filled with water;

Also the porcelains called *Yao-pien*, whose tints are transmuted by the alchemy of fire; for they enter blood-crimson into the heat, and change there to lizard-green, and at last come forth azure as the cheek of the sky;

Also the *Ki-tcheou-yao*, which are all violet as a summer's night; and the *Hing-yao* that sparkle with the sparklings of mingled silver and snow;

Also the *Sieouen-yao*, – some ruddy as iron in the furnace, some diaphanous and ruby-red, some granulated and yellow as the rind of an orange, some softly flushed as the skin of a peach;

Also the *Tsoui-khi-yao*, crackled and green as ancient ice is; and the *Tchou-fou-yao*, which are the Porcelains of Emperors, with dragons wriggling and snarling in gold; and those *yao* that are pink-ribbed and have their angles serrated as the claws of crabs are;

Also the *Ou-ni-yao*, black as the pupil of the eye, and as lustrous; and the *Hou-tien-yao*, darkly yellow as the faces of men of India; and the *Ou-kong-yao*, whose color is the dead-gold of autumn-leaves;

Also the *Long-kang-yao*, green as the seedling of a pea, but bearing also paintings of sun-silvered cloud, and of the Dragons of Heaven;

Also the *Tching-hoa-yao*, – pictured with the amber bloom of grapes and the verdure of vine-leaves and the blossoming of poppies, or decorated in relief with figures of fighting crickets;

Also the *Khang-hi-nien-ts'ang-yao*, celestial azure sown with star-dust of gold; and the *Khien-long-nien-thang-yao*, splendid in sable and silver as a fervid night that is flashed with lightnings.

Not indeed the *Long-Ouang-yao*, – painted with the lascivious *Pi-hi*, with the obscene *Nan-niu-ssé-sie*, with the shameful *Tchun-hoa*, or "Pictures of Spring"; abominations created by command of the wicked Emperor Moutsong, though the Spirit of the Furnace hid his face and fled away;

But all other vases of startling form and substance, magically articulated, and ornamented with figures in relief, in cameo, in transparency, – the vases with orifices belled like the cups of flowers, or cleft like the bills of birds, or fanged like the jaws of serpents, or pink-lipped as the mouth of a girl; the vases flesh-colored and purple-veined and dimpled, with ears and with earrings; the vases in likeness of mushrooms, of lotos-flowers, of lizards, of horse-footed dragons woman-faced; the vases strangely translucid, that simulate the white glimmering of grains of prepared rice, that counterfeit the vapory lace-work of frost, that imitate the efflorescences of coral; –

Also the statues in porcelain of divinities: the Genius of the Hearth; the Long-pinn who are the Twelve Deities of Ink; the blessed Lao-tseu, born with silver hair; Kong-fu-tse, grasping the scroll of written wisdom; Kouan-in, sweetest Goddess of Mercy, standing snowy-footed upon the heart of her golden lily; Chi-nong, the god who taught men how to cook; Fo, with long eyes closed in meditation, and lips smiling the mysterious smile of Supreme Beatitude; Cheou-lao, god of Longevity, bestriding his aërial steed, the white-winged stork; Pou-t'ai, Lord of Contentment and of Wealth, obese and dreamy; and that fairest Goddess of Talent, from whose beneficent hands eternally streams the iridescent rain of pearls.

And though many a secret of that matchless art that Pu bequeathed unto men may indeed have been forgotten and lost forever, the story of the Porcelain-God is remembered; and I doubt not that any of the aged *Jeou-yen-liao-kong*, any one of the old blind men of the great potteries, who sit all day grinding colors in the sun, could tell you Pu was once a humble Chinese workman, who grew to be a great artist by dint of tireless study and patience and by the inspiration of Heaven. So famed he became that some deemed him an alchemist, who possessed the secret called *White-and-Yellow*, by which stones might be turned into gold; and others thought him a magician, having the ghastly power of murdering men with horror of nightmare, by hiding charmed effigies of them under the tiles of their own roofs; and others, again, averred that he was an astrologer who had discovered the mystery of those Five Hing which influence all things,

– those Powers that move even in the currents of the star-drift, in the milky *Tien-ho*, or River of the Sky. Thus, at least, the ignorant spoke of him; but even those who stood about the Son of Heaven, those whose hearts had been strengthened by the acquisition of wisdom, wildly praised the marvels of his handicraft, and asked each other if there might be any imaginable form of beauty which Pu could not evoke from that beauteous substance so docile to the touch of his cunning hand.

And one day it came to pass that Pu sent a priceless gift to the Celestial and August: a vase imitating the substance of ore-rock, all aflame with pyritic scintillation, – a shape of glittering splendor with chameleons sprawling over it; chameleons of porcelain that shifted color as often as the beholder changed his position. And the Emperor, wondering exceedingly at the splendor of the work, questioned the princes and the mandarins concerning him that made it. And the princes and the mandarins answered that he was a workman named Pu, and that he was without equal among potters, knowing secrets that seemed to have been inspired either by gods or by demons. Whereupon the Son of Heaven sent his officers to Pu with a noble gift, and summoned him unto his presence.

So the humble artisan entered before the Emperor, and having performed the supreme prostration, – thrice kneeling, and thrice nine times touching the ground with his forehead, – awaited the command of the August.

And the Emperor spake to him, saying: "Son, thy gracious gift hath found high favor in our sight; and for the charm of that offering we have bestowed upon thee a reward of five thousand silver *liang*. But thrice that sum shall be awarded thee so soon as thou shalt have fulfilled our behest. Hearken, therefore, O matchless artificer! it is now our will that thou make for us a vase having the tint and the aspect of living flesh, but – mark well our desire! – *of flesh made to creep by the utterance of such words as poets utter, – flesh moved by an Idea, flesh horripilated by a Thought!* Obey, and answer not! We have spoken."

Now Pu was the most cunning of all the *P'ei-se-kong*, – the men who marry colors together; of all the *Hoa-yang-kong*, who draw the shapes of vase-decoration; of all the *Hoei-sse-kong*, who paint in enamel; of all the *T'ien-thsai-kong*, who brighten color; of all the *Chao-lou-kong*, who watch the furnace-fires and the porcelain-ovens. But he went away sorrowing from the Palace of the Son of Heaven, notwithstanding the gift of five thousand silver *liang* which had been given to him. For he thought to himself: "Surely the mystery of the comeliness of flesh, and the mystery of that by which it is moved, are the secrets of the Supreme Tao. How shall man lend the aspect of sentient life to dead clay? Who save the Infinite can give soul?"

Now Pu had discovered those witchcrafts of color, those surprises of grace, that make the art of the ceramist. He had found the secret of the *feng-hong*, the wizard flush of the Rose; of the *hoa-hong*, the delicious incarnadine; of the mountain-green called *chan-lou*; of the pale soft yellow termed *hiao-hoang-yeou*; and of the *hoang-kin*, which is the blazing beauty of gold. He had found those eel-tints, those serpent-greens, those pansy-violets, those furnace-crimsons, those carminates and lilacs, subtle as spirit-flame, which our enamellists of the Occident long sought without success to reproduce. But he trembled at the task assigned him, as he returned to the toil of his studio, saying: "How shall any miserable man render in clay the quivering of flesh to an Idea, – the inexplicable horripilation of a Thought? Shall a man venture to mock the magic of that Eternal Moulder by whose infinite power a million suns are shapen more readily than one small jar might be rounded upon my wheel?"

Yet the command of the Celestial and August might never be disobeyed; and the patient workman strove with all his power to fulfil the Son of Heaven's desire. But vainly for days, for weeks, for months, for season after season, did he strive; vainly also he prayed unto the gods to aid him; vainly he besought the Spirit of the Furnace, crying: "O thou Spirit of Fire, hear me, heed me, help me! how shall I, – a miserable man, unable to breathe into clay a living soul, – how shall I render in this inanimate substance the aspect of flesh made to creep by the utterance of a Word, sentient to the horripilation of a Thought?"

For the Spirit of the Furnace made strange answer to him with whispering of fire: "*Vast thy faith, weird thy prayer! Has Thought feet, that man may perceive the trace of its passing? Canst thou measure me the blast of the Wind?*"

Nevertheless, with purpose unmoved, nine-and-forty times did Pu seek to fulfil the Emperor's command; nine-and-forty times he strove to obey the behest of the Son of Heaven. Vainly, alas! did he consume his substance; vainly did he expend his strength; vainly did he exhaust his knowledge: success smiled not upon him; and Evil visited his home, and Poverty sat in his dwelling, and Misery shivered at his hearth.

Sometimes, when the hour of trial came, it was found that the colors had become strangely transmuted in the firing, or had faded into ashen pallor, or had darkened into the fuliginous hue of forest-mould. And Pu, beholding these misfortunes, made wail to the Spirit of the Furnace, praying: "O thou Spirit of Fire, how shall I render the likeness of lustrous flesh, the warm glow of living color, unless thou aid me?"

And the Spirit of the Furnace mysteriously answered him with murmuring of fire: "*Canst thou learn the art of that Infinite Enameller who hath made beautiful the Arch of Heaven, – whose brush is Light; whose paints are the Colors of the Evening?*"

Sometimes, again, even when the tints had not changed, after the pricked and labored surface had seemed about to quicken in the heat, to assume the vibratility of living skin, – even at the last hour all the labor of the workers proved to have been wasted; for the fickle substance rebelled against their efforts, producing only crinklings grotesque as those upon the rind of a withered fruit, or granulations like those upon the skin of a dead bird from which the feathers have been rudely plucked. And Pu wept, and cried out unto the Spirit of the Furnace: "O thou Spirit of Flame, how shall I be able to imitate the thrill of flesh touched by a Thought, unless thou wilt vouchsafe to lend me thine aid?"

And the Spirit of the Furnace mysteriously answered him with muttering of fire: "*Canst thou give ghost unto a stone? Canst thou thrill with a Thought the entrails of the granite hills?*"

Sometimes it was found that all the work indeed had not failed; for the color seemed good, and all faultless the matter of the vase appeared to be, having neither crack nor wrinkling nor crinkling; but the pliant softness of warm skin did not meet the eye; the flesh-tinted surface offered only the harsh aspect and hard glimmer of metal. All their exquisite toil to mock the pulpiness of sentient substance had left no trace; had been brought to nought by the breath of the furnace. And Pu, in his despair, shrieked to the Spirit of the Furnace: "O thou merciless divinity! O thou most pitiless god! – thou whom I have worshipped with ten thousand sacrifices! – for what fault hast thou abandoned me? for what error hast thou forsaken me? How may I, most wretched of men! ever render the aspect of flesh made to creep with the utterance of a Word, sentient to the titillation of a Thought, if thou wilt not aid me?"

And the Spirit of the Furnace made answer unto him with roaring of fire: "*Canst thou divide a Soul? Nay!... Thy life for the life of thy work! – thy soul for the soul of thy Vase!*"

And hearing these words Pu arose with a terrible resolve swelling at his heart, and made ready for the last and fiftieth time to fashion his work for the oven.

One hundred times did he sift the clay and the quartz, the *kao-ling* and the *tun*; one hundred times did he purify them in clearest water; one hundred times with tireless hands did he knead the creamy paste, mingling it at last with colors known only to himself. Then was the vase shapen and reshapen, and touched and retouched by the hands of Pu, until its blandness seemed to live, until it appeared to quiver and to palpitate, as with vitality from within, as with the quiver of rounded muscle undulating beneath the integument. For the hues of life were upon it and infiltrated throughout its innermost substance, imitating the carnation of blood-bright tissue, and the reticulated purple of the veins; and over all was laid the envelope of sun-colored *Pe-kia-ho*, the lucid and glossy enamel, half diaphanous, even like the substance that it counterfeited, – the polished skin of a woman. Never since the making of the world had any work comparable to this been wrought by the skill of man.

Then Pu bade those who aided him that they should feed the furnace well with wood of *tcha*; but he told his resolve unto none. Yet after the oven began to glow, and he saw the work of his hands blossoming and blushing in the heat, he bowed himself before the Spirit of Flame, and murmured: "O thou Spirit and Master of Fire, I know the truth of thy words! I know that a Soul may never be divided! Therefore my life for the life of my work! – my soul for the soul of my Vase!"

And for nine days and for eight nights the furnaces were fed unceasingly with wood of *tcha*; for nine days and for eight nights men watched the wondrous vase crystallizing into being, rose-lighted by the breath of the flame. Now upon the coming of the ninth night, Pu bade all his weary comrades retire to, rest, for that the work was well-nigh done, and the success assured. "If you find me not here at sunrise," he said, "fear not to take forth the vase; for I know that the task will have been accomplished according to the command of the August." So they departed.

But in that same ninth night Pu entered the flame, and yielded up his ghost in the embrace of the Spirit of the Furnace, giving his life for the life of his work, – his soul for the soul of his Vase.

And when the workmen came upon the tenth morning to take forth the porcelain marvel, even the bones of Pu had ceased to be; but lo! the Vase lived as they looked upon it: seeming to be flesh moved by the utterance of a Word, creeping to the titillation of a Thought. And whenever tapped by the finger it uttered a voice and a name, – the voice of its maker, the name of its creator: PU.

And the son of Heaven, hearing of these things, and viewing the miracle of the vase, said unto those about him: "Verily, the Impossible hath been wrought by the strength of faith, by the force of obedience! Yet never was it our desire that so cruel a sacrifice should have been; we sought only to know whether the skill of the matchless artificer came from the Divinities or from the Demons, – from heaven or from hell. Now, indeed, we discern that Pu hath taken his place among the gods." And the Emperor mourned exceedingly for his faithful servant.

But he ordained that godlike honors should be paid unto the spirit of the marvellous artist, and that his memory should be revered forevermore, and that fair statues of him should be set up in all the cities of the Celestial Empire, and above all the toiling of the potteries, that the multitude of workers might unceasingly call upon his name and invoke his benediction upon their labors.

The Tradition of the Tea-Plant

Lafcadio Hearn

"Good is the continence of the eye;
Good is the continence of the ear;
Good is the continence of the nostrils;
Good is the continence of the tongue;
Good is the continence of the body;
Good is the continence of speech;
Good is all...."

Again the Vulture of Temptation soared to the highest heaven of his contemplation, bringing his soul down, down, reeling and fluttering, back to the World of Illusion. Again the memory made dizzy his thought, like the perfume of some venomous flower. Yet he had seen the bayadere for an instant only, when passing through Kasí upon his way to China, – to the vast empire of souls that thirsted after the refreshment of Buddha's law, as sun-parched fields thirst for the life-giving rain. When she called him, and dropped her little gift into his mendicant's bowl, he had indeed lifted his fan before his face, yet not quickly enough; and the penally of that fault had followed him a thousand leagues, – pursued after him even into the strange land to which he had come to hear the words of the Universal Teacher. Accursed beauty! surely framed by the Tempter of tempters, by Mara himself, for the perdition of the just! Wisely had Bhagavat warned his disciples: "O ye Çramanas, women are not to be looked upon! And if ye chance to meet women, ye must not suffer your eyes to dwell upon them; but, maintaining holy reserve, speak not to them at all. Then fail not to whisper unto your own hearts, 'Lo, we are Çramanas, whose duty it is to remain uncontaminated by the corruptions of this world, even as the Lotos, which suffereth no vileness to cling unto its leaves, though it blossom amid the refuse of the wayside ditch.'" Then also came to his memory, but with a new and terrible meaning, the words of the Twentieth-and-Third of the Admonitions: –

"Of all attachments unto objects of desire, the strongest indeed is the attachment to form. Happily, this passion is unique; for were there any other like unto it, then to enter the Perfect Way were impossible."

How, indeed, thus haunted by the illusion of form, was he to fulfil the vow that he had made to pass a night and a day in perfect and unbroken meditation? Already the night was beginning! Assuredly, for sickness of the soul, for fever of the spirit, there was no physic save prayer. The sunset was swiftly fading out. He strove to pray: –

"*O the Jewel in the Lotos!*

"Even as the tortoise withdraweth its extremities into its shell, let me, O Blessed One, withdraw my senses wholly into meditation!

"*O the Jewel in the Lotos!*

"For even as rain penetrateth the broken roof of a dwelling long uninhabited, so may passion enter the soul uninhabited by meditation.

"*O the Jewel in the Lotos!*

"Even as still water that hath deposited all its slime, so let my soul, O Tathâgata, be made pure! Give me strong power to rise above the world, O Master, even as the wild bird rises from its marsh to follow the pathway of the Sun!

"*O the Jewel in the Lotos!*

"By day shineth the sun, by night shineth the moon; shineth also the warrior in harness of war; shineth likewise in meditations the Çramana. But the Buddha at all times, by night or by day, shineth ever the same, illuminating the world.

"*O the Jewel in the Lotos!*

"Let me cease, O thou Perfectly Awakened, to remain as an Ape in the World-forest, forever ascending and descending in search of the fruits of folly. Swift as the twining of serpents, vast as the growth of lianas in a forest, are the all-encircling growths of the Plant of Desire.

"*O the Jewel in the Lotos*!"

Vain his prayer, alas! vain also his invocation! The mystic meaning of the holy text – the sense of the Lotos, the sense of the Jewel – had evaporated from the words, and their monotonous utterance now served only to lend more dangerous definition to the memory that tempted and tortured him. *O the jewel in her ear!* What lotos-bud more dainty than the folded flower of flesh, with its dripping of diamond-fire! Again he saw it, and the curve of the cheek beyond, luscious to look upon as beautiful brown fruit. How true the Two Hundred and Eighty-Fourth verse of the Admonitions! – "So long as a man shall not have torn from his heart even the smallest rootlet of that liana of desire which draweth his thought toward women, even so long shall his soul remain fettered." And there came to his mind also the Three Hundred and Forty-Fifth verse of the same blessed book, regarding fetters:

"In bonds of rope, wise teachers have said, there is no strength; nor in fetters of wood, nor yet in fetters of iron. Much stronger than any of these is the fetter of *concern for the jewelled earrings of women*."

"Omniscient Gotama!" he cried, – "all-seeing Tathâgata! How multiform the Consolation of Thy Word! how marvellous Thy understanding of the human heart! Was this also one of Thy temptations? – one of the myriad illusions marshalled before Thee by Mara in that night when the earth rocked as a chariot, and the sacred trembling passed from sun to sun, from system to system, from universe to universe, from eternity to eternity?"

O the jewel in her ear! The vision would not go! Nay, each time it hovered before his thought it seemed to take a warmer life, a fonder look, a fairer form; to develop with his weakness; to gain force from his enervation. He saw the eyes, large, limpid, soft, and black as a deer's; the pearls in the dark hair, and the pearls in the pink mouth; the lips curling to a kiss, a flower-kiss; and a fragrance seemed to float to his senses, sweet, strange, soporific, – a perfume of youth, an odor of woman. Rising to his feet, with strong resolve he pronounced again the sacred invocation; and he recited the holy words of the *Chapter of Impermanency*:

"Gazing upon the heavens and upon the earth ye must say, *These are not permanent*. Gazing upon the mountains and the rivers, ye must say, *These are not permanent*. Gazing upon the forms and upon the faces of exterior beings, and beholding their growth and their development, ye must say, *These are not permanent*."

And nevertheless! how sweet illusion! The illusion of the great sun; the illusion of the shadow-casting hills; the illusion of waters, formless and multiform; the illusion of – Nay, nay I what impious fancy! Accursed girl! yet, yet! why should he curse her? Had she ever done aught to merit the malediction of an ascetic? Never, never! Only her form, the memory of her, the beautiful phantom of her, the accursed phantom of her! What was she? An illusion creating illusions, a mockery, a dream, a shadow, a vanity, a vexation of spirit! The fault, the sin, was in himself, in his rebellious thought, in his untamed memory. Though mobile as water, intangible as vapor, Thought, nevertheless, may be tamed by the Will, may be harnessed to the chariot of Wisdom – must be! – that happiness be found. And he recited the blessed verses of the "Book of the Way of the Law": –

"*All forms are only temporary.*" When this great truth is fully comprehended by any one, then is he delivered from all pain. This is the Way of Purification.

"*All forms are subject unto pain.*" When this great truth is fully comprehended by any one, then is he delivered from all pain. This is the Way of Purification.

"*All forms are without substantial reality.*" When this great truth is fully comprehended by any one, then is he delivered from all pain. This is the way of ...

Her form, too, unsubstantial, unreal, an illusion only, though comeliest of illusions? She had given him alms! Was the merit of the giver illusive also, – illusive like the grace of the supple fingers that gave? Assuredly there were mysteries in the Abhidharma impenetrable, incomprehensible!... It was a golden coin, stamped with the symbol of an elephant, – not more of an illusion, indeed, than the gifts of Kings to the Buddha! Gold upon her bosom also, less fine than the gold of her skin. Naked between the silken sash and the narrow breast-corslet, her young waist curved glossy and pliant as a bow. Richer the silver in her voice than in the hollow *pagals* that made a moonlight about her ankles! But her smile! – the little teeth like flower-stamens in the perfumed blossom of her mouth!

O weakness! O shame! How had the strong Charioteer of Resolve thus lost his control over the wild team of fancy! Was this languor of the Will a signal of coming peril, the peril of slumber? So strangely vivid those fancies were, so brightly definite, as about to take visible form, to move with factitious life, to play some unholy drama upon the stage of dreams! "O Thou Fully Awakened!" he cried aloud, "help now thy humble disciple to obtain the blessed wakefulness of perfect contemplation! let him find force to fulfil his vow! suffer not Mara to prevail against him!" And he recited the eternal verses of the Chapter of Wakefulness: –

"*Completely and eternally awake are the disciples of Gotama!* Unceasingly, by day and night, their thoughts are fixed upon the Law.

"*Completely and eternally awake are the disciples of Gotama!* Unceasingly, by day and night, their thoughts are fixed upon the Community.

"*Completely and eternally awake are the disciples of Gotama!* Unceasingly, by day and night, their thoughts are fixed upon the Body.

"*Completely and eternally awake are the disciples of Gotama!* Unceasingly, by day and night, their minds know the sweetness of perfect peace.

"*Completely and eternally awake are the disciples of Gotama!* Unceasingly, by day and night, their minds enjoy the deep peace of meditation."

There came a murmur to his ears; a murmuring of many voices, smothering the utterances of his own, like a tumult of waters. The stars went out before his sight; the heavens darkened their infinities: all things became viewless, became blackness; and the great murmur deepened, like the murmur of a rising tide; and the earth seemed to sink from beneath him. His feet no longer touched the ground; a sense of supernatural buoyancy pervaded every fibre of his body: he felt himself floating in obscurity; then sinking softly, slowly, like a feather dropped from the pinnacle of a temple. Was this death? Nay, for all suddenly, as transported by the Sixth Supernatural Power, he stood again in light, – a perfumed, sleepy light, vapory, beautiful, – that bathed the marvellous streets of some Indian city. Now the nature of the murmur became manifest to him; for he moved with a mighty throng, a people of pilgrims, a nation of worshippers. But these were not of his faith; they bore upon their foreheads the smeared symbols of obscene gods! Still, he could not escape from their midst; the mile-broad human torrent bore him irresistibly with it, as a leaf is swept by the waters of the Ganges. Rajahs were there with their trains, and princes riding upon elephants, and Brahmins robed in their vestments, and swarms of voluptuous dancing-girls, moving to chant of *kabit* and *damâri*. But whither, whither? Out of the city into the sun they passed, between avenues of banyan, down colonnades of palm. But whither, whither?

Blue-distant, a mountain of carven stone appeared before them, – the Temple, lifting to heaven its wilderness of chiselled pinnacles, flinging to the sky the golden spray of its decoration. Higher it grew with approach, the blue tones changed to gray, the outlines sharpened in the light. Then each detail became visible: the elephants of the pedestals standing upon tortoises of rock; the great grim faces of the capitals; the serpents and monsters writhing among the friezes; the many-headed gods of basalt in their galleries of fretted niches, tier above tier; the pictured foulnesses, the painted lusts, the divinities of abomination. And, yawning in the sloping precipice of sculpture, beneath a frenzied swarming of gods and Gopia, – a beetling pyramid of limbs and bodies interlocked, – the Gate, cavernous and shadowy as the mouth of Siva, devoured the living multitude.

The eddy of the throng whirled him with it to the vastness of the interior. None seemed to note his yellow robe, none even to observe his presence. Giant aisles intercrossed their heights above him; myriads of mighty pillars, fantastically carven, filed away to invisibility behind the yellow illumination of torch-fires. Strange images, weirdly sensuous, loomed up through haze of incense. Colossal figures, that at a distance assumed the form of elephants or garuda-birds, changed aspect when approached, and revealed as the secret of their design an interplaiting of the bodies of women; while one divinity rode all the monstrous allegories, – one divinity or demon, eternally the same in the repetition of the sculptor, universally visible as though self-multiplied. The huge pillars themselves were symbols, figures, carnalities; the orgiastic spirit of that worship lived and writhed in the contorted bronze of the lamps, the twisted gold of the cups, the chiselled marble of the tanks....

How far had he proceeded? He knew not; the journey among those countless columns, past those armies of petrified gods, down lanes of flickering lights, seemed longer than the voyage of a caravan, longer than his pilgrimage to China! But suddenly, inexplicably, there came a silence as of cemeteries; the living ocean seemed to have ebbed away from about him, to have been engulfed within abysses of subterranean architecture! He found himself alone in some strange crypt before a basin, shell-shaped and shallow, bearing in its centre a rounded column of less than human height, whose smooth and spherical summit was wreathed with flowers. Lamps similarly formed, and fed with oil of palm, hung above it. There was no other graven image, no visible divinity. Flowers of countless varieties lay heaped upon the pavement; they covered its surface like a carpet, thick, soft; they exhaled their ghosts beneath his feet. The perfume seemed to penetrate his brain, – a perfume sensuous, intoxicating, unholy; an unconquerable languor mastered his will, and he sank to rest upon the floral offerings.

The sound of a tread, light as a whisper, approached through the heavy stillness, with a drowsy tinkling of *pagals*, a tintinnabulation of anklets. All suddenly he felt glide about his neck the tepid smoothness of a woman's arm. *She, she!* his Illusion, his Temptation; but how transformed, transfigured! – preternatural in her loveliness, incomprehensible in her charm! Delicate as a jasmine-petal the cheek that touched his own; deep as night, sweet as summer, the eyes that watched him. "*Heart's-thief*," her flower-lips whispered, – "*heart's-thief, how have I sought for thee! How have I found thee! Sweets I bring thee, my beloved; lips and bosom; fruit and blossom. Hast thirst? Drink from the well of mine eyes! Wouldst sacrifice? I am thine altar! Wouldst pray? I am thy God!*"

Their lips touched; her kiss seemed to change the cells of his blood to flame. For a moment Illusion triumphed; Mara prevailed!... With a shock of resolve the dreamer awoke in the night, – under the stars of the Chinese sky.

Only a mockery of sleep! But the vow had been violated, the sacred purpose unfulfilled! Humiliated, penitent, but resolved, the ascetic drew from his girdle a keen knife, and with unfaltering hands severed his eyelids from his eyes, and flung them from him. "O

Thou Perfectly Awakened!" he prayed, "thy disciple hath not been overcome save through the feebleness of the body; and his vow hath been renewed. Here shall he linger, without food or drink, until the moment of its fulfilment." And having assumed the hieratic posture, – seated himself with his lower limbs folded beneath him, and the palms of his hands upward, the right upon the left, the left resting upon the sole of his upturned foot, – he resumed his meditation.

Dawn blushed; day brightened. The sun shortened all the shadows of the land, and lengthened them again, and sank at last upon his funeral pyre of crimson-burning cloud. Night came and glittered and passed. But Mara had tempted in vain. This time the vow had been fulfilled, the holy purpose accomplished.

And again the sun arose to fill the World with laughter of light; flowers opened their hearts to him; birds sang their morning hymn of fire worship; the deep forest trembled with delight; and far upon the plain, the eaves of many-storied temples and the peaked caps of the city-towers caught aureate glory. Strong in the holiness of his accomplished vow, the Indian pilgrim arose in the morning glow. He started for amazement as he lifted his hands to his eyes. What! was everything a dream? Impossible! Yet now his eyes felt no pain; neither were they lidless; not even so much as one of their lashes was lacking. What marvel had been wrought? In vain he looked for the severed lids that he had flung upon the ground; they had mysteriously vanished. But lo! there where he had cast them two wondrous shrubs were growing, with dainty leaflets eyelid-shaped, and snowy buds just opening to the East.

Then, by virtue of the supernatural power acquired in that mighty meditation, it was given the holy missionary to know the secret of that newly created plant, – the subtle virtue of its leaves. And he named it, in the language of the nation to whom he brought the Lotos of the Good Law, "*TE*"; and he spake to it, saying: –

"Blessed be thou, sweet plant, beneficent, life-giving, formed by the spirit of virtuous resolve! Lo! the fame of thee shall yet spread unto the ends of the earth; and the perfume of thy life be borne unto the uttermost parts by all the winds of heaven! Verily, for all time to come men who drink of thy sap shall find such refreshment that weariness may not overcome them nor languor seize upon them; – neither shall they know the confusion of drowsiness, nor any desire for slumber in the hour of duty or of prayer. Blessed be thou!"

And still, as a mist of incense, as a smoke of universal sacrifice, perpetually ascends to heaven from all the lands of earth the pleasant vapor of TE, created for the refreshment of mankind by the power of a holy vow, the virtue of a pious atonement.

The God of the City

Rev. J. Macgowan

One evening in the distant past a fisherman anchored his boat near the bank of a stream which flowed close by a great city, whose walls could be seen rising grey and rugged in the near distance. The sound of life fell upon his ear and kept him from feeling lonely. Coolies, with bamboo carrying-poles on their shoulders, tired out with the heavy work of the day, hurried by afraid lest the darkness should overtake them before they reached their homes. The bearers of sedan-chairs, which they had carried for many a weary mile, strode by with quickened step and with an imperious shout at the foot passengers to get out of their way and not block up the narrow road by which they would gain the city walls before the great gates were closed for the night.

By the time that the afterglow had died out of the sky and the distant hills were blotted out of the horizon, the fisherman had finished the cooking of his evening meal. The rice sent a fragrant odour from the wide-mouthed pan in which it lay white and appetizing. A few of the very small fish he had caught in the river had been fried to a brown and savoury-looking colour, and he was just about to sit down and enjoy his supper when, happening to look round, he saw a stranger sitting in the after part of the boat.

He was greatly amazed and was about to express his surprise, when something about the appearance of this unexpected visitor kept him spell-bound. For the stranger had a fine scholarly look about him, and the air of a man belonging to a good family. He had, moreover, a benevolent, kindly face, which could not fail to win the confidence of anyone who gazed upon it.

Whilst the fisherman was wondering who his visitor was and how he had managed to come so mysteriously into the boat, the stranger said: "Allow me to explain who I am and to apologise for intruding on you without first having got your permission to do so. I am the spirit of a man who two years ago was drowned not very far from where your boat is now anchored. Many attempts have I made to inveigle others into the river, so that I might be free to leave the spot to which my miserable fate binds me until another unhappy wretch shall take my place."

The spirit of a drowned person is condemned to hover round the spot where his life was lost, until, either by accident or by the wiles of the sufferer, someone else perishes in the water and thus takes the place of the spirit, which then travels with lightning speed to the Land of Shadows.

"I was so dull this evening," continued the stranger, "that I felt impelled to come and have a chat with you for a short time. So I hope you will take my visit in good part, and allow me to sit in your boat until it is time for you to go to bed."

The fisherman, who was greatly taken with his courtly visitor, expressed his great pleasure in receiving him, and invited him to share his evening meal and to make himself quite at home for as long as he liked.

After this the solitary spirit of the river used frequently to come and spend an evening with the fisherman, until quite a friendship sprang up between them. One evening this ghostly visitor appeared with a face covered with smiles and with a glad note of joy in his voice. No sooner had he sat down than he said, "This is the last evening I shall be able to spend with you. The long weary time of waiting is now nearly at an end, and tomorrow another victim to the river will give me my release and you will see me no more."

Now, the fisherman was a deeply benevolent man, and he was most anxious to see what unhappy person was to be drowned on the morrow. About midday, as he was watching by the river-side, he saw a poor woman, weeping and sobbing, come rushing with hasty steps towards the water. Her hair was dishevelled, and her eyes red with tears, and frequent cries of sorrow burst from her lips. Straight as an arrow she made for the stream, and was just preparing to throw herself into it, when the fisherman in a loud and commanding voice told her to stop.

He then asked her what was the matter and what reason there was for her to sacrifice her life in the river.

"I am a most unhappy woman," she replied. "On my way home just now I was waylaid by a footpad, who robbed me of some money that I was taking back to my husband. This money was to pay a debt we owed to a man who threatens us with the severest penalties if we do not give it to him today. Far rather would I face death than see the sorrow which would overwhelm my husband if I told him my sorrowful story."

Having asked her how much money had been taken from her, the fisherman presented the woman with the exact amount, and soon she was proceeding with joyful footsteps in the direction of her home.

That same evening the fisherman was again visited by the spirit who had bidden him an eternal farewell the previous evening.

"What did you mean," asked the visitor, "by depriving me of the one chance I had of gaining my freedom?"

"I could not bear to see the sorrow of the poor woman," replied the fisherman, "nor to think of the tragedy to her home had she perished in the stream, and so I saved her." With eloquent lips he proceeded to describe the beauty of benevolence, and urged upon his guest the nobler course of trying to save life even at the expense of his own happiness. In the end the latter was so deeply moved that he promised never again to make any attempt to gain his liberty through another's death, even though this should mean that he would have to spend long ages of misery in the fatal stream.

Years went by, and yet for the imprisoned spirit there came no release. Cases of suicide or accidental drowning in the flowing stream ceased altogether. Many a life that would have perished was saved from destruction by mysterious warnings which came from the sullen water, and which terrified away the would-be suicides as they were about to hurl themselves into it.

At length Kwan-yin, the Goddess of Mercy, moved by the sight of such a generous sacrifice of self in order to save the souls of unfortunate people who had become weary of life, released this noble spirit from its watery prison. Moreover, as she felt convinced that such a man could safely be entrusted with the destinies of those who might appear before his tribunal, she made him a god and decreed that temples should be erected to him in every town and city of the Empire, so that all who were suffering wrong or injustice could have their causes righted at the shrine of one who had shown such profound devotion and sympathy for others in distress.

Such is the story of the God of the City.

Since he is regarded as the representative of the dread ruler of the Land of Shadows, his temple has been erected very much in the same style as the courts of the Mandarins. Its main entrance is large and imposing, and the great gates suggest those of the yamen of some high official.

Within these is an immense courtyard, paved with slabs of granite, and on each side of this there are six life-size statues of the "runners," or policemen, of the god, who stand ready to carry out his decisions, and to pursue and capture by invisible and mysterious processes those whom he has condemned as guilty. The faces of these figures are distorted by passion, and their attitudes are such as men might be conceived to assume in apprehending some notorious criminal whom Yam-lo had ordered to be seized.

At the end of this spacious courtyard is the shrine of the god, but he is so hidden behind a yellow curtain that it is impossible to catch a glimpse of his image. In front of him are statues of his two secretaries, who, with huge pens in their hands, stand ready day and night to take down the petitions and indictments laid before the god by those who are in sorrow or who are suffering wrong.

One afternoon the peace of such a temple was suddenly disturbed by a noisy clamour outside, and the sound of hurried footsteps as of a crowd rushing through the main gates. Two men advanced with rapid, excited strides straight past the demon policeman at the door, who seemed to scowl with added ferocity as they gazed at the actors in a scene with which they would have much to do by-and-by.

The two men were quite young, a little over twenty; and behind them followed a string of idlers and loafers and street arabs, who seem to spring up like magic when anything unusual happens. One of the young men was slightly ahead of the crowd. His face was flushed and his black eyes sparkled with excitement, whilst in his left hand he carried a large white cock. He was the complainant, and his purpose in coming to the temple was to appeal to the god to vindicate his honour.

He took his stand in front of the idol, and the secretaries, with pens in their hands, seemed to put on a strained look of attention as the young fellow produced a roll of paper and began to read the statement he had drawn up. It was diffuse and wordy, as most of such documents are, but the main facts were quite plain.

The two young men were assistants in a shop in the city. Some little time before, the master of the shop, without telling either of them, concealed in a chosen place a sum of one hundred dollars, which he wished to have in readiness in order to pay for certain goods he had purchased. The previous day, when he went to get the money on the presentation of the bill, he found to his horror that it had disappeared. He had told no one of this secret hoard, not even his wife; and therefore he felt convinced that in some way or other one of his two assistants had discovered his hiding-place. For some reason his suspicions became aroused against the man who was now detailing his grievances, and who was appealing to the god to set in motion all the tremendous forces at his command, not only to proclaim his innocence but also to bring condign punishment on the real culprit.

The scene was a weird and fascinating one, and became most exciting as the young man neared the end of his appeal. He called upon the god to hurl all the pains and penalties in his unseen armoury against the man who had really stolen the money.

"Let his life be one long torture," he cried with uplifted hands. "May every enterprise in which he engages end in disaster; may his father and mother die, and let him be left desolate; may a subtle and incurable disease lay its grip upon him; may misfortune pursue him in every shape and form; may he become a beggar with ulcered legs and sit on the roadside and beseech the passers-by, in sunshine and in storm, for a few cash that will just help to keep him alive; may he never have a son to perpetuate his name or to make offerings to his spirit in the Land of Shadows; may madness seize upon him so that his reason shall fly and he shall be a source of terror to his fellow-men; and finally, may a tragic and horrible death bring his life to a sudden end, even as I bring to an end the life of this white cock that I have brought with me."

As he uttered these last words he grasped a chopper, and with one sharp and vicious blow cut off the head of the struggling animal, which wildly fluttered its wings in the agonies of death, whilst its life-blood poured out in a stream on the ground.

He then took his petition, and advancing close up to the secretaries, who seemed for the moment to gaze down upon him with a look of sympathy on their faces, he set fire to it and burned it to ashes. In this way it passed into the hands of the god, who would speedily set in motion unseen machinery to bring down upon the head of the guilty one the judgments which had just been invoked.

The sympathies of the crowd were with the man who had sworn a solemn oath that he was innocent of the theft. The other young fellow, who had said little or nothing during the proceedings, was believed to be the real culprit, but there was no evidence upon which he could be convicted. The god knew, however, and every one was satisfied that in due time punishment would descend upon the transgressor.

In a few minutes the temple resumed its normal aspect, for with the disappearance of the two principal actors in the scene, the idlers from the street slowly dispersed, each one loudly expressing his opinion as to the merits of the question in dispute. With the dissolving of the crowd, it would have seemed to the casual observer that no further proceedings were to be taken in the matter. The god's face wore its usually placid look, unmoved by the shifting panorama of human life which ebbed and flowed in front of him from morning till night. The ghastly-looking policemen, with their grinning visages and ferocious scowls and contorted bodies, remained in the same unchanging postures by the main entrance.

A week or two had gone by since the appeal had been made to the god, when those who were following the case and were looking out for some grim evidence that the god was at work in bringing retribution on the man whom everyone suspected of being the thief, were startled by a heartrending catastrophe.

This man had a sister, just bursting into womanhood, who was the very light of her home. Her merry laugh could be heard throughout the day, so that sadness could not long abide in the same house. Her face, too, seemed to have been formed to match her sunny smiles, and was a constant inspiration that never failed to give those who looked upon it a brighter view of life.

One morning she went down to the river-bank with several of her neighbours to do the household washing. The stream was strong and rapid in the centre, but the place which these women had selected for their work had always been considered perfectly safe, for it was outside the current and no accident had ever happened there.

They had finished all that they had purposed to do, and were ascending the bank to return home, when they heard an agonized cry and turning swiftly round they perceived that this young girl had stumbled and fallen into the river. They were so horrified at the accident that they lost all presence of mind and allowed the fast-flowing stream to get a grip of her and drag her into the current. When help at last came, her body could just be seen floating on the troubled waters, and before a boat could be launched it had disappeared in the waves of the sea which tumbled and roared about a quarter of a mile further down.

This terrible disaster, which brought unutterable gloom and sorrow upon the home, was unquestionably the work of the god. With bated breath people talked of the tragic end of this beautiful girl, who had won her way into the hearts of all who knew her; but they recognized that her death had been caused by no mere accident, but by the mysterious power of the invisible forces which are always at work to bring punishment upon those who have violated the Righteousness of Heaven.

About a month after this calamity, the monsoon rains began to fall. The clouds gathered in dense masses upon the neighbouring hills, and poured down such copious showers that the mountain streams were turned into roaring avalanches, tearing their way down to the sea with an impetuosity that nothing could resist.

One of these streams, which used to run by the side of the ancestral property of the family of the man who was believed to have stolen the hundred dollars, overflowed its banks and rushing along with mad and headlong speed it swept away their fields, so that when the rains ceased not a trace of them was to be found, but only sand and gravel, from which no crop could ever be gathered in the future. The consequence was that the family was utterly ruined.

This second disaster falling on the homestead was a clear indication to everyone who knew the story of the stolen money that the god was still at work in bringing retribution on the sinner. The fact that other farms had come out of the flood undamaged was proof positive of this.

From this time, too, the young man who really was the culprit began to be troubled in his mind because of the calamities that had fallen on his family. The death of his sister by drowning, and the utter destruction of his home by the flood, which had injured no other farmer in the neighbourhood, were plain indications that the curses which his falsely accused fellow-assistant had prayed the god to bring down on the head of the guilty party were indeed coming fast and thick upon him.

A dread of coming evil took possession of him, and this so preyed upon his mind that he began to lose his reason. He would go about muttering to himself, and declaring that he saw devils. These fits grew upon him, until at last he became raving mad, and had to be seized and bound with ropes to prevent him doing injury to himself or to others. At times he suffered from violent spasms of mania, while at others, again, though undoubtedly insane, he was quiet and subdued. He would then talk incessantly to himself, and bemoan the sad fact that the dread God of the City was sending evil spirits to torment him because he had purloined the hundred dollars belonging to his master.

By-and-by these random confessions attracted the attention of his heart-broken father, who used to sit watching by his side, and they became so frequent and so circumstantial, describing even where the money had been hidden, that at last he determined to examine into the matter. Investigations were made, and the whole sum was found in the very place which the young man had mentioned in his delirium, and was at once returned to the shopkeeper.

As the money had been given back, and the father and mother were dependent upon their only son to provide for them in their old age, the man who had entered the accusation before the god was entreated again to appear before him in his temple and withdraw the charges that he had previously made against his fellow-assistant. Only in this formal and legal way could the god have official knowledge of the fact that reparation had been made for the offence which had been committed; and if this were not done he would still continue to send sorrow after sorrow until the whole family were involved in absolute ruin or death.

Out of pity for the old couple the other young man consented to take the necessary steps. He accordingly presented a petition to the god, stating that he wished to withdraw the accusation which he had made against a certain man who had been suspected of theft. The stolen money had been returned to its owner, and the god was now besought to stay all further proceedings and forgive the culprit for the wrong he had done.

It was evident that this petition was granted, for at once the young man began to recover, and soon all signs of madness left him. He had, however, learned a lesson which he never forgot; and as long as he lived he never committed another offence such as the theft which had brought such serious consequences upon himself and his family.

The Tragedy of the Yin Family

Rev. J. Macgowan

In a certain district in one of the central provinces of China, there lived a man of the name of Yin. He was possessed of considerable property, with a great ambition to become distinguished in life. The one desire of his heart, which seemed to master every other, was that his family should become an aristocratic one.

So far as he knew, none of his immediate predecessors had ever been a conspicuous scholar, or had gained any honour in the great triennial examinations. The result was that his family was a plebeian one, from which no mandarin had ever sprung. In what way, then, could he secure that the fame and dignities, which had come to some of the clans in the region in which he lived, should descend upon his home and upon his grandsons?

He was a rich man, it is true, but he was entirely illiterate, and all his money had been made in trade. As a lad his education had been neglected, for his early life had been spent in the mere struggle for existence. He had been more than successful, but the honours of the student never could be his, and never could he act as one of the officials of the Empire. It occurred to him, however, that though it was impossible that he himself should ever be classed amongst the great scholars of China, his sons and grandsons might be so honoured. In that case the glory of their success would be reflected upon him, and men would talk of him as the head of a family which had become distinguished for scholarship and high dignities in the State.

He finally came to the conclusion that the most effectual way of accomplishing this was to secure a lucky burying-ground in which he could lay the bodies of his father and his grandfather, who had departed this life some years before. The universal belief that in some mysterious way the dead have the power of showering down wealth and honours and prosperity upon the surviving members of their families, was held most tenaciously by Mr. Yin. This belief pointed out to him how he could emerge from the common and dreary road along which his ancestors had travelled, into the one where royal favours and official distinction would mark out his posterity in the future.

As he had retired from business, he was able to spend nearly the whole of his time in searching the country for the spots where certain unseen forces are supposed to collect with such dominant and overmastering power that the body of any person laid to rest amongst them will be found to dispense untold riches and dignities upon his nearest relatives. Accordingly, attended by a professor of the art, whose study of this intricate science enable him to detect at a glance the places which fulfilled the required conditions, Yin made frequent excursions in the regions around his home.

The valleys through which the streams ran, and where the sound of the running waters could be heard day and night as they sang their way to the sea, were all explored. Wherever water and hills were to be found in a happy conjunction, there these two men were to be seen peering over the ground, and with the aid of a compass which the professor carried with him in a cloth bag, marking whether the lines upon which they ran indicated that the mysterious Dragon had his residence beneath.

Innumerable places were carefully examined, and whilst some of them would have been admirably suited for a person of ordinary ambition, they did not satisfy the large expectations for the future which were cherished by Mr. Yin. The rising knolls and winding streams and far-off views of hills lying in the mist-like distance, showed perhaps that moderate prosperity would be the lot of those whose kindred might be buried there; but there were no signs of preëminence in scholarship, or of mandarins riding on horseback or in sedan-chairs, with great retinues attending them, as they proceeded in haughty dignity through the streets of the city in which they lived as rulers. Such places were therefore rejected as unsuitable.

Days and months went by in this search for a spot with which the fortunes of the Yin family were to be linked for many generations yet to come; but every place failed in some one or two particulars which would have marred the splendid prospect that ambition had pictured before the vision of this wealthy man.

At last, as they were sauntering along one day with eyes keen and alert, they stayed for a moment to rest on the top of a low hill which they had just ascended. Hardly had they cast a rapid glance over the beautiful scenery that lay stretched out before them, before the professor, with flashing eyes and unusual enthusiasm, exclaimed with excitement in his voice, "See! this is the very place we have been looking for all these days!

"No more suitable spot could have been found in the whole of China than this. We stand, as it were, in the centre of a great amphitheatre in which have been gathered the finest forces of Fung-Shuy. Behind us the hill rises in a graceful semi-circular form to shield the spot, where the dead shall lie buried, from the northern blasts, and from the fierce and malignant spirits that come flying on the wings of the great gales which blow with the touch of the ice and snow in them.

"On the plain in front of us, scattered over its surface, are gentle risings showing where the Dragon lies reposing, waiting to dispense its favours to all who come within its magic influence. And then, behold how the river winds in and out, seemingly unwilling to leave a place where unseen influences are at work to enrich the homes and gladden the hearts of the men and women of this region. See how it flows out with a hasty rush towards the sea beyond, and how it threads its way round yonder cape and is lost to view. Then mark again how it would seem as though some force it could not control had swung it round in its course, for it winds back upon the plain with gleaming eyes and joyous looks as if it were glad to return once more towards the distant mountains from whence it took its rise.

"The meaning of all this is," he continued, "that the prosperity, which the Dragon will bestow upon the living through the ministry of the dead lying within its domain, shall not soon pass away, but like the river that we see meandering before us, shall stay and comfort for many a long year those to whom it has been granted.

"That riches will come is certain, and official rank, and honours as well; for cast your eyes upon yonder ridge gleaming in the morning sun, and note the figure which rises up distinct and well-defined from its summit. It is simply a rock, it is true, but mark well its contour and you will note how the outline grows upon your vision until it assumes the form of a mandarin in full official robes standing with his face towards us.

"I would strongly advise you," concluded the professor, "to secure this plot of land on which we stand, whatever it may cost you, for every ambition that has ever filled your soul shall in time be satisfied by the wealth and honours which not only the Dragon but all his attendant spirits shall combine to pour into your home."

Yin was entranced with the prospect which was pictured before him in such glowing language by the man at his side, and he heartily agreed with the proposal that he should stay his search and purchase the ground on which they were standing as a cemetery for his family.

Just at this moment a man came sauntering along to see what these two strangers were doing in this out-of-the-way place, to which no road ran and from which no by-paths led to the villages beyond.

"Can you tell me, my man," asked Yin, "to whom this piece of land belongs?"

"Yes, I can easily do that," he replied. "Do you see that dilapidated-looking cottage down by the riverside? Well, it is occupied by a man named Lin, together with his wife and a daughter about nineteen years of age. They are exceedingly poor, as you can see by their house. The only property Lin possesses is this plot of ground, which has come down to him from his forefathers, and which he hopes one day to dispose of to some well-to-do person as a burying-ground that may bring him good luck."

"I am very willing to buy the land, if I can only get it at a reasonable price," replied Yin, "and I shall be glad if you will consent to act as middleman and negotiate the matter for me. You might go at once and see Lin, and find out what are the terms upon which he is willing to transfer the property to me."

On the morrow the middle-man returned and reported to Yin that Lin would on no consideration consent to let him have the ground. "The fact is," he continued, "that Lin has a settled purpose in his mind with which this particular plot of land has a good deal to do. He and his wife are getting on in years, and when the daughter is married off he is afraid that his branch of the family will become extinct; so he plans to get a husband for her who will come into the home and act the part of a son as well as that of son-in-law."

So determined, however, was Yin to gain possession of this particular piece of land that after considerable negotiations during which it seemed as though the old father would never be moved from his settled purpose, it was finally agreed that his daughter should be married to Yin's eldest son, Shung, and that her father and mother should remove to rooms in Yin's family mansion, where they should be maintained by him in ease and comfort as long as they lived. Had Yin been a large-hearted and generous person, this plan would have been an ideal one, but seeing that he was by nature a stingy, money-grubbing individual, it was attended with the most tragic results.

No sooner had the deeds of the coveted plot of ground been passed over to him than Yin had the body of his father, who had been buried in a place far removed from the influence of the Dragon, transferred to this new location, where he would be in touch with the higher spirits of the Underworld. Here, also, he could catch the eye of the mandarin, who day and night would have his face turned towards him, and who from the very fact of the sympathy that would grow up between them, must in time give him the mysterious power of turning his grandsons, and their sons after them, into scholars, who would obtain high positions in the service of the State.

In the meanwhile preparations were being made for the marriage of the young maiden of low degree to a man in a much higher social position than she could ever have aspired to in the ordinary course of events. Pearl was a sweet, comely-looking damsel, who would have made a model wife to one of her own station in life, but who was utterly unsuited for the new dignity which would be thrust upon her as soon as she crossed the threshold of the wealthy family of Yin. She was simply a peasant girl, without education and without refinement. Her days had been passed amidst scenes of poverty, and though she was a thoroughly good girl, with the high ideals that the commonest people in China everywhere have, her proper position was after all amongst the kind of people with whom she had lived all her life.

Her father and mother had indeed all along been doubtful about the propriety of marrying their daughter into a family so much above them as the Yins, and for a long time they had stood out against all the arguments in favour of it. Finally, overborne by the impetuosity of Yin, and dazzled with the prospects which such an alliance offered not only to the girl herself but also to themselves by the agreement to keep them in comfort for the rest of their lives, they had given an unwilling consent.

In order that Pearl should suffer as little disgrace as possible when she appeared amongst her new relations, her father sold all his available belongings in order to procure suitable wedding-garments for her. His idea, however, of the fitness of things had been gathered from the humble surroundings in which he had lived all his days, and the silks and satins and expensive jewellery that adorn the brides of the wealthy had never come within the vision of his dreams. Still Pearl was a pretty girl, and with her piercing black eyes which always seemed to be suffused with laughter, and with a smile which looked like a flash from a summer sky, she needed but little adornment, and would have won the heart of any man who had the soul to appreciate a true woman when he saw one.

At last the day came, hurried on by the eager desire of Yin to have the whole thing settled, when the humble home was to be given up and its inmates transferred to the rich house that lay just over a neighbouring hill.

A magnificent bridal chair, whose brilliant crimson colour made it a conspicuous object on the grey landscape, wound its way towards the cottage where the bride was attired all ready to step into it the moment it appeared at the door.

In front of it there marched a band, making the country-side resound with weird notes which seemed to fly on the air with defiance in their tones, and to send their echoes mounting to the tops of the hills and piercing down into the silent valleys. There were also crowds of retainers and dependants of the wealthy man. These were dressed in semi-official robes, and flocked along with smiling faces and joyous shouts. The occasion was a festal one, and visions of rare dishes and of generous feasting, kept up for several days, filled the minds of the happy procession as it went to meet the bride.

The return of the party was still more boisterous in its merriment. The members of the band seemed inspired by the occasion and sent forth lusty strains, whilst the instruments, as if aware how much depended upon them, responded to the efforts of the performers and filled the air with joyful notes.

A distinguished company had assembled to receive the bride, as she was led by her husband from the crimson chair and advanced with timid steps and faltering heart into the room that had been prepared for her reception. As she entered the house something in the air struck a chill into her heart and caused the hopes of happiness, which she had been cherishing, to die an almost instant death.

Shung, her husband, was a man of ignoble mind, and had always objected to marrying a woman so far beneath him. The sight of his bride, with her rustic air, and the ill-made commonplace-looking clothes in which she was dressed, made his face burn with shame, for he knew that a sneer was lurking on the face of everyone who had gathered to have a look at her.

A profound feeling of hatred entered his narrow soul, and as the days went by the one purpose of his life was to humiliate this sweet-tempered woman, who had been sacrificed simply to further the ambitious schemes of her designing father-in-law, Mr. Yin. For a few weeks he simply ignored her, but by degrees he treated her so cruelly that many a time she had serious thoughts of putting an end to her life. It soon turned out that a systematic attempt was being made by both father and son to get rid of the whole family.

The old father and mother, whom Yin had agreed to provide for during the rest of their lives, found things so intolerable that they voluntarily left the miserable quarters assigned to them and returned to their empty cottage. Every stick of furniture had been sold in order to buy their daughter's wedding garments, so that when they reached their old home they found absolutely nothing in it. With a few bundles of straw they made up a bed on the floor, but there was no food to eat, and not a single thing to comfort them in this their hour of darkest misery.

Sorrow for their daughter, and disappointment and anguish of heart at the thought of how they had been tricked and cheated by Mr. Yin in order that he might gain possession of their bit of land, so told upon their spirits that they both fell ill of a low fever, which laid them prostrate on their bed of straw. As they lived remote from other people, for some time no one knew that they were sick. Days went by without anyone visiting them, and when at last one kindly-hearted farmer came to make enquiries, he found to his horror that both husband and wife lay dead, side by side, in their miserable cabin.

The news of their death produced the greatest pleasure in the mind of the wretched man who was really the cause of it. He was now freed from the compact compelling him to provide for them during their life, and so there would be an actual saving of the money which he would have had to spend in providing them with food and clothing. A cruel, wintry smile lingered on his hard face for several days after the poor old couple had been lain to rest on the hillside near their cottage, and this was the only look of mourning his features ever assumed.

From this time Pearl's life became more and more of a burden to her. Love, the one element which would have filled her heart with happiness, was the one thing that was never offered her. Instead of affection there were cruel, cutting words and scornful looks and heavy blows – all these were plentifully bestowed upon her by the soulless man who was called her husband.

At length, to show his utter contempt and abhorrence of her, he arranged with the connivance of his father to bring a concubine into his home. This lady came from a comparatively good family, and was induced to take this secondary position because of the large sum of money that was paid to her father for her. The misery of Pearl was only intensified by her appearance on the scene. Following the lead of her husband, and jealous of the higher position in the family that the law gave her rival, she took every means that a spiteful woman could devise to make her life still more miserable.

The death of her parents had filled Pearl's heart with such intense grief and sorrow that life had lost all its charm for her. She saw, moreover, from the sordid rejoicing that was openly made at their tragic end, that the Yins would never be satisfied until she too had followed them into the Land of Shadows. She would therefore anticipate the cruel purposes of her husband and his father, and so deliver herself from a persecution that would only cease with her death. So one midnight, when all the rest of the family were asleep, and nothing was heard outside but the moaning of the wind which seemed as though it was preparing to sing a requiem over her, she put an end to all her earthly troubles by hanging herself in her own room.

When the body was found next day, suspended from a hook in one of the beams, a great cry of delight was uttered by Yin and his son. Without any violence on their part they had been set free from their alliance with this low-class family, and at a very small cost they had obtained firm possession of the land which was to enrich and ennoble their descendants.

And so whilst the poor girl lay dead, driven to an untimely end by spirits more fierce and malignant than any that were supposed to be flying with hatred in their hearts in the air around, smiles and laughter and noisy congratulations were indulged in by the living ghouls whose persecution had made this sweet-tempered woman's life unbearable.

But retribution was at hand. Heaven moves slowly in the punishment of the wicked, but its footsteps are sure and they travel irresistibly along the road that leads to vengeance on the wrongdoer.

One dark night, when the sky was overcast and neither moon nor stars were to be seen, and a storm of unusual violence was filling the air with a tumult of fierce and angry meanings, a weird and gruesome scene was enacted at the grave where the father of Yin had been buried. Hideous sounds of wailing and shrieking could be heard, as though all the demons of the infernal regions had assembled there to hold a night of carnival. Louder than the storm, the cries penetrated through the shrillest blasts, and people in their homes far away were wakened out of their sleep by the unearthly yells which froze their blood with terror. At last a thunderbolt rolled from the darkened heavens, louder than ever mortal man had heard. The lightnings flashed, and concentrating all their force upon the grave just where the coffin lay, they tore up a huge chasm in the earth, and gripping the coffin within their fiery fingers, they tossed it with disdain upon a hillside a mile away.

After a long search, Yin discovered it next day in the lonely spot where it had been cast, and was returning to make arrangements for its interment, when in a lonely part of the road two unearthly figures suddenly rose up before him. These, to his horror, he recognized as the spirits of Pearl's father and mother who had practically been done to death by him, and whom Yam-lo had allowed to revisit the earth in order to plague the man who was the author of their destruction. So terrified was Yin at their wild and threatening aspect, that he fell to the ground in a swoon, and thus he was found, hours afterwards, by his son, who had come out in search of him.

For several days he was tended with the greatest care, and the most famous physicians were called in to prescribe for him. He never rallied, however, and there was always a vague and haunted look in his eyes, as though he saw some terrible vision which frightened away his reasoning powers and prevented him from regaining consciousness. In this condition he died, without a look of recognition for those he loved, and without a word of explanation as to the cause of this tragic conclusion of a life that was still in its prime.

The eldest son was now master of his father's wealth; but instead of learning a lesson from the terrible judgment which had fallen on his home because of the injustice and wrong that had been committed on an innocent family, he only became more hard-hearted in his treatment of those who were within his power. He never dreamed of making any reparation for the acts of cruelty by which he had driven his wife to hang herself in order to escape his tyranny. But the steps of Fate were still moving on towards him. Leaden-footed they might be and slow, but with unerring certainty they were travelling steadily on to carry out the vengeance of the gods.

By-and-by the room in which Pearl had died became haunted. Her spectral figure could be seen in the gloaming, flitting about and peering out of the door with a look of agony on her face. Sometimes she would be seen in the early dawn, restless and agitated, as though she had been wandering up and down the whole night; and again she would flit about in the moonlight and creep into the shadow of the houses, but always with a ghost of the old look that had made her face so winning and so charming when she was alive.

When it was realized that it was her spirit which was haunting the house, the greatest alarm and terror were evinced by every one in it. There is nothing more terrible than the appearance of the spirits of those who have been wronged, for they always come with some vengeful purpose. No matter how loving the persons themselves may have been in life, with death their whole nature changes and they are filled with the most passionate desire to inflict injury and especially death upon the object of their hatred.

The course of ill-usage which her husband Shung had cruelly adopted in order to drive Pearl to commit suicide was known to every one, and that she should now appear to wreak vengeance on him was not considered at all wonderful; but still every one was mortally afraid lest they should become involved in the punishment that was sure to be meted out.

As the ghost continued to linger about and showed no signs of disappearing, Shung was at last seized with apprehension lest some calamity was about to fall upon his house. In order to protect himself from any unexpected attack from the spirit that wandered and fluttered about in the darkest and most retired rooms in his home, he provided himself with a sword which he had ground down to a very sharp edge and which he carried in his hand ready uplifted to lunge at Pearl should she dare to attack him.

One evening, unaware that his concubine was sitting in a certain room on which the shadows had thickly fallen, he was entering it for some purpose, when the spirit of his late wife gripped his hand with an overmastering force which he felt himself unable to resist, and forced him to strike repeated blows against the poor defenceless woman. Not more than a dozen of these had been given before she was lying senseless on the ground, breathing out her life from the gaping wounds through which her life-blood was flowing in streams.

When the grip of the ghost had relaxed its hold upon him and he felt himself free to look at what he had done, Shung was horrified beyond measure as he gazed with staring eyes upon the dreadful sight before him, and realized the judgment that had come upon him for the wrongs he had done to Pearl and her family.

As soon as the news of the murder of the woman was carried to her father, he entered a complaint before the nearest mandarin, who issued a warrant for Shung's apprehension. At his trial he attempted to defend himself by declaring that it was not he who had killed his concubine, but an evil spirit which had caught hold of his arm and had directed the blows that had caused her death.

The magistrate smiled at this extraordinary defence, and said that Shung must consider him a great fool if he thought for a moment that he would be willing to accept such a ridiculous excuse for the dreadful crime he had committed.

As Shung was a wealthy man and had the means of bribing the under-officials in the yamen, his case was remanded in order to see how much money could be squeezed out of him before the final sentence was given. The murder – apparently without reason or provocation – of a woman who had been a member of a prominent family in society, produced a widespread feeling of indignation, and public opinion was strong in condemnation of Shung. Every one felt that there ought to be exemplary punishment in his case; otherwise any man who had only money enough might be able to defy all the great principles established by Heaven for the government of society and for the prevention of crime.

In order to make it easy for Shung whilst he was in prison, his mother had to spend large sums in bribing every one connected with the yamen. Never before had such an opportunity for reaping a golden harvest been presented to the avaricious minions entrusted by the Emperor with the administration of justice amongst his subjects. In her anxiety for her son the poor woman sold field after field to find funds wherewith to meet the demands of these greedy officials. Dark hints had simply to be thrown out by some of these that Shung was in danger of his life, and fresh sales would be made to bribe the mandarin to be lenient in his judgment of him.

At length the property had all been disposed of, and when it was known that no further money could be obtained, sentence was given that Shung should be imprisoned for life. This was a cruel blow to his mother, who had all along hoped that he might be released. Full of sorrow and absolutely penniless in a few weeks she died of a broken heart, whilst the son, seeing nothing but a hopeless imprisonment before him, committed suicide and thus ended his worthless life.

This tragic extinction of a family, which only a short year before was in the highest state of prosperity, was accepted by every one who heard the story as a just and righteous punishment from Heaven. For Heaven is so careful of human life that any one who destroys it comes under the inevitable law that he too shall in his turn be crushed under the wheels of avenging justice.

Kwang-Jui and the God of River

Rev. J. Macgowan

China is a land where the great masses of the people have to toil and struggle incessantly in order to obtain even the bare necessities of daily existence. Unnumbered multitudes never enjoy a sufficiency of food, but have to be contented with whatever Heaven may send them; and profoundly thankful they are when they can be sure of two meals a day to stave off the pangs of hunger from themselves and their children.

How many there are who cannot by the severest toil obtain even these two meals is evident from the organized beggar communities, which are to be found in connection with every great city in the Empire, and from the vast numbers of tramps, who wander over the country on the highways and byways with pale and sodden faces and with garments nearly falling to pieces, picking up a scanty livelihood from the benevolent as they pass from village to village.

Whatever may be their inmost thoughts, the Chinese bear their terrible hardships and privations with a splendid heroism, with little complaining, with no widespread outbreaks of robbery, and with no pillaging of rice-shops and public granaries by organized mobs driven mad by hunger.

There is one beautiful feature about the Chinese that has been an important factor in steadying the nation. They are imbued with at least one great ideal, which touches their common life in every direction. Every man in the Empire, rich or poor, learned or unlearned, has a profound respect for what he calls Tien-Li, or Divine Righteousness. By this the Chinese judge all actions. It is the standard by which Kings and Princes and common people direct their conduct, whether in the highest affairs of state, or in the ordinary engagements of common every-day life.

In addition to this, the minds of the Chinese are filled with romance and poetry, so that to them the invisible world is peopled with fairies and all kinds of spirits, both good and bad, the former relieving in mysterious ways the dull greyness that sorrow and disaster often shed upon the lives of men.

The story of Kwang-Jui is a remarkable evidence of the unbounded faith which the Chinese have in the intervention of these mysterious beings to deliver men from calamities which would otherwise prove fatal to them.

When we first meet with Kwang-Jui, he is living with his widowed mother in a retired part of the country. His father had been dead for some time, and Kwang-Jui was now the only one upon whom the fortunes of the home could be built. He was a very studious lad, and was possessed of remarkable abilities, the result being that he successfully passed the various Imperial Examinations, even the final one in the capital, where the Sovereign himself presided as examiner.

After this last examination, as the men were waiting outside the Hall for the names of those who had satisfied the Emperor to be read out a considerable crowd had collected. Most of these people had come from mere curiosity to see the Imperial Edict, and to discover who the scholar was that stood first on the list. The excitement was intense, and speculation ran rife as to which of the candidates, who had come from almost every province in the Empire, was going to obtain the place of honour which was the dream and the ambition of every scholar in the land.

At last every breath was hushed, and every voice stilled in silence, as one of the high officials of the Palace, attended by an imposing retinue, came out of the great central doors, which had been flung wide open at his approach. In a clear voice he began to read the list. It was headed by the name of Kwang-Jui.

At this precise moment occurred an incident which was destined to change the whole current of Kwang-Jui's career. As he was standing overcome with emotion in consequence of the supreme honour which had been conferred upon him by the Emperor's Edict, a small round ball, beautifully embroidered, was thrown from an upper window of a house across the way, and struck him on the shoulder.

It may here be explained that it was a custom in the early days of the history of China to allow any young maiden who was reluctant to have her husband chosen for her by her parents, to make use of what was called "The throwing of the embroidered ball" in order to discover the man whom the gods intended her to marry. This ball was made of some soft material, wrapped round with a piece of red silk which was covered with variegated figures, worked by the damsel's own hands and emblematic of the love by which the hearts of husband and wife are bound indissolubly to each other. It was firmly believed by every maiden of this romantic type that the man who was struck by the ball from her fair hands was the one whom Heaven had selected as her husband; and no parent would ever dream of refusing to accept a choice made in this way.

Whilst Kwang-Jui was gazing in amused wonder at the symbol which he understood so well, a messenger from the house from which it had been thrown requested him in respectful tones to accompany him to his master, who desired to discuss with him a most important subject.

As Kwang-Jui entered the house, he discovered to his astonishment that it belonged to the Prime Minister, who received him with the utmost cordiality, and after a long conversation declared that he was prepared to submit to the will of the gods, and to accept him as his son-in-law. Kwang-Jui was of course in raptures at the brilliant prospects which were suddenly opening up before him. The day, indeed, was a red-letter one – an omen, he hoped, that fate was preparing to pour down upon him good fortune in the future. In one brief day he had been hailed as the most distinguished scholar in the Empire, and he had also been acknowledged as the son-in-law of the Empire's greatest official, who had the power of placing him in high positions where he could secure not only honours but also wealth sufficient to drive poverty away for ever from his home.

As there was no reason for delay, the hand of the beautiful daughter who had thrown the embroidered ball, and who was delighted that Heaven had chosen for her such a brilliant husband, was bestowed upon him by her parents. Times of great rejoicing succeeded, and when Kwang-Jui thought of the quiet and uninteresting days when he was still unknown to fame, and contrasted them with his present life, it seemed to him as though he were living in fairy-land. His wildest dreams in the past had never conjured up anything so grand as the life he was now leading. In one bound he had leaped from comparative poverty to fame and riches.

After a time, through the influence of his father-in-law, and with the hearty consent of the Emperor, who remembered what a brilliant student he had been, Kwang-Jui was appointed to be Prefect of an important district in the centre of China.

Taking his bride with him, he first of all proceeded to his old home, where his mother was waiting with great anxiety to welcome her now famous son. The old lady felt rather nervous at meeting her new daughter-in-law, seeing that the latter came from a family which was far higher in rank and far more distinguished than any in her own clan. As it was very necessary that Kwang-Jui should take up his office as Prefect without any undue delay, he and his mother and his bride set out in the course of a few days on the long journey to the distant Prefecture, where their lives were destined to be marred by sorrow and disaster.

They had travelled the greater part of the way, and had reached a country market-town that lay on their route, when Kwang-Jui's mother, worn out with the toilsome journey, fell suddenly ill. The doctor who was called in shook his head and pronounced that she was suffering from a very serious complaint, which, whilst not necessarily fatal, would necessitate a complete rest for at least two or three months. Any further travelling must therefore be abandoned for the present, as it might be attended with the most serious consequences to the old lady.

Both husband and wife were greatly distressed at the unlucky accident which placed them in such an awkward position at this wayside inn. They were truly grieved at the serious sickness of their mother, but they were still more puzzled as to what course they should pursue in these most trying circumstances. The Imperial Rescript appointing Kwang-Jui to his office as Prefect commanded him to take up his post on a certain definite date. To delay until his mother would again be able to endure the fatigues of travel was out of the question, as disobedience to the Emperor's orders would be attended by his grave displeasure. Eventually his mother suggested that he and his wife should go on ahead, and that after taking up the duties of his office he should then delegate them for a time to his subordinates and return to take her home.

This advice Kwang-Jui decided to carry out; though with great reluctance, as he was most unwilling to abandon his mother to the care of strangers. He accordingly made all the arrangements he possibly could for her comfort whilst they were parted from each other; he had servants engaged to attend upon her, and he left sufficient money with her to meet all her expenses during his absence.

With a mind full of consideration for his mother, and wishing to show how anxious he was to give her pleasure, he went out into the market of the town to see if he could buy a certain kind of fish of which she was passionately fond. He had hardly got outside the courtyard of the inn, when he met a fisherman with a very fine specimen of the very fish that he wished to purchase.

As he was discussing the price with the man, a certain something about the fish arrested his attention. There was a peculiar look in its eyes that seemed full of pathos and entreaty. Its gaze was concentrated upon him, so human-like and with such intensity, that he instinctively felt it was pleading with him to do something to deliver it from a great disaster. This made him look at it more carefully, and to his astonishment the liquid eyes of the fish were still fixed upon him with a passionate regard that made him quiver with excitement.

"Fisherman," he said, "I want to buy this fish, and here is the price that you ask for it. I have but one stipulation to make, and that is that you take it to the river from which you caught it, and set it free to swim away wherever it pleases. Remember that if you fail to carry out this part of the bargain, great sorrow will come upon you and your home."

Little did either of them dream that the fish was the presiding God of the River, who for purposes of his own had transformed himself into this form, and who, while swimming up and down the stream had been caught in the net of the fisherman.

After travelling for some hours Kwang-Jui and his wife came to the bank of a considerable river, where they hired a large boat to convey them to their destination.

The boatman they engaged was a man of very low character. He had originally been a scholar and of good family, but, utterly depraved and immoral, he had gradually sunk lower and lower in society, until at last he had been compelled to fly from his home to a distant province, and there to engage in his present occupation in order to earn his living. The large amount of property which Kwang-Jui had with him seemed to arouse the worst passions in this man, and while the boat was being carried along by a fair wind and a flowing tide, he planned in his mind how he was to become the possessor of it. By the time that they reached the place where they were to anchor for the night, he had already decided what measures he should adopt.

A little after midnight, accordingly, he crept stealthily towards the place where Kwang-Jui was sleeping, stabbed him to the heart and threw his body into the fast-flowing river. He next threatened the wife that if she dared to utter a sound, he would murder her also and send her to join her husband in the Land of Shadows. Paralyzed with terror, she remained speechless, only a stifled sob and groan now and again breaking from her agonized heart. Her first serious idea was to commit suicide, and she was preparing to fling herself into the water that gurgled along the sides of the boat, when she was restrained by the thought that if she destroyed herself, she would never be able to avenge her husband's death or bring punishment upon the villain who had just murdered him.

It was not mere robbery, however, that was in the mind of the man who had committed this great crime. He had bigger ideas than that. He had noticed that in personal appearance he very much resembled his victim, so he determined to carry out the daring project of passing himself off as Kwang-Jui, the mandarin whom the Emperor had despatched to take up the appointment of Prefect.

Having threatened the widow that instant death would be her portion if she breathed a word to anyone about the true state of the case, and having arrayed himself in the official robes of the man whom he had stabbed to death, the boatman appeared at the yamen, where he presented the Imperial credentials and was duly installed in his office. It never entered his mind that it was not cowardice which kept the widow silent, but the stern resolve of a brave and high-minded woman that she would do her part to see that vengeance should in time fall upon the man who had robbed her of a husband whom she looked upon as the direct gift of Heaven.

Now, immediately after the body of Kwang-Jui had been cast into the water, the customary patrol sent by the God of the

River to see that order was kept within his dominions, came upon it, and conveyed it with all speed into the presence of the god himself.

The latter looked at it intently for a moment, and then exclaimed in great excitement, "Why, this is the very person who only yesterday saved my life, when I was in danger of being delivered over to a cruel death! I shall now be able to show my gratitude by using all the power I possess to serve his interests. Bring him to the Crystal Grotto," he continued, "where only those who have distinguished themselves in the service of the State have ever been allowed to lie. This man has a claim upon me such as no one before him ever possessed. He is the saviour of my life, and I will tenderly care for him until the web of fate has been spun, and, the vengeance of Heaven having been wreaked upon his murderer, he shall once more rejoin the wife from whom he has been so ruthlessly torn."

With the passing of the months, the widow of Kwang-Jui gave birth to a son, the very image of his father. It was night-time when he was born, and not long after his birth, a mysterious voice, which could not be traced, was heard distinctly saying, "Let the child be removed without delay from the yamen, before the return of the Prefect, as otherwise its life will not be safe."

Accordingly, on the morrow, the babe, about whose destiny even Heaven itself seemed concerned, was carefully wrapped round with many coverings to protect it against the weather. Inside the inmost dress, there was enclosed a small document, telling the child's tragic story and describing the danger from a powerful foe which threatened its life. In order to be able to identify her son, it might be after the lapse of many years, the mother cut off the last joint of the little finger of his left hand; and then, with tears and sighs, and with her heart full of unspoken agony, she took a last, lingering look upon the face of the little one.

A confidential slave woman carried him out of her room, and by devious ways and secret paths finally laid him on the river's bank. Casting a final glance at the precious bundle to see that no danger threatened it, she hurried back in the direction of the city, with the faint cries of the abandoned infant still sounding in her ears.

And now the child was in the hands of Heaven. That this was so was evident from the fact that in a few minutes the abbot of the monastery, which could be seen crowning the top of a neighbouring hill, passed along the narrow pathway by the side of the river. Hearing a baby's cry, he hastened towards the place from which the sounds came, and picking up the little bundle, and realizing that the infant had been deserted, he carried it up to the monastery and made every arrangement for its care and comfort. Fortunately he was a man of a deeply benevolent nature, and no more suitable person could have been found to take charge of the child.

We must now allow eighteen years to pass by. The child that had been left on the margin of the river had grown up to be a fine, handsome lad. The abbot had been his friend ever since the day when his heart had been touched by his cries, and his love for the little foundling had grown with the years. The boy had become a kind of son to him, and in order not to be parted from him he had taught him the temple duties, so that he was now a qualified priest in the service of the gods.

One morning the young man, whose name was Sam-Choang, came to the abbot with a restless, dissatisfied look on his face, and begged to be told who his father was, and who his mother. The old priest, who had long been aware of the tragic story of Kwang-Jui's murder, felt that the time had come when the lad ought to know what he had hitherto concealed from him. Taking out the document which he had found upon him as a baby, he read it to him, and then the great secret was out. After this a long and serious discussion took place between the two as to the wisest methods to be adopted for bringing the Prefect to justice and delivering the lad's mother from the humiliating position which she had so heroically borne for all these eighteen years.

The next day a young priest, with shaven head and dressed in the usual slate-coloured gown, appeared at the yamen of the Prefect to solicit subscriptions for the neighbouring monastery. As the Prefect was absent on some public business, he was ushered into the reception-room, where he was received by his mother, who had always been a generous supporter of the Goddess of Mercy.

At the first sight of this striking-looking young bonze, she found her heart agitated in a strange and powerful way, such as she had not experienced for many a long year; and when she noticed that the little finger on his left hand was without the last joint, she trembled with the utmost excitement.

After a few words about the object for which he had come, the young priest slipped into her hand the very paper which she had written eighteen years ago; and as she looked at her own handwriting and then gazed into his face and saw the striking likeness to the man at whom she had thrown the embroidered ball, the mother-instinct within her flashed suddenly out, and she recognized that this handsome lad was her own son. The joy of the mother as she looked upon the face of Sam-Choang was reflected in the sparkling eyes and glowing look of pleasure that lit up his whole countenance.

Retiring for a short time his mother returned with a letter which she handed to him. In a low voice she told him that it was to her father, who still lived in the capital, and to whom he was to take it without any delay. In order to prevent suspicion on the part of the Prefect, he was to travel as a priest, who was endeavouring to obtain subscriptions for his monastery. He was to be sure, also, to visit the place where his grandmother had been left, and to try and find out what had become of her. In order to defray his expenses she gave him a few bars of gold, which he could exchange for the current money at the banks on the way.

When Sam-Choang arrived at the inn where his father had parted with his grandmother, he could find no trace of her. A new landlord was in possession, who had never even heard her name; but on enquiring amongst the shopkeepers in the neighbourhood, he found to his horror that she was now a member of the beggars' camp, and that her name was enrolled amongst that degraded fraternity.

On reaching the wretched hovel where she was living, he discovered that when her money was exhausted and no remittance came to her from her son, she had been driven out on to the street by the innkeeper, and from that time had tramped the country, living on the scraps and bits which were bestowed upon her by the benevolent. Great was her joy when her grandson led her away to the best inn in the place, and on his departure gave her an ample supply of money for all her needs until they should meet again.

When Sam-Choang reached the capital and handed his mother's letter to his grandfather, the most profound excitement ensued. As soon as the Emperor was officially informed of the case, he determined that the severest punishment should be inflicted upon the man who had not only committed a cruel murder, but through it had dared to usurp a position which could only be held at the Sovereign's command. An Imperial Edict was accordingly issued ordering the Prime Minister to take a considerable body of troops and proceed with all possible speed to the district where such an unheard-of crime had been committed, and there to hand over the offender to immediate execution.

By forced marches, so as to outstrip any private intelligence that might have been sent from the capital, the avenging force reached the city a little before the break of day. Here they waited in silence outside the city gates, anxiously listening for the boom of the early gun which announces the dawn, and at the same time causes the gates to be flung wide open for the traffic of the day to commence.

As soon as the warders had admitted the waiting crowd outside, the soldiers, advancing at a run, quickly reached the yamen, and arrested the Prefect. Without form of trial but simply with a curt announcement from the Prime Minister that he was acting upon instructions from the Emperor, the mandarin was dragged unceremoniously through the gaping crowds that rushed from their doors to see the amazing spectacle.

The feet of Fate had marched slowly but with unerring certainty, and had at last reached the wretched criminal.

But where was he being taken? This road did not lead to the execution ground, where malefactors were doomed to end their careers in shame. Street after street was passed, and still the stern-faced soldiers forced the mandarin down the main thoroughfares, whose sides had often been lined with respectful crowds as he swept by with his haughty retinue. At last they reached the city gate, through which they marched, and then on towards the river, which could be seen gleaming like a silver thread in the distance.

Arrived at its bank, the troops formed into a square with the prisoner in the centre. Addressing him, the Prime Minister said, "I have selected this spot rather than the public execution ground where criminals are put to death. Your crime has been no common one; and so today, in the face of high Heaven whose righteousness you have dared to violate, and within sound of the flowing waters of the stream that witnessed the murder, you shall die."

Half a dozen soldiers then threw him violently to the ground, and in a few minutes the executioner had torn his bleeding heart from his bosom. Then, standing with it still in his hand, he waited by the side of the Prime Minister, who read out to the great multitude the indictment which had been drawn up against the Prefect. In this he described his crimes, and at the same time appealed to Heaven and to the God of the River to take measures to satisfy and appease the spirit of him who had been cut off in the prime of life by the man who had just been executed.

As soon as the reading of the document had been concluded, it was set fire to and allowed to burn until only the blackened ashes remained. These, together with the criminal's heart, were then cast into the river. They were thus formally handed over to the god, who would see that in the Land of Shadows there should come a further retribution on the murderer for the crimes he had committed on earth.

The water patrol happened to pass by soon after the ashes and heart had been flung into the river, and picking them up most carefully, they carried them to the official residence of the god. The indictment was at once formally entered amongst the archives of the office, to be used as evidence when the case was in due time brought before the notice of Yam-lo: and after looking at the heart with the intensest scrutiny for some little time, the god exclaimed, "And so the murderer has at last received some part of the punishment he so richly deserved. It is now time for me to awake the sleeping husband, so that he may be restored to the wife from whom he has been separated for eighteen years."

Passing into the Crystal Grotto, where the unconscious form of Kwang-Jui had reposed for so many years, the god touched the body gently with his hand, and said: – "Friend, arise! Your wife awaits you, and loving ones who have long mourned you. Many years of happiness are still before you, and the honours that your Sovereign will bestow upon you shall place you amongst the famous men of the State. Arise, and take your place once more amongst the living!"

The Prime Minister was sitting with his daughter, listening to the sad story of the years of suffering through which she had passed, when the door was silently opened, and the figure of her long-lost husband glided in. Both started up in fear and amazement, for they believed that what they saw was only a restless spirit which had wandered from the Land of Shadows and would speedily vanish again from their sight. In this, however, they were delightfully disappointed. Kwang-Jui and his wife were once more reunited, and for many a long year their hearts were so full of gladness and contentment, that the sorrows which they had endured gradually became effaced from their memories. They always thought with the deepest gratitude of the God of the River, who for eighteen years had kept the unconscious husband alive and had finally restored him to his heart-broken wife.

The Beautiful Daughter of Liu-Kung

Rev. J. Macgowan

In one of the central provinces of this long-lived Empire of China, there lived in very early times a man of the name of Chan. He was a person of a bright, active nature which made him enjoy life, and caused him to be popular amongst his companions and a favourite with every one who knew him. But he was also a scholar, well-versed in the literature of his country, and he spent every moment that he could spare in the study of the great writings of the famous men of former days.

In order that he might be interrupted as little as possible in his pursuit of learning, he engaged a room in a famous monastery some miles away from his own home. The only inhabitants of this monastery were a dozen or so of Buddhist priests, who, except when they were engaged in the daily services of the temple, lived a quiet, humdrum, lazy kind of existence which harmonized well with the solitude and the majestic stillness of the mountain scenery by which they were surrounded.

This monastery was indeed one of the most beautiful in China. It was situated on the slope of a hill, looking down upon a lovely valley, where the natural solitude was as complete as the most devoted hermit could desire. The only means of getting to it were the narrow hill footpaths along which the worshippers from the great city and the scattered villages wound in and out on festal days, when they came trooping to the temple to make their offerings to the famous God enshrined within.

Chan was a diligent student, and rarely indulged in recreation of any kind. Occasionally, when his mind became oppressed with excessive study he would go for a quiet walk along the hillside; but these occasions were few and far between, for he made up for every hour he spent away from his beloved books by still closer application to them in the hours that followed.

One day he was strolling in an aimless kind of way on the hillside, when suddenly a party of hunters from the neighbouring city of Eternal Spring came dashing into view. They were a merry group and full of excitement, for they had just sighted a fox which Chan had seen a moment before flying away at its highest speed in mortal dread of its pursuers.

Prominent amongst the hunters was a young girl, who was mounted on a fiery little steed, so full of spirit and so eager to follow in the mad chase after the prey, that its rider seemed to have some difficulty in restraining it. The girl herself was a perfect picture. Her face was the loveliest that Chan had ever looked upon, and her figure, which her trim hunting dress showed off to the utmost advantage, was graceful in the extreme. As she swept by him with her face flushed with excitement and her features all aglow with health, Chan felt at once that he had lost his heart and that he was deeply and profoundly in love with her.

On making enquiries, he found that she was named Willow, that she was the daughter of the chief mandarin of the town in which she lived, and that she was intensely fond of the chase and delighted in galloping over the hills and valleys in the pursuit of the wild animals to be found there. So powerfully had Chan's mind been affected by what he had seen of Willow, that he had already begun to entertain serious thoughts of making her his wife; but while his mind was full of this delightful prospect he was plunged into the deepest grief by hearing that she had suddenly died. For some days he was so stricken with sorrow that he lost all interest in life, and could do nothing but dwell on the memory of her whom he had come to love with all the devotion of his heart.

A few weeks after the news of her death, the quiet of the retreat was one day broken by a huge procession which wound its way along the mountain path leading to the monastery doors. On looking out, Chan saw that many of the men in this procession were dressed in sackcloth, and that in front of it was a band of musicians producing weird, shrill notes on their various instruments.

By these signs Chan knew that what he saw was a funeral, and he expected to see the long line of mourners pass on to some spot on the hillside where the dead would be buried. Instead of that, however, they entered through the great gates of the monastery, and the coffin, the red pall of which told him that it contained the body of a woman, was carried into an inner room of the building and laid on trestles that had been made ready for it.

After the mourners had dispersed, Chan asked one of the priests the name of the woman who had died, and how it was that the coffin was laid within the precincts of the temple instead of in the house of the deceased, where it could be looked after by her relatives and where the customary sacrifices to the spirit of the dead could be offered more conveniently than in the monastery.

The bonze replied that this was a peculiar case, calling for special treatment.

"The father of the poor young girl who died so suddenly," he said, "was the mandarin of the neighbouring city of Eternal Spring. Just after the death of his daughter an order came from the Emperor transferring him to another district, a thousand miles from here.

"The command was very urgent that he should proceed without delay to take up his post in the far-off province, and that he was to allow nothing to hinder him from doing so. He could not carry his daughter's body with him on so long a journey, and no time was permitted him to take the coffin to his home, where she might be buried amongst her own kindred. It was equally impossible to deposit the coffin in the yamen he was about to leave, for the new mandarin who was soon to arrive would certainly object to have the body of a stranger in such close proximity to his family. It might bring him bad luck, and his career as an official might end in disaster.

"Permission was therefore asked from our abbot to allow the coffin to be placed in one of our vacant rooms, until the father some day in the future can come and bear the body of his beloved daughter to the home of his ancestors, there to be laid at rest amongst his own people.

"This request was readily granted, for whilst he was in office the mandarin showed us many favours, and his daughter was a beautiful girl who was beloved by everyone; and so we were only too glad to do anything in our power to help in this unhappy matter."

Chan was profoundly moved when he realized that the woman whom he had loved as his own life lay dead within a chamber only a few steps away from his own. His passion, instead of being crushed out of his heart by the thought that she was utterly beyond his reach, and by no possibility could ever be more to him than a memory, seemed to grow in intensity as he became conscious that it was an absolutely hopeless one.

On that very same evening, about midnight, when silence rested on the monastery, and the priests were all wrapped in slumber, Chan, with a lighted taper in his hand, stole with noiseless footsteps along the dark passages into the chamber of death where his beloved lay. Kneeling beside the coffin with a heart full of emotion, in trembling accents he called upon Willow to listen to the story of his passion.

He spoke to her just as though she were standing face to face with him, and he told her how he had fallen in love with her on the day on which he had caught a glimpse of her as she galloped in pursuit of the fox that had fled through the valley from the hunters. He had planned, he told her, to make her his wife, and he described, in tones through which the tears could be heard to run, how heart-broken he was when he heard of her death.

"I want to see you," he continued, "for I feel that I cannot live without you. You are near to me, and yet oh! how far away. Can you not come from the Land of Shadows, where you are now, and comfort me by one vision of your fair face, and one sound of the voice that would fill my soul with the sweetest music?"

For many months the comfort of Chan's life was this nightly visit to the chamber where his dead love lay. Not a single night passed without his going to tell her of the unalterable and undying affection that filled his heart; and whilst the temple lay shrouded in darkness, and the only sounds that broke the stillness were those inexplicable ones in which nature seems to indulge when man is removed by sleep from the scene, Chan was uttering those love notes which had lain deeply hidden within his soul, but which now in the utter desolation of his heart burst forth to ease his pain by their mere expression.

One night as he was sitting poring over his books, he happened to turn round, and was startled to see the figure of a young girl standing just inside the door of his room. It seemed perfectly human, and yet it was so ethereal that it had the appearance of a spirit of the other world. As he looked at the girl with a wondering gaze, a smile lit up her beautiful features, and he then discovered to his great joy that she was none other than Willow, his lost love whom he had despaired of ever seeing again.

With her face wreathed in smiles, she sat down beside him and said in a timid, modest way: – "I am here tonight in response to the great love which has never faltered since the day I died. That is the magnet which has had the power of drawing me from the Land of Shadows. I felt it there, and many speak about it in that sunless country. Even Yam-lo, the lord of the spirits of that dreary world, has been moved by your unchanging devotion; so much so that he has given me permission to come and see you, in order that I might tell you how deeply my heart is moved by the profound affection that you have exhibited for me all these months during which you never had any expectation of its being returned."

For many months this sweet intercourse between Chan and his beloved Willow was carried on, and no one in the whole monastery knew anything of it. The interviews always took place about midnight, and Willow, who seemed to pass with freedom through closed doors or the stoutest walls, invariably vanished during the small hours of the morning.

One evening whilst they were conversing on topics agreeable to them both, Willow unburdened her heart to Chan, and told him how unhappy she was in the world of spirits.

"You know," she said, "that before I died I was not married, and so I am only a wandering spirit with no place where I can rest, and no friends to whom I can betake myself. I travel here and there and everywhere, feeling that no one cares for me, and that there are no ties to bind me to any particular place or thing. For a young girl like me, this is a very sad and sorrowful state of things.

"There is another thing that adds to my sorrow in the Land of Shadows," she went on to say, with a mournful look on her lovely countenance. "I was very fond of hunting when I was in my father's home, and many a wild animal was slain in the hunting expeditions in which I took an active part. This has all told against me in the world in which I am now living, and for the share I took in destroying life I have to suffer by many pains and penalties which are hard for me to endure.

"My sin has been great," she said, "and so I wish to make special offerings in this temple to the Goddess of Mercy and implore her to send down to the other world a good report of me to Yam-lo, and intercede with him to forgive the sins of which I have been guilty. If you will do this for me, I promise that after I have been born again into the world I will never forget you, and if you like to wait for me I shall willingly become your wife and serve you with the deepest devotion of which my heart is capable, as long as Heaven will permit you and me to live together as husband and wife."

From this time, much to the astonishment of the priests in the monastery, Chan began to show unwonted enthusiasm for the service of the Goddess, and would sometimes spend hours before her image and repeat long prayers to her. This was all the more remarkable, as the scholar had rarely if ever shown any desire to have anything to do with the numerous gods which were enshrined in various parts of the temple.

After some months of this daily appeal to the Goddess of Mercy, Willow informed him that his prayers had been so far successful that the misery of her lot in the Land of Shadows had been greatly mitigated. The pleadings of the Goddess with Yam-lo had so influenced his heart towards Willow that she believed her great sin in the destruction of animal life had been forgiven, and there were signs that the dread ruler of the Underworld was looking upon her with kindness.

Chan was delighted with this news, and his prayers and offerings became still more frequent and more fervent. He little dreamed that his devotion to the Goddess would be the means of his speedy separation from Willow, but so it was. One evening she came as usual to see him, but instead of entering with smiling face and laughter in her eyes, she was weeping bitterly as though she were in the direst sorrow.

Chan was in the greatest distress when he saw this and asked her to explain the reason for her grief. "The reason for my tears," she said, "is because after this evening I shall not see you again. Your petitions to the Goddess have had such a powerful effect upon her mind that she has used all her influence with Yam-lo to induce him to set me free from the misery of the Land of Shadows, and so I am to leave that sunless country and to be born again into life in this upper world."

As she uttered these words her tears began to flow once more and her whole frame was convulsed with sobbing.

"I am glad," she said, "that I am to be born once more and live amongst men, but I cannot bear the thought of having to be separated for so long from you. Let us not grieve too much, however. It is our fate, and we may not rebel against it. Yam-lo has been kinder to me than he has ever been to any one in the past, for he has revealed to me the family into which I am to be born and the place where they live, so if you come to me in eighteen years you will find me waiting for you. Your love has been so great that it has entered into my very soul, and there is nothing that can ever efface it from my heart. A thousand re-births may take place, but never shall I love any one as I love you."

Chan professed that he was greatly comforted by this confession of her love, but all the same he felt in despair when he thought of the future.

"When next I shall see you," he said with a sigh, "I shall be getting so old that you, a young girl in the first flush of womanhood, will not care to look at me. My hair will have turned grey and my face will be marked with wrinkles, and in the re-birth you will have forgotten all that took place in the Land of Shadows, and the memory of me will have vanished from your heart for ever."

Willow looked with loving but sorrowful eyes upon her lover as he was expressing his concern about the future, but quickly assured him that nothing in the world would ever cause her to cease to remember him with the tenderest affection.

"In order to comfort you," she said, "let me tell you of two things that the dread Yam-lo, out of consideration for your love for me, has granted me – two things which he has never bestowed upon any other mortal who has come within the region of his rule. The first is, he has allowed me to inspect the book of Life and Death, in which is recorded the history of every human being, with the times of their re-births and the places in which they are to be born. I want you this very minute to write down the secret which has been revealed to me as to my new name and family and the place where I shall reside, so that you will have no difficulty in finding me, when eighteen years hence you shall come to claim me as your wife.

"The next is a gift so precious that I have no words in which to express my gratitude for its having been bestowed upon me. It is this. I am given the privilege of not forgetting what has taken place during my stay in the Land of Shadows, and so when I am re-born into another part of China, with a new father and mother, I shall hold within my memory my recollection of you. The years will pass quickly, for I shall be looking for you, and this day eighteen years hence will be the happiest in my life, for it will bring you to me never more to be separated from me.

"But I must hasten on," she hurriedly exclaimed, "for the footsteps of fate are moving steadily towards me. In a few minutes the gates of Hades will have closed against me, and Willow will have vanished, and I shall be a babe once more with my new life before me. See, but a minute more is left me, and I seem to have so much to say. Farewell! Never forget me! I shall ever remember you, but my time is come!"

As she uttered these words, a smile of ineffable sweetness flashed across, her beautiful face, and she was gone.

Chan was inexpressibly sad at the loss he had sustained by the re-birth of Willow, and in order to drive away his sorrow he threw his heart and soul into his studies. His books became his constant companions, and he tried to find in them a solace for the loneliness which had come upon him since the visits of Willow had ceased. He also became a diligent worshipper of the idols, and especially of the

Goddess of Mercy, who had played such an important part in the history of his beloved Willow.

The years went slowly by, and Chan began to feel that he was growing old. His hair became dashed with silver threads, and wrinkles appeared in his forehead and under his eyes. The strain of waiting for the one woman who had taken complete possession of his heart had been too much for him. As the time drew near, too, when he should go to meet her, a great and nervous dread began to fill him with anxiety. Would she recognize him? And would she, a young girl of eighteen, be content to accept as a husband a man so advanced in years as he now was? These questions were constantly flashing through his brain.

At last only a few months remained before he was to set out on his journey to the distant province where Yam-lo had decided that Willow was to begin her new life on earth.

He was sitting one evening in his study, brooding over the great problem that would be solved before long, when a man dressed in black silently entered the room. Looking on Chan with a kindly smile which seemed to find its way instantly to his heart, he informed him that he was a fairy from the Western Heaven and that he had been specially deputed by the rulers there to render him all the assistance in his power at this particular crisis, when they knew his heart was so full of anxiety.

"We have all heard in that far-off fairyland," he continued, "of the devotion you have shown to Willow, and how during all the years which have intervened since you saw her last you have never faltered in your love for her. Such affection is rare among mortals, and the dwellers in fairyland would like to help in bringing together two such loving hearts; for let me assure you that however strong your feeling for the one whom you are so anxious to see again, she on her part is just as deeply in love with you, and is now counting the days until she will be able to see you and until you need never again be parted from each other. In order to assist in this happy consummation, I want you to take a short trip with me. It will only take a few hours, and you will then find that something has happened to remove all your fears as to how you will be received by Willow."

The fairy man then led Chan to the door, and gave a wave of his hand in the direction of the sky. Instantly the sound of the fluttering and swish of wings was heard, and in a moment a splendid eagle landed gracefully at their feet. Taking their seats upon its back, they found themselves flashing at lightning speed away through the darkness of the night. Higher and higher they rose, till they had pierced the heavy masses of clouds which hung hovering in the sky. Swift as an arrow the eagle still cleft its way upward until the clouds had vanished to an infinite distance below them; and still onward they were borne in the mighty stillness of an expanse where no human being had ever travelled before.

Chan felt his heart throb with a nervousness which he could not control. What if the bird should tire, he thought, and he should be dropped into the fathomless abyss below? Life's journey would then come to a tragic end. Where, too, was he being carried and how should he be ever able to return to his far-off home on the earth? He was becoming more and more agitated, when the fairy took hold of his hand and in a voice which at once stilled his fears, assured him that there was not the least danger in this journey through the air.

"We are as safe here," he assured him, "as though we were standing upon a mountain whose roots lie miles below the surface of the earth. And see," he continued, pointing to something in the distance, "we shall arrive at our destination in the course of a few seconds."

True enough, he had hardly finished speaking when a land, fairer than Chan had ever seen on earth or pictured in imagination, loomed up suddenly in front of them; and before he could gather together his astonished thoughts, the eagle had landed them on its shores, and with outspread wings was soaring into the mystery of the unknown beyond.

The fairy now led Chan along a road surrounded by the most bewildering beauty. Rare flowers, graceful trees, and birds which made the groves resound with the sweetest music, were objects that kept his mind in one continual state of delight. Before long they arrived in front of a magnificent palace, so grand and vast that Chan felt afraid to enter within its portals, or even tread the avenue leading up to it.

Once more his companion relieved Chan's anxiety by assuring him that he was an expected guest, and that the Queen of this fairy country had sent him to earth specially to invite him to come and visit her, in order that she might bestow upon him a blessing which would enrich the whole of his life and would enable him to spend many happy years with her whom he had loved with such devotion.

Chan was ushered into a large reception hall, where he was met by a very stately lady, with a face full of benevolence, whom he at once recognized, from the images he had often worshipped, as the Goddess of Mercy. He was startled when he discovered in what august presence he was standing, and began to tremble with excitement as he realized that here in actual life was the famous personage whose image was worshipped by the millions of China, and whose influence spread even into the Land of Shadows.

Seeing Chan's humility and evident terror of her, the Goddess spoke to him in a gentle, loving voice, and told him to have no fear, for she had summoned him to her presence not to rebuke but to comfort him.

"I know your story," she said, "and I think it is a beautiful one. Before I was raised to the high position I now occupy I was at one time a woman like Willow, and I can sympathize with her in her devotion to you because of the wonderful love you have shown her from the first moment that you saw her.

"I know, too, your anxiety about your age, and your fear lest when

Willow sees you with the marks of advancing years upon you, her love

may die out and you will be left with your heart broken and in despair.

I have foreseen this difficulty, and I am going to have it removed.

"The fairy who brought you here," she continued, "will now take you round the palace grounds, and if you will carry out my wishes, the fears which have been troubling you for years shall entirely vanish. You will then meet Willow with a heart as light as that of any man in the flush of youth, who awaits the coming of the bridal chair which bears his future wife to his home."

Chan at once, without any hesitation, followed his guide through the spacious grounds which surrounded the palace, and was finally led to the edge of a beautiful little lake embowered amongst trees and ferns, and rare and fragrant flowers. It was the most exquisite scene on which his vision had ever rested.

With a kindly look at his companion, the fairy said, "This beautiful piece of water goes by the name of the 'Fountain of Eternal Youth,' and it is the Queen's express desire that you should bathe in it."

Quickly undressing, Chan plunged into the pool and for a moment sank beneath the surface of the waters. Emerging quickly from them, a delightful feeling of new-born strength seemed to be creeping in at every pore of his body. The sense of advancing age passed away, and the years of youth appeared to come back to him again. He felt as though he were a young man once more; for the weary doubts, which for some years past had made his footsteps lag, had gone with his first plunge into those fragrant waters.

By-and-by he came out of this "Fountain of Eternal Youth" with the visions and ambitions of his young manhood rushing through his brain. His powers, which seemed of late to have become dull and sluggish, had recovered the impetus which in earlier years had carried him so successfully through many a severe examination. His thoughts, too, about Willow had so completely changed that instead of dreading the day when he should stand before her, his one passionate desire now was to start upon his journey to keep his appointment with her.

Chan and the fairy then proceeded to the edge of the vast and boundless expanse which bordered the palace of the Goddess, and found a magnificent dragon waiting to convey them back to earth. No sooner had they taken their seats on its back than it fled with the swiftness of the wind through the untrodden spaces of the air, until at length the mountains came looming out of the dim and shadowy distance, and with a rush Chan found himself safely landed at the door of the temple from which he had taken his departure for his amazing journey to the Western Heaven.

Whilst these wonderful things were taking place, Willow – or rather Precious Pearl, as she had been named by her new parents, who of course had no knowledge of her previous history – had grown up to be a most beautiful and fascinating woman.

During all these years she had never ceased to look forward with an anxious heart to the day when she would once more meet the man to whom she had betrothed herself eighteen years ago. Latterly she had begun to count the days that must still elapse before she could see him again. She never forgot the night in the temple when she bade him "Good-bye" just before she was reborn into this world. The day and the hour had been stamped upon her memory, and since then the years had seemed to travel with halting, leaden feet, as though they were loth to move on. But now only a few months remained, and no doubt ever entered her brain that Chan would fail her.

Just about this time her mother had an offer of marriage for her from a very wealthy and distinguished family, and contrary to the usual custom of mothers in China she asked her daughter what she thought of the proposal. Pearl was distressed beyond measure, and prayed and entreated her mother on no account to broach the subject to her again, as she could never entertain any proposition of the kind.

Amazed at such a statement, her mother begged her to explain her reason for such strange views. "Girls at your age," she said, "are usually betrothed and are thinking of having homes of their own. This is the universal custom throughout the Empire, and therefore there must be some serious reason why you will not allow me to make arrangements for your being allied to some respectable family."

Pearl had been feeling that the time was drawing near when she would have to divulge the secret of her love affair, and she considered that now was the best opportunity for doing so. To the astonishment therefore of her mother, who believed that she was romancing, she told her the whole story of the past; how Chan had fallen in love with her, and how after she had died and had come under the control of Yam-lo in the Land of Shadows, that dread lord had permitted her spirit to visit her lover in the temple where her body had been laid until a lucky resting-place could be found for it on the hillside. She also explained how it had been agreed between them that she was to wait for him until after the lapse of eighteen years, when she would be old enough to become his wife. "In a few months the time will be up," she concluded, "and so I beseech you not to speak of my being betrothed to any one else, for I feel that if I am compelled to marry any other than Chan I shall die."

The mother was thunderstruck at this wonderful story which her daughter told her. She could only imagine that Pearl had in some way or another been bewitched, and was under a fatal delusion that she was in love with some hero of romance, to whom she believed she was betrothed. Still, her daughter had always been most loving and devoted to her, and had shown more brightness and ability than Chinese girls of her age usually possessed. Her mother did not like, therefore, to reprove her for what she considered her ridiculous ideas, so she determined to try another plan to cure her of her folly.

"What age was this man Chan," she asked, "when you entered into this engagement with him?"

"He was just thirty," Pearl replied. "He was of very good family and a scholar, and had distinguished himself for his proficiency in the ancient literature of China."

"Oh! then he must be nearly fifty now. A fine mate he would make for you, a young girl of only eighteen! But who knows how he may have changed since last you saw him? His hair must be turning grey, and his teeth may have fallen out; and for anything you know he may have been dead and buried so long ago that by this time they have taken up his bones, and nothing is left of him but what the funeral urn may contain of his ashes."

"Oh! I do pray that nothing of that kind has happened to him," cried Pearl, in a tone of voice which showed the anguish she was suffering. "Let us leave the question for a few months, and then when he comes for me, as I know he will, you will find by personal knowledge what a splendid man he is, and how entirely worthy he is of being your son-in-law."

On the day which had been appointed under such romantic circumstances eighteen years before, Chan arrived in the town, and after taking a room in an inn and making certain enquiries, he made his way to the home where he believed that Willow resided. On his arrival, however, he was roughly told by the servant that no such person as Willow lived there, and that they did not like strangers coming about the house. Indeed he was given plainly to understand that the sooner he left, the better everyone would be pleased. This treatment was of course part of a scheme devised by Pearl's parents to frustrate any plans that Chan might have formed for seeing her. They were determined not to give their daughter to a man so old as he must be, and therefore they decided that an interview between the two must be prevented at all hazards.

Chan was greatly distressed at the rebuff which he had received. Had Willow after all made a mistake eighteen years ago when she gave him the name of this town as the place where her new home was to be? He had carefully written it down at her dictation, and it had been burned into his brain all the years since. No, there could be no mistake on that point. If there were any, then it was one that had been made purposely by Yam-lo in order to deceive them both. That idea, however, was unthinkable, and so there must be something else to account for his not finding Willow as he had expected. He at once made enquiries at the inn at which he was staying, and found that there was a daughter at the very house to which he had gone, and that in almost every particular the description he was given of her corresponded with his beloved Willow.

In the meantime, poor Pearl was in a state of the greatest anxiety. The eventful day on which she was to meet her lover had opened for her with keen expectation of meeting him after their long and romantic separation. She had never for one moment doubted that he would keep his engagement with her. An instinct which she could not explain made her feel certain that he was still alive, and that nothing in the world would prevent him from meeting her, as had been agreed upon between them at that eventful parting in the temple eighteen years before.

As the day wore on, however, and there were no signs of Chan, Pearl's distress became exceedingly pitiful; and when night came and her mother declared that nothing had been seen of him, she was so stricken with despair that she lost all consciousness, and had to be carried to bed, where she lay in a kind of trance from which, for some time, it seemed impossible to arouse her.

When at last she did regain consciousness, her mother tried to comfort her by saying that perhaps Chan was dead, or that he had forgotten her in the long course of years, and that therefore she must not grieve too much. "You are a young girl," she said, "and you have a long life before you. Chan is an old man by this time; no doubt he has long ago married, and the home ties which he has formed have caused him to forget you. But you need not be broken-hearted on that account. There are many other men who will be more suitable for you than he could possibly be. By-and-by we shall arrange a marriage for you, and then life will appear to you very different from what it does now."

Instead of being comforted, however, Pearl was only the more distressed by her mother's words. Her love, which had begun in the Land of Shadows, and which had been growing in her heart for the last eighteen years, was not one to be easily put aside by such plausible arguments as those she had just listened to. The result was that she had a relapse, and for several days her life was in great danger.

The father and mother, fearing now that their daughter would die, determined, as there seemed no other remedy, to bring Chan to their home, and see whether his presence would not deliver Pearl from the danger in which the doctor declared she undoubtedly was.

The father accordingly went to the inn where he knew Chan was staying, and to his immense surprise he found him to be a young man of about twenty-five, highly polished in manner, and possessed of unusual intelligence. For some time he utterly refused to believe that this handsome young fellow was really the man with whom Pearl was so deeply in love, and it was not until Chan had told him the romantic story of his life that he could at all believe that he was not being imposed upon. Eventually, however, he was so taken with Chan that he became determined to do all in his power to bring about his marriage with his daughter.

"Come with me at once," he said, "and see if your presence will not do more than the cleverest doctors in the town have been able to accomplish. Pearl has been so distressed at not seeing you that she is now seriously ill, and we have been afraid that she would die of a broken heart."

When they arrived at the house Chan was taken into the sick-room, and the girl gazed into his face with a look of wonderment. "I do not seem to recognize you," she said in a feeble voice. "You are much younger than Chan, and although there is something about you that reminds me of him, I cannot realize that you are the same person with whom my spirit eighteen years ago held fellowship in the monastery where my body lay unburied."

Chan proceeded to explain the mystery. "For years," he said, "my mind was troubled about the difference between our ages. I was afraid that when you saw me with grey hairs and with wrinkles on my face, your love would receive a shock, and you might regret that you had ever pledged yourself to me. Although you had vanished from my sight, my prayers still continued to be offered to the Goddess of Mercy. She had heard them for you, you remember, when you were in the Land of Shadows, and through her intercession Yam-lo had forgiven your sins, and had made life easier for you in that gloomy country.

"I still continued to pray to her, hoping in some vague way that she would intervene to bring about the desire of my heart, and that when in due time I should meet you again, every obstacle to our mutual love would be for ever removed.

"One day a fairy came into the very room where your spirit had often conversed with me. He carried me away with him to the Western Heaven and brought me into the very presence of the Goddess of Mercy. She gave directions for me to bathe in the 'Fountain of Eternal Youth,' and I became young again. That is why you see me now with a young face and a young nature, but my heart in its love for you has never changed, and never will as long as life lasts."

As he was telling this entrancing story, a look of devoted love spread over the beautiful countenance of Pearl. She gradually became instinct with life, and before he had finished speaking, the lassitude and exhaustion which had seemed to threaten her very life entirely disappeared. A rosy look came over her face, and her coal-black eyes flashed with hidden fires.

"Now I know," she cried, "that you are Chan. You are so changed that when I first caught sight of you my heart sank within me, for I had pictured an older man, and I could not at once realize that you were the same Chan who showed such unbounded love for me in the years gone by.

"It was not that I should have loved you less even though you had really been older. My heart would never have changed. It was only my doubt as to your reality that made me hesitate, but now my happiness is indeed great; for since through the goodness of the Goddess you have recovered your youth, I need not fear that the difference between our years may in the near future bring to us an eternal separation."

In a few days Pearl was once more herself again. Her parents, delighted with the romantic turn that things had taken and highly pleased with Chan himself, arranged for the betrothal of their daughter to him; and in the course of a few months, the loving couple were united in marriage. And so, after years of waiting, the happy consummation was accomplished, which Heaven and the Goddess of Mercy and even the dread Ruler of the Land of Shadows had each taken a share in bringing about; and for many and many a long year the story of Chan and his wife was spread abroad throughout the region in which they lived.

The Vengeance of the Goddess

Rev. J. Macgowan

In a certain temple in the northern part of the Empire, there once lived a famous priest named Hien-Chung, whose reputation had spread far and wide, not merely for the sanctity of his life, but also for the supernatural powers which he was known to possess, and which he had exhibited on several remarkable occasions. Men would have marvelled less about him had they known that the man dressed in the long slate-coloured robe, with shaven head, and saintly-looking face, over which no one had ever seen a smile flicker, was in reality a pilgrim on his way to the Western Heaven, which he hoped to reach in time, and to become a fairy there.

One night Hien-Chung lay asleep in a room opening out of the main hall in which the great image of the Goddess of Mercy, with her benevolent, gracious face, sat enshrined amidst the darkness that lay thickly over the temple. All at once, there stood before him a most striking and stately-looking figure. The man had a royal look about him, as though he had been accustomed to rule. On his head there was a crown, and his dress was such as no mere subject would ever be allowed to wear.

Hien-Chung gazed at him in wonder, and was at first inclined to believe that he was some evil spirit who had assumed this clever disguise in order to deceive him. As this thought flashed through his mind, the man began to weep. It was pitiable indeed to see this kingly person affected with such oppressive grief that the tears streamed down his cheeks, and with the tenderness that was distinctive of him Hien-Chung expressed his deep sympathy for a sorrow so profound.

"Three years ago," said his visitor, "I was the ruler of this 'Kingdom of the Black Flower.' I was indeed the founder of my dynasty, for I carved my own fortune with my sword, and made this little state into a kingdom. For a long time I was very happy, and my people were most devoted in their allegiance to me. I little dreamed of the sorrows that were coming on me, and the disasters which awaited me in the near future.

"Five years ago my kingdom was visited with a very severe drought. The rains ceased to fall; the streams which used to fall down the mountain-sides and irrigate the plains dried up; and the wells lost the fountains which used to fill them with water. Everywhere the crops failed, and the green herbage on which the cattle browsed was slowly blasted by the burning rays of the sun.

"The common people suffered in their homes from want of food, and many of the very poorest actually died of starvation. This was a source of great sorrow to me, and every day my prayers went up to Heaven, that it would send down rain upon the dried-up land and so deliver my people from death. I knew that this calamity had fallen on my kingdom because of some wrong that I had done, and so my heart was torn with remorse.

"One day while my mind was full of anxiety, a man suddenly appeared at my palace and begged my ministers to be allowed to have an audience with me. He said that it was of the utmost importance that he should see me, for he had come to propose a plan for the deliverance of my country.

"I gave orders that he should instantly be brought into my presence, when I asked him if he had the power to cause the rain to descend upon the parched land.

"'Yes,' he replied, 'I have, and if you will step with me now to the front of your palace I will prove to you that I have the ability to do this, and even more.'

"Striding out to a balcony which overlooked the capital, and from which one could catch a view of the hills in the distance, the stranger lifted up his right hand towards the heavens and uttered certain words which I was unable to understand.

"Instantly, and as if by magic, a subtle change crept through the atmosphere. The sky became darkened, and dense masses of clouds rolled up and blotted out the sun. The thunder began to mutter, and vivid flashes of lightning darted from one end of the heavens to the other, and before an hour had elapsed the rain was descending in torrents all over the land, and the great drought was at an end.

"My gratitude to this mysterious stranger for the great deliverance he had wrought for my kingdom was so great that there was no favour which I was not willing to bestow upon him. I gave him rooms in the palace, and treated him as though he were my equal. I had the truest and the tenderest affection for him, and he seemed to be equally devoted to me.

"One morning we were walking hand in hand in the royal gardens. The peach blossoms were just out, and we were enjoying their perfume and wandering up and down amongst the trees which sent forth such exquisite fragrance.

"As we sauntered on, we came by-and-by upon a well which was hidden from sight by a cluster of oleander trees. We stayed for a moment to peer down its depths and to catch a sight of the dark waters lying deep within it. Whilst I was gazing down, my friend gave me a sudden push and I was precipitated head first into the water at the bottom. The moment I disappeared, he took a broad slab of stone and completely covered the mouth of the well. Over it he spread a thick layer of earth, and in this he planted a banana root, which, under the influence of the magic powers he possessed, in the course of a few hours had developed into a full-grown tree. I have lain dead in the well now for three years, and during all that time no one has arisen to avenge my wrong or to bring me deliverance."

"But have your ministers of State made no efforts during all these three years to discover their lost king?" asked Hien-Chung. "And what about your wife and family? Have they tamely submitted to have you disappear without raising an outcry that would resound throughout the whole kingdom? It seems to me inexplicable that a king should vanish from his palace and that no hue and cry should be raised throughout the length and breadth of the land until the mystery should be solved and his cruel murder fully avenged."

"It is here," replied the spirit of the dead king, "that my enemy has shown his greatest cunning. The reason why men never suspect that any treason has been committed is because by his enchantments he has transformed his own appearance so as to become the exact counterpart of myself. The man who called down the rain and saved my country from drought and famine has simply disappeared, so men think, and I the King still rule as of old in my kingdom. Not the slightest suspicion as to the true state of things has ever entered the brain of anyone in the nation, and so the usurper is absolutely safe in the position he occupies today."

"But have you never appealed to Yam-lo, the ruler of the Land of Shadows?", asked Hien-Chung. "He is the great redresser of the wrongs and crimes of earth, and now that you are a spirit and immediately within his jurisdiction, you should lay your complaint before him and pray him to avenge the sufferings you have been called upon to endure."

"You do not understand," the spirit hastily replied. "The one who has wrought such ruin in my life is an evil spirit. He has nothing in common with men, but has been let loose from the region where evil spirits are confined to punish me for some wrong that I have committed in the past. He therefore knows the ways of the infernal regions, and is hand in glove with the rulers there, and even with Yam-lo himself. He is, moreover, on the most friendly terms with the tutelary God of my capital, and so no complaint of mine would ever be listened to for a moment by any of the powers who rule in the land of the dead.

"There is another very strong reason, too, why any appeal that I might make for justice would be disregarded. My soul has not yet been loosed from my body, but is still confined within it in the well. The courts of the Underworld would never recognize me, because I still belong to this life, over which they have no control.

"Only today," he continued, "a friendly spirit whispered in my ear that my confinement in the well was drawing to a close, and that the three years I had been adjudged to stay there would soon be up. He strongly advised me to apply to you, for you are endowed, he said, with powers superior to those possessed by my enemy, and if you are only pleased to exercise them I shall speedily be delivered from his evil influence."

Now the Goddess of Mercy had sent Hien-Chung a number of familiar spirits to be a protection to him in time of need. Next morning, accordingly, he summoned the cleverest of these, whose name was Hing, in order to consult with him as to how the king might be delivered from the bondage in which he had been held for the three years.

"The first thing we have to do," said Hing, "is to get the heir to the Throne on our side. He has often been suspicious at certain things in the conduct of his supposed father, one of which is that for three years he has never been allowed to see his mother. All that is needed now is to get some tangible evidence to convince him that there is some mystery in the palace, and we shall gain him as our ally.

"I have been fortunate," he continued, "in obtaining one thing which we shall find very useful in inducing the Prince to listen to what we have to say to him about his father. You may not know it, but about the time when the King was thrown into the well, the seal of the kingdom mysteriously disappeared and a new one had to be cut.

"Knowing that you were going to summon me to discuss this case, I went down into the well at dawn this morning, and found the missing seal on the body of the King. Here it is, and now we must lay our plans to work on the mind of the son for the deliverance of the father. Tomorrow I hear that the Prince is going out hunting on the neighbouring hills. In one of the valleys there is a temple to the Goddess of Mercy, and if you will take this seal and await his coming there, I promise you that I will find means to entice him to the shrine."

Next morning the heir to the Throne of the "Kingdom of the Black Flower" set out with a noisy retinue to have a day's hunting on the well-wooded hills overlooking the capital. They had scarcely reached the hunting grounds when great excitement was caused by the sudden appearance of a remarkable-looking hare. It was decidedly larger than an ordinary hare, but the curious feature about it was its colour, which was as white as the driven snow.

No sooner had the hounds caught sight of it, than with loud barkings and bayings they dashed madly in pursuit. The hare, however, did not seem to show any terror, but with graceful bounds that carried it rapidly over the ground, it easily out-distanced the fleetest of its pursuers. It appeared, indeed, as though it were thoroughly enjoying the facility with which it could outrun the dogs, while the latter grew more and more excited as they always saw the quarry before them and yet could never get near enough to lay hold upon it.

Another extraordinary thing was that this hare did not seem anxious to escape. It took no advantage of undergrowth or of clumps of trees to hide the direction in which it was going. It managed also to keep constantly in view of the whole field; and when it had to make sudden turns in the natural windings of the road which led to a valley in the distance, where there stood a famous temple, it hesitated for a moment and allowed the baying hounds to come perilously near, before it darted off with the speed of lightning and left the dogs far behind it.

Little did the hunters dream that the beautiful animal which was giving them such an exciting chase was none other than the fairy Hing, who had assumed this disguise in order to bring the Prince to the lonely temple in the secluded valley, where, beyond the possibility of being spied upon by his father's murderer, the story of treachery could be told, and means be devised for his restoration to the throne.

Having arrived close to the temple, the mysterious hare vanished as suddenly as it had appeared, and not a trace was left to enable the dogs, which careered wildly round and round, to pick up the scent.

The Prince, who was a devoted disciple of the Goddess of Mercy, now dismounted and entered the temple, where he proceeded to burn incense before her shrine and in muttered tones to beseech her to send down blessings upon him.

After a time, he became considerably surprised to find that the presiding priest of the temple, instead of coming forward to attend upon him and to show him the courtesies due to his high position, remained standing in a corner where the shadows were darkest, his eyes cast upon the ground and with a most serious look overspreading his countenance.

Accordingly, when he had finished his devotions to the Goddess, the Prince approached the priest, and asked him in a kindly manner if anything was distressing him.

"Yes," replied Hien-Chung, "there is, and it is a subject which materially affects your Royal Highness. If you will step for a moment into my private room, I shall endeavour to explain to you the matter which has filled my mind with the greatest possible anxiety."

When they entered the abbot's room, Hien-Chung handed the Prince a small box and asked him to open it and examine the article it contained.

Great was the Prince's amazement when he took it out and cast a hurried glance over it. A look of excitement passed over his face and he cried out, "Why, this is the great seal of the kingdom which was lost three years ago, and of which no trace could ever be found! May I ask how it came into your possession and what reason you can give for not having restored it to the King, who has long wished to discover it?"

"The answer to that is a long one, your Highness, and to satisfy you, I must go somewhat into detail."

Hien-Chung then told the Prince of the midnight visit his father had made him, and the tragic story of his murder by the man who was now posing as the King, and of his appeal to deliver him from the sorrows of the well in which he had been confined for three years.

"With regard to the finding of the seal," he continued, "my servant Hing, who is present, will describe how by the supernatural powers with which he is endowed, he descended the well only this very morning and discovered it on the body of your father."

"We have this absolute proof," he said, "that the vision I saw only two nights ago was not some imagination of the brain, but that it was really the King who appealed to me to deliver him from the power of an enemy who seems bent upon his destruction.

"We must act, and act promptly," he went on, "for the man who is pretending to be the ruler of your kingdom is a person of unlimited ability, and as soon as he gets to know that his secret has been divulged, he will put into operation every art he possesses to frustrate our purpose.

"What I propose is that your Highness should send back the greater part of your retinue to the palace, with an intimation to the effect that you are going to spend the night here in a special service to the Goddess, whose birthday it fortunately happens to be today. After night has fallen upon the city, Hing shall descend into the well and bring the body of your father here. You will then have all the proof you need of the truth of the matter, and we can devise plans as to our future action."

A little after midnight, Hing having faithfully carried out the commission entrusted to him by Hien-Chung, arrived with the body of the King, which was laid with due ceremony and respect in one of the inner rooms of the temple. With his marvellous wonder-working powers and with the aid of invisible forces which he had been able to summon to his assistance, he had succeeded in transporting it from the wretched place where it had lain so long to the friendly temple of the Goddess of Mercy.

The Prince was deeply moved by the sight of his father's body. Fortunately it had suffered no change since the day when it was thrown to the bottom of the well. Not a sign of decay could be seen upon the King's noble features. It seemed as though he had but fallen asleep, and presently would wake up and talk to them as he used to do. The fact that in some mysterious way the soul had not been separated from the body accounted for its remarkable preservation. Nevertheless to all appearance the King was dead, and the great question now was how he could be brought back to life, so that he might be restored to his family and his kingdom.

"The time has come," said Hien-Chung, "when heroic measures will have to be used if the King is ever to live again. Two nights ago he made a passionate and urgent request to me to save him, for one of the gods informed him that I was the only man who could do so. So far, we have got him out of the grip of the demon that compassed his death, and now it lies with me to provide some antidote which shall bring back the vital forces and make him a living man once more.

"I have never had to do with such a serious case as this before, but I have obtained from the Patriarch of the Taoist Church a small vial of the Elixir of Life, which has the marvellous property of prolonging the existence of whoever drinks it. We shall try it on the King and, as there is no sign of vital decay, let us hope that it will be effective in restoring him to life."

Turning to a desk that was kept locked, he brought out a small black earthenware bottle, from which he dropped a single drop of liquid on to the lips of the prostrate figure. In a few seconds a kind of rosy flush spread over the King's features. Another drop, and a look of life flashed over the pallid face. Still another, and after a short interval the eyes opened and looked with intelligence upon the group surrounding his couch. Still one more, and the King arose and asked how long he had been asleep, and how it came about that he was in this small room instead of being in his own palace.

He was soon restored to his family and to his position in the State, for the usurper after one or two feeble attempts to retain his power ignominiously fled from the country.

A short time after, Hien-Chung had a private interview with the King. "I am anxious," he said, "that your Majesty should understand the reason why such a calamity came into your life.

"Some years ago without any just reason you put to death a Buddhist priest. You never showed any repentance for the great wrong you had done, and so the Goddess sent a severe drought upon your Kingdom. You still remained unrepentant, and then she sent one of her Ministers to afflict you, depriving you of your home and your royal power. The man who pushed you down the well was but carrying out the instructions he had received from the Goddess. Your stay down the well for three years was part of the punishment she had decreed for your offence, and when the time was up, I was given the authority to release you.

"Kings as well as their subjects are under the great law of righteousness, and if they violate it they must suffer like other men. I would warn your Majesty that unless you show some evidence that you have repented for taking away a man's life unjustly, other sorrows will most certainly fall upon you in the future."

The Wonderful Man

Rev. J. Macgowan

There is a certain Prefectural city in the south of China, which has earned a reputation distinguishing it from all such towns throughout the Empire.

In outward appearance this city is very much like every other of similar size. The streets are narrow, and the houses are crowded close up to each other. Every foot of land has been utilized, and no room has been left for sanitation, or for parks and open spaces, where the people may breathe the pure air of heaven. These things are modern inventions of the West and have never yet touched the thought or the life of the East, where sullen heat, fetid atmosphere, and stifling surroundings are the natural inheritance of the men and women who throng the cities and crowd and elbow each other in the great battle of life.

There was one thing, however, for which this city was deservedly celebrated. It had a great reputation for learning, and was famous as the abode of scholars.

In the main thoroughfares, where men with a dexterity begotten of long experience just managed to evade jostling each other, the long-gowned students were conspicuous by their numbers. Their pale intellectual faces, and their gleaming black eyes burning with hidden fires, marked them out distinctly from the farmers and artisans and coolies, with their coarser, heavier features, who moved along side by side with them. And down the narrow alley-ways, where fetid smells and impure airs floated the live-long day, one's ear would catch the shrill tones of more youthful students, who in unhealthy rooms were mastering aloud the famous classics of China, in order that in time they might compete in the triennial examinations for the prizes offered by the Empire to its scholars.

The ambition for learning was in the air, and a belated wayfarer, wandering down the labyrinth of streets in the early hours of the morning, would hear the solemn stillness broken into by the voices of the students, as in their highest tones they repeated the writings of the great sages.

The town was therefore dear to the God of Literature, who has ever been ready to champion the cause of his scholars, whenever anyone has dared to lay a hand upon their privileges.

A legend in which there is widespread belief declares that on one occasion, when the scholars of five counties had assembled at a triennial examination, the Imperial Examiner, who for some reason or other had conceived a spite against the competitors from this particular city, determined that not one of them should pass.

As their essays came into his hands, he carefully laid them in a pile close beside him on the table. The God of Literature, who was sitting in his shrine at the far end of the room, became indignant at the insult that was about to be put on his favourites, and breathed some classic phrases under his breath, to the effect that he would never allow such a wrong to be perpetrated as long as he had power to prevent it.

The last paper had been examined and laid carefully on the top of the others, when, as if by a flash of lightning, the examiner was seized with a stroke of paralysis, and fell to the ground unconscious. That was the answer of the God to his evil schemes.

The greatest dismay was exhibited by the under-officials of the examination. Thousands of students were waiting outside for the list to be issued of those who had passed, but the only man who had the power to prepare this list lay helpless in the grip of paralysis. Yet something must be done, and that speedily. As they looked over the manuscripts lying on the table, a little pile was discovered, evidently placed there by the examiner for some purpose of his own. One of the officials at once suggested that these must belong to the men who had gained their degrees. The idea was enthusiastically accepted as the correct one. There was no need for further delay. The names of the writers were hurriedly copied out and pasted up on the board in front of the Examination Hall.

To the amazement of all the assembled scholars, the only men who had got their degrees were those belonging to the city favoured of the God. This was the God's second answer to the examiner, who would unjustly have excluded them from the honours of the day.

There was another thing for which the people of this city were noted, and that was the pleasure taken by the leaders of society in recognizing those who displayed conspicuous civic virtues.

Outside one of the four gates, and well beyond the streets and houses which had grown up as an overflow from the great city, there was a considerable open space, through the middle of which the main road meandered on its way to the countless towns and villages in the regions beyond, and finally to the far-off capital, Peking, thousands of miles away in the extreme north. It was a busy, much-frequented road, and the tread of human feet and the sound of the voices of passing travellers never ceased from early dawn until darkness had fallen and driven men to the shelter of the city.

The striking feature about the long stretch of uninhabited land which bordered one side of this road was a magnificent series of memorial arches built in close succession to each other for a considerable distance. They were composed of granite slabs, some very plain in their design, whilst others were highly artistic, and had evidently been produced by men who were masters of their craft. The general plan and execution were the same in all, but the ornamentation in some was most elaborate, and filled one with pleasure and delight to look at it.

Every one of these arches had been erected to commemorate some person who had already passed away, but whose virtues in life had been so conspicuous that the community had determined that they should not be forgotten, but that a record of them should be handed down to posterity, not only to keep their memory fragrant, but also to provide beautiful examples for succeeding generations.

Amongst the virtues recorded on these granite slabs, the most common was that of filial piety. A son had distinguished himself by his devotion to his parents, and had sacrificed his very life in faithful service to them. In undying words the story was carved into the stone; and the two mystic characters, "Holy Will," in the centre of the middle arch showed that the Emperor had given his permission for the erection of this memorial to a virtue so admired by the whole Chinese nation.

Other arches, almost as numerous as those raised to dutiful sons, were those setting forth the virtues of widows who had refused to marry again after their husbands had died.

In one case a widow had been left in great straits, and had been compelled to struggle with poverty and privations of every kind. All these she might have avoided had she been willing to listen to the offers of marriage that were made to her. Nothing, however, could make her forget the allegiance which she believed she still owed to the man who had first won her heart, or induce her to neglect her duty to the children of her marriage. She could never consent to let them become the property of another man, who might despise and ill-treat them, and who at any rate would never have for them the kind of affection which would lead him to make the sacrifices necessary to help them towards gaining a better position in life. Accordingly, she struggled on, enduring the greatest sufferings in order to provide for the needs of her sons as they gradually grew up; and eventually, owing to the hardships which she had borne so heroically, they all passed with honour through their examinations into the service of the Emperor.

On her death her story was forwarded to the capital, and his Majesty was so much moved by it that he gave his sanction for an arch to be erected to her memory, in order that for ages to come the crowds passing daily under its shadow might read the record of her self-sacrifice, and might learn how an admiring community had built this imperishable memorial of her wifely and motherly virtues.

But of all the numerous arches spanning the road there was one which attracted more attention than any other in the long line.

This was not because the virtues of the person, in whose honour it was raised, were so conspicuous, or because they so far outrivalled those recorded on the other arches, that men were constrained to stop and ponder over a life so remarkable for its heroism.

On the contrary, no virtues of any kind were mentioned. On the central arch, in large letters cut into the granite stone, were the words: "The Wonderful Man"; and that was all. Not a word of explanation was given as to who this wonderful man was; not a hint as to the special story of his life.

Scholars passing along the dusty road would catch a sight of this brief but cryptic inscription, and would at once be set wondering what a phrase so unclassical and so mysterious could possibly mean. They would walk round to the other side of the arch, to see if any explanation were afforded there. But no, the inscription was simply repeated in the same cold and veiled language; and so they would pass on, no wiser than before.

Farmers, with produce of their own growing suspended from their shoulders on stout bamboo poles, would come along at their accustomed trot, and would gaze at these words, "The wonderful man," with a curious look on their faces. They were not profound scholars, for on account of their poverty they had been compelled to leave school before they had mastered the ancient characters which make up the Chinese written language; but they knew enough to read such simple words as these. But what did the words really mean? They would laugh and joke with each other about them as they sped on their way, and many a witty suggestion would be merrily thrown out as a solution of the mystery.

The story that really lay behind this strange inscription was after all a most romantic and a most pathetic one.

Many years before, in a village beyond the hills skirting the plain on which the city was built, there lived a family of three; that is to say, a man and his wife and their little son. It was a supremely happy home. The husband and wife were devotedly attached to each other, and the ambition of every family amongst the four hundred millions of China had been granted them; for they had a son, who in the future would perpetuate the father's name, and present at his grave sacrificial offerings which would reach him in the Land of Shadows and keep him from starvation there.

The one great sorrow of the home was its poverty. There was no question but that they were exceedingly poor; and every morning, as the dawn broke upon them, they felt that they stood close up to the line beyond which lay hunger and even starvation.

But China is full of homes in such a situation. In this respect, indeed, the country is a land of heroes and heroines, for with vast masses of the people it is a daily struggle for food. Millions scattered throughout the Empire never or very rarely get enough to eat, and yet with splendid and pathetic patience they set themselves to suffer and to die, sternly and uncomplainingly, as becomes an Imperial race such as the Chinese are.

All that this particular family had to live upon were a few diminutive fields, which under the most favourable circumstances could produce barely enough sweet potatoes to keep body and soul together, and a scanty supply of vegetables with which to season them. If the rains failed and the potato vines were parched and blasted in their ridges by the great red-hot sun, then the husband had to look out for some other means of earning enough money to provide the bare necessaries of life for his little home.

Sometimes he would engage himself as a porter to carry the produce of the larger farmers to the great market-town which lay ten miles distant; but even then he could earn only just enough to provide the most meagre fare for his family for a week or two at the very most.

At other times he would secure better-paid employment by carrying a sedan-chair to some distant place, which would take him from home for several days at a time. He would return, it is true, with some goodly strings of cash, which would make his wife's eyes gleam with satisfaction at the possibilities they contained for at least another month of better food for them all; but it was dearly earned money. The man had not been trained as a chairbearer, and so had not learned the knack of manipulating the cross-bars, which rested on his shoulders, in such a way as to make the heavy burden less distressing to him. The result was that every time he returned from one of these expeditions, he was so seriously knocked up that for several days he had to lie in bed and refrain from all work.

Time went on, and the severe strain of his labour, and the poor quality of the food upon which he had to live, and the constant wear and tear of a constitution that never had been very strong, told upon the poor, overworked father. Gradually he became a confirmed invalid, so that he could not perform even the lightest work on his little farm. The shadows of coming misfortune grew darker and blacker every day. Hope began to abandon the hearts of husband and wife, and the sound of the footsteps of cruel Fate could almost be heard, as they drew nearer and nearer. Still these two heroic souls uttered no complaints, and there were no signs of heartbreak, except occasionally when the wife's eyes overflowed with tears, which she brushed hastily away lest her husband should see them and be distressed.

One night the storm was blowing a north-east gale outside, and the wind howled and moaned in such weird and doleful tones around the cottage, that it seemed as though some troubled spirit had been let loose to wail out a solemn requiem over a departing soul.

The Chinese believe that the air is filled with demons who have a mortal hatred of human beings, and who are ever on the watch to compass their destruction. These evil spirits gather round when disaster is about to fall on a home. They stand with invisible forms and peer into the darkened room, where some one lies dying, and they breathe out their delight in unholy sounds that strike terror into the hearts of the watchers.

In her anxiety about her husband the wife had not been able to sleep. Her heart throbbed with an infinite pain, and suppressed sobs now and again showed the anguish of her spirit. She began to realize, during this dreadful night, that her husband was exceedingly ill and might very probably die. The storm which raged outside, and the furious blasts and the uncanny sounds in the air, had terrified her and made her nervous.

It was true that only that day she had gone to the nearest temple, and had been assured by the god that her husband was going to recover; but he had been growing steadily weaker and weaker, and now the tempest had broken her courage and filled her with an unspeakable dread. What a tumult there was outside! Whose were the hideous voices that shrieked round the building, and whose were the hands that tore at the doors and windows until they shook and rattled under their grasp?

At last she could stand it no longer. She felt she must get up and see whether the mad and furious spirits, who had evidently gathered in force around the dwelling, were going to prove to be true prophets of evil.

The room was in darkness, so she lit the tiny wick that lay in a saucer of oil, and, peering into her husband's face, she looked with all her heart in her eyes into his sunken features. He seemed to know her, for a wan and wintry smile flickered round his lips and died out in a moment. She gazed at him with an almost breaking heart, for her instinct told her that the greyness of his face and the sudden paling of his lips were the forerunners of death. A long-drawn sigh, and a sob or two, and the one who was the dearest to her in all the world had left her forever.

After the funeral, which swallowed up everything she possessed, even to the very fields, which she had been compelled to sell in order to meet the expenses, the widow was left almost destitute. She was a woman, however, with a very strong character, and she realized the absolute necessity of making up her mind at once as to her course of action. That she should marry again seemed to every one the only course open to her; but this she determined she would never do. The memory of her dead husband was too precious to her, and besides it was her duty to rear up her little son to manhood, so that he might take his place amongst the scholars and thinkers of the Empire.

Soon a scheme, as original as it was daring, sprang up within her brain. No one must ever learn what it was. It must be the secret of her life, which she should bury within her own bosom, and which not even her own son should ever know, if she could possibly help it.

Having sold her cottage, she moved away to a quiet suburb outside the great city which was so renowned for learning. Then she discarded her woman's attire and dressed herself as a man. In no other way could she support herself and her child, for in China a woman is always under great disadvantages in the way of earning her own living. As a man, she knew that she could hold her own in any of the unskilled employments which she was capable of taking up. And so it turned out. She could carry as heavy a load as any of the men with whom she had to compete, and she was so civil and so well-behaved and so free from the use of profane language, that employers unaware of her sex used to pick her out in preference to others who offered themselves.

The years went by, and her little son was growing up to be a fine young man. The mother had determined that he should be a scholar. This was the one ambition of her life, and for this she slaved and toiled and denied herself almost the very necessaries of life.

Twenty years had passed since that stormy night. In the neighbouring city, the triennial examinations were just finished and the excitement was intense amongst the thousands of students who gathered round the Examination Hall to learn the names of the successful candidates.

By-and-by the son came home with a light step and with his eyes flashing with delight. His excitement was so great that he could hardly utter distinctly the words which rushed from his lips.

"Father," he cried, "the great desire of your heart and of mine has been granted to us today. I have passed, and that too with honours, for my name stands at the very top of the list of those who have been adjudged successful. And now, my beloved father, there will be no more hard work for you. My name will soon be flashed throughout the Province and will be posted in every Confucian guild, and scholars everywhere will speak with admiration of the great success I have won. My fortune has indeed been made, and it is due entirely to your self-denial, and to the sufferings and hardships you have consented to endure, during the long years of the past, that I have at length come into my kingdom, and that I need not be a labouring man, earning but a few cash a day, as you, my dear father, have been willing to do for the love of me."

All the time her son was talking, the mother's face shone with delight, for the hopes and wishes of a lifetime had come to her with a rush that almost overpowered her.

"Ah! if only my husband could have been with us now," she thought, "to share with us the supreme joy of this moment!" And her memory wandered back to that dreadful night, the blackest she had ever known in her life; and the roar of the storm which had thundered round the poor little shanty of a home and the ominous wailings of the spirits of evil which had struck a chill into her very blood, once more sounded in her ears as though the tragedy had happened only the night before.

In the fulness of the new joy which had suddenly transformed his life, the son went on to talk of the plans that he had been mapping out for the future. There would be no lack of money any more, he said, for employment would open up to him in all directions. He would be invited by the wealthy men of the city to teach their sons. He was a notable scholar now, and men of means would compete with each other to secure his services.

Before long too, he would be certain to obtain a government appointment which would bring riches into the home; and then his father would be a gentleman, and would live with him in his yamen, and be treated by all with honour and respect. And so with glowing face and glistening eyes, as the visions of the future rose up before him, the boy talked on with the enthusiasm of youth, whilst his mother gazed at him with admiring eyes.

At last he suddenly stopped. The laughter died out of his countenance, and with a grave and solemn face he exclaimed, "Father, I want you to tell me where my mother is buried. I must arrange to go to her grave and make the proper offerings to her spirit, and tell her how her son has prospered, and how grateful he is to her. That is my duty as a filial son, and I must not delay in performing it."

The young fellow did not notice the deadly pallor that spread over his parent's face as he uttered these words. He did not know that they produced a feeling of despair in the heart of his mother, for she now felt that she had come to the end of her life. She was a true and noble woman, with a high ideal of what a woman's life ought to be, and she dared not face the opinion of the world when it was discovered that she had lived as a man, and for many years had freely mingled with men. She had violated the laws of etiquette which regulate the conduct of women in every grade of society, and now the only thing left for her to do was to die.

Next morning, at sunrise, when the son entered his father's room, as was his daily custom, he found him lying upon his bed, dead, but marvellous to say, dressed in a woman's clothes. That the death was not accidental could be seen at a glance. The body lay prepared as if for a funeral. The clothes and the dressing of the hair, and the other minute details necessary in laying out a body for burial, had all been attended to. No outside hands need touch her, and no curious or unsympathetic eyes be gratified by peering too deeply into the mystery of her life.

The story spread with wonderful rapidity from the suburbs into the city. There it was discussed in every home, gentle and simple. The universal feeling was one of intense admiration for the devotion and heroism which had caused the mother to sacrifice her life for her son, and the mandarins and scholars petitioned the Emperor to issue an edict permitting an arch to be erected in order that the memory of such a noble woman should be kept alive for ever.

This petition was granted; and it was decided that the inscription to be carved upon the arch should consist simply of these words: "THE WONDERFUL MAN."

Sam-Chung and the Water-Demon

Rev. J. Macgowan

Sam-chung was one of the most famous men in the history of the Buddhist Church, and had distinguished himself by the earnestness and self-denial with which he had entered on the pursuit of eternal life. His mind had been greatly exercised and distressed at the pains and sorrows which mankind were apparently doomed to endure. Even those, however, terrible as they were, he could have managed to tolerate had they not ended, in the case of every human being, in the crowning calamity which comes upon all at the close of life.

Death was the great mystery which cast its shadow on every human being. It invaded every home. The sage whose virtues and teachings were the means of uplifting countless generations of men came under its great law. Men of infamous and abandoned character seemed often to outlive the more virtuous of their fellow-beings; but they too, when the gods saw fit, were hurried off without any ceremony. Even the little ones, who had never violated any of the laws of Heaven, came under this universal scourge; and many of them, who had only just commenced to live were driven out into the Land of Shadows by this mysterious force which dominates all human life.

Accordingly Sam-Chung wanted to be freed from the power of death, so that its shadow should never darken his life in the years to come.

After careful enquiry, and through friendly hints from men who, he had reason to believe, were fairies in disguise and had been sent by the Goddess of Mercy to help those who aspired after a higher life, he learned that it was possible by the constant pursuit of virtue to arrive at that stage of existence in which death would lose all its power to injure, and men should become immortal. This boon of eternal life could be won by every man or woman who was willing to pay the price for so precious a gift. It could be gained by great self-denial, by willingness to suffer, and especially by the exhibition of profound love and sympathy for those who were in sorrow of any kind. It appeared, indeed, that the one thing most imperatively demanded by the gods from those who aspired to enter their ranks was that they should be possessed of a divine compassion, and that their supreme object should be the succouring of distressed humanity. Without this compassion any personal sacrifice that might be made in the search for immortality would be absolutely useless.

Sam-Chung was already conscious that he was a favourite of the gods, for they had given him two companions, both with supernatural powers, to enable him to contend against the cunning schemes of the evil spirits, who are ever planning how to thwart and destroy those whose hearts are set upon higher things.

One day, accompanied by Chiau and Chu, the two attendants commissioned by the Goddess of Mercy to attend upon him, Sam-Chung started on his long journey for the famous Tien-ho river, to cross which is the ambition of every pilgrim on his way to the land of the Immortals. They endured many weeks of painful travelling over high mountains and through deep valleys which lay in constant shadow, and across sandy deserts where men perished of thirst or were struck down by the scorching heat of the sun, before they met any of the infernal foes that they expected to be lying in wait for them.

Weary and footsore, they at last arrived one evening on the shores of the mighty Tien-ho, just as the sun was setting. The glory of the clouds in the west streamed on to the waters of the river, and made them sparkle with a beauty which seemed to our wearied travellers to transform them into something more than earthly. The river here was so wide that it looked like an inland sea. There was no sign of land on the distant horizon, nothing but one interminable vista of waters, stretching away as far as the eye could reach.

One thing, however, greatly disappointed Sam-Chung and his companions, and that was the absence of boats. They had planned to engage one, and by travelling across the river during the night, they hoped to hurry on their way and at the same time to rest and refresh themselves after the fatigues they had been compelled to endure on their long land journey.

It now became a very serious question with them where they were to spend the night. There was no sign of any human habitation round about. There was the sandy beach along which they were walking, and there was the wide expanse of the river, on which the evening mists were slowly gathering; but no appearance of life. Just as they were wondering what course they should pursue, the faint sound of some musical instruments came floating on the air and caught their ear. Hastening forward in the direction from which the music came, they ascended a piece of rising ground, from the top of which they were delighted to see a village nestling on the hillside, and a small temple standing on the very margin of the river.

With hearts overjoyed at the prospect of gaining some place where they could lodge for the night, they hurried forward to the hamlet in front of them. As they drew nearer, the sounds of music became louder and more distinct. They concluded that some festival was being observed, or that some happy gathering amongst the people had thrown them all into a holiday mood. Entering the village, they made their way to a house which stood out prominently from the rest, and which was better built than any others they could see. Besides, it was the one from which the music issued, and around its doors was gathered a number of people who had evidently been attending some feast inside.

As the three travellers came up to the door, a venerable-looking old man came out to meet them. Seeing that they were strangers, he courteously invited them to enter; and on Sam-Chung asking whether they could be entertained for the night, he assured them that there was ample room for them in the house, and that he gladly welcomed them to be his guests for as long as it was their pleasure to remain.

"In the meanwhile you must come in," he said, "and have some food, for you must be tired and hungry after travelling so far, and the tables are still covered with the good things which were prepared for the feast today."

After they had finished their meal, they began to talk to the old gentleman who was so kindly entertaining them. They were greatly pleased with his courtesy and with the hearty hospitality which he had pressed upon them. They noticed, however, that he was very absent-minded, and looked as if some unpleasant thought lay heavy on his heart.

"May I ask," said Sam-Chung, "what was the reason for the great gathering here today? There is no festival in the Chinese calendar falling on this date, so I thought I would take the liberty of enquiring what occasion you were really commemorating."

"We were not commemorating anything," the old man replied with a grave face. "It was really a funeral service for two of my grand-children, who, though they are not yet dead, will certainly disappear out of this life before many hours have passed."

"But how can such a ceremony be performed over persons who are still alive?" asked Sam-Chung with a look of wonder in his face.

"When I have explained the circumstances to you, you will then be no longer surprised at this unusual service," replied the old man.

"You must know," he continued, "that this region is under the control of a Demon of a most cruel and bloodthirsty disposition. He is not like the ordinary spirits, whose images are enshrined in our temples, and whose main aim is to protect and guard their worshippers. This one has no love for mankind, but on the contrary the bitterest hatred, and his whole life seems to be occupied in scheming how he may inflict sorrow and disaster on them. His greatest cruelty is to insist that every year just about this time two children, one a boy and the other a girl, shall be conveyed to his temple by the river side to be devoured by him. Many attempts have been made to resist this barbarous demand, but they have only resulted in increased suffering to those who have dared to oppose him. The consequence is that the people submit to this cruel murder of their children, though many a heart is broken at the loss of those dearest to them."

"But is there any system by which the unfortunate people may get to know when this terrible sacrifice is going to be demanded from them?" asked Sam-Chung.

"Oh yes," replied the man. "The families are taken in rotation, and when each one's turn comes round, their children are prepared for the sacrifice. Moreover, that there may be no mistake, the Demon himself appears in the home a few days before, and gives a threatening command to have the victims ready on such a date. Only the day before yesterday, this summons came to us to have our children ready by tomorrow morning at break of day. That is why we had a feast today, and performed the funeral rites for the dead, so that their spirits may not be held under the control of this merciless Damon, but may in time be permitted to issue from the Land of Shadows, and be born again under happier circumstances into this world, which they are leaving under such tragic circumstances."

"But what is the Demon like?" enquired Sam-Chung.

"Oh, no one can ever tell what he is like," said the man. "He has no bodily form that one can look upon. His presence is known by a strong blast of wind which fills the place with a peculiar odour, and with an influence so subtle that you feel yourself within the grip of a powerful force, and instinctively bow your head as though you were in the presence of a being who could destroy you in a moment were he so disposed."

"One more question and I have finished," said Sam-Chung. "Where did this Demon come from, and how is it that he has acquired such an overmastering supremacy over the lives of men, that he seems able to defy even Heaven itself, and all the great hosts of kindly gods who are working for the salvation of mankind?"

"This Demon," the man replied, "was once an inhabitant of the Western Heaven, and under the direct control of the Goddess of Mercy. He must, however, have been filled with evil devices and fiendish instincts from the very beginning, for he seized the first opportunity to escape to earth, and to take up his residence in the grottoes and caverns that lie deep down beneath the waters of the Tien-ho. Other spirits almost as bad as himself have also taken up their abode there, and they combine their forces to bring calamity and disaster upon the people of this region."

Sam-Chung, whose heart was filled with the tenderest feelings of compassion for all living things, so much so that his name was a familiar one even amongst the Immortals in the far-off Western Heaven, felt himself stirred by a mighty indignation when he thought of how innocent childhood had been sacrificed to minister to the unnatural passion of this depraved Demon. Chiau and Chu were as profoundly indignant as he, and a serious consultation ensued as to the best methods to be adopted to save the little ones who were doomed to destruction on the morrow, and at the same time to break the monster's rule so that it should cease for ever.

Chiau, who was the more daring of the two whom I the goddess had deputed to protect Sam-Chung, at length cried out with flashing eyes, "I will personate the boy, Chu shall act the girl, and together we will fight the Demon and overthrow and kill him, and so deliver the people from his dreadful tyranny."

Turning to the old man, he said, "Bring the children here so that we may see them, and make our plans so perfect that the Demon with all his cunning will not be able to detect or frustrate them."

In a few moments the little ones were led in by their grandfather. The boy was seven and the girl was one year older. They were both of them nervous and shy, and clung timidly to the old man as if for protection.

They were very interesting-looking children. The boy was a proud, brave-spirited little fellow, as one could see by the poise of his head as he gazed at the strangers. If anything could be predicted from his looks, he would one day turn out to be a man of great power, for he had in his youthful face all the signs which promise a life out of the common. The girl was a shy little thing, with her hair done up in a childlike fashion that well became her. She was a dainty little mortal. Her eyes were almond-shaped, and with the coyness of her sex she kept shooting out glances from the corners of them at the three men who were looking at her. Her cheeks were pale, with just a suspicion of colour painted into them by the deft hand of nature; whilst her lips had been touched with the faintest dash of carmine, evidently just a moment ago, before she left her mother's side.

"Now, my boy," said Chiau to the little fellow, "keep your eyes fixed on me, and never take them from me for a moment; and you, little sister," addressing the girl, "do the same to the man next to me, and you will see something that will make you both laugh."

The eyes of them both were at once riveted on the two men, and a look of amazement slowly crept into their faces. And no wonder, for as they gazed they saw the two men rapidly changing, and becoming smaller and smaller, until they were the exact size and image of themselves. In their features and dress, and in every minute detail they were the precise pattern of the children, who with staring eyes were held spellbound by the magic change which had taken place in front of them.

"Now," said Chiau to the old gentleman, "the transformation is complete. Take the children away and hide them in the remotest and most inaccessible room that you have in your house. Let them be seen by no chattering woman or servant who might divulge our secret, so that in some way or other it might reach the ears of the Demon, and put him on his guard. Remember that from this moment these little ones are not supposed to exist, but that we are your grand-children who are to be taken to the temple tomorrow morning at break of day."

Just as the eastern sky showed the first touch of colour, two sedan-chairs were brought up to the door to carry the two victims away to be devoured by the Demon. A few frightened-looking neighbours peered through the gloom to catch a last glimpse of the children, but not one of them had the least suspicion that the boy and girl were really fairies who were about to wage a deadly battle with the Demon in order to deliver them from the curse under which they lived.

No sooner had the children been put into the temple, where a dim rush-light did but serve to disclose the gloom, and the doors had been closed with a bang, than the chair-bearers rushed away in fear for their very lives.

An instant afterwards a hideous, gigantic form emerged from an inner room and advanced towards the children. The Demon was surprised, however, to find that on this occasion the little victims did not exhibit any signs of alarm, as had always been the case hitherto, but seemed to be calmly awaiting his approach. There was no symptom of fear about them, and not a cry of terror broke from their lips; but with a fearless and composed mien they gazed upon him as he advanced.

Hesitating for a moment, as if to measure the foe which he began to fear might lie concealed beneath the figures of the boy and girl before him, the Demon's great fiery eyes began to flash with deadly passion as he saw the two little ones gradually expand in size, until they were transformed into beings as powerful and as mighty as himself. He knew at once that he had been outwitted, and that he must now battle for his very life; so, drawing a sword which had always stood him in good stead, he rushed upon the two who faced him so calmly and with such apparent confidence in themselves.

Chiau and Chu were all ready for the fray, and with weapons firmly gripped and with hearts made strong by the consciousness of the justice of their cause, they awaited the onslaught of the Demon.

And what a battle it was that then ensued in the dim and shadowy temple! It was a conflict of great and deadly significance, waged on one side for the deliverance of helpless childhood, and on the other for the basest schemes that the spirits of evil could devise. It was a battle royal, in which no quarter was either asked or given. The clash of weapons, and sounds unfamiliar to the human ear, and groans and cries which seemed to come from a lost soul, filled the temple with their hideous uproar.

At last the Demon, who seemed to have been grievously wounded, though by his magic art he had caused his wounds to be instantly healed, began to see that the day was going against him. One more mighty lunge with his broadsword, and one more furious onset, and his craven heart failed him. With a cry of despair he fled from the temple, and plunged headlong into the river flowing by its walls.

Great were the rejoicings when Chiau and Chu returned to report to Sam-Chung the glorious victory they had gained over the Demon. Laughter and rejoicing were heard in every home, and men and women assembled in front of their doors and at the corners of the narrow alley-ways to congratulate each other on the great deliverance which that day had come to them and to their children. The dread of the Demon had already vanished, and a feeling of freedom so inspired the men of the village that as if by a common impulse, they rushed impetuously down to where the temple stood, and in the course of a few hours every vestige of it had disappeared beneath the waters into which the Demon had plunged.

After his great defeat the baffled spirit made his way to the grotto beneath the waters, where he and the other demons had taken up their abode. A general council was called to devise plans to wipe out the disgrace which had been sustained, and to regain the power that had slipped from the Demon's grasp. They wished also to visit Sam-Chung with condign punishment which would render him helpless for the future.

"We must capture him," said one wicked-looking imp, who always acted as counsellor to the rest. "I have been told that to devour some of his flesh would ensure the prolongation of life for more than a thousand years."

The suggestion to seize Sam-Chung was unanimously accepted as a very inspiration of genius, and the precise measures which were to be adopted in order to capture him were agreed to after a long discussion.

On the very next morning, a most violent snowstorm set in, so that the face of the river and the hills all round about, and the very heavens themselves were lost in the blinding snow-drifts that flew before the gale. Gradually the cold became so intense that the Ice King laid his grip upon the waters of the Tien-ho, and turned the flowing stream into a crystal highway, along which men might travel with ease and safety. Such a sight had never been seen before by any of the people who lived upon its banks, and many were the speculations as to what such a phenomenon might mean to the welfare of the people of the region. It never occurred to any one that this great snow-storm which had turned into ice a river that had never been known to freeze before, was all the work of demons determined on the destruction of Sam-Chung.

Next day the storm had passed, but the river was one mass of ice which gleamed and glistened in the morning rays. Much to the astonishment of Sam-Chung and his two companions, they caught sight of a number of people, who appeared to be merchants, moving about on the bank of the river, together with several mules laden with merchandise. The whole party seemed intent on their preparations for crossing the river, which they were observed to test in various places to make sure that it was strong enough to bear their weight. This they seemed satisfied about, for in a short time the men and animals set forward on their journey across the ice.

Sam-Chung immediately insisted upon following their example, though the plan was vigorously opposed by the villagers, who predicted all kinds of dangers if he entered on such an uncertain and hazardous enterprise. Being exceedingly anxious to proceed on his journey, however, and seeing no prospect of doing so if he did not take advantage of the present remarkable condition of the river, he hastened to follow in the footsteps of the merchants, who by this time had already advanced some distance on the ice.

He would have been less anxious to enter on this perilous course, had he known that the innocent-looking traders who preceded him were every one of them demons who had changed themselves into the semblance of men in order to lure him to his destruction.

Sam-Chung and his companions had not proceeded more than five or six miles, when ominous symptoms of coming disaster began to manifest themselves. The extreme cold in the air suddenly ceased, and a warm south wind began to blow. The surface of the ice lost its hardness. Streamlets of water trickled here and there, forming great pools which made walking exceedingly difficult.

Chiau, whose mind was a very acute and intelligent one, became terrified at these alarming symptoms of danger, especially as the ice began to crack, and loud and prolonged reports reached them from every direction. Another most suspicious thing was the sudden disappearance of the company of merchants, whom they had all along kept well in sight. There was something wrong, he was fully convinced, and so with all his wits about him, he kept himself alert for any contingency. It was well that he did this, for before they had proceeded another mile, the ice began to grow thinner, and before they could retreat there was a sudden crash and all three were precipitated into the water.

Hardly had Chiau's feet touched the river, than with a superhuman effort he made a spring into the air, and was soon flying with incredible speed in the direction of the Western Heaven, to invoke the aid of the Goddess of Mercy to deliver Sam-Chung from the hands of an enemy who would show him no quarter.

In the meanwhile Sam-Chung and Chu were borne swiftly by the demons, who were eagerly awaiting their immersion in the water, to the great cave that lay deep down at the bottom of the mighty river. Chu, being an immortal and a special messenger of the Goddess, defied all the arts of the evil spirits to injure him, so that all they could do was to imprison him in one of the inner grottoes and station a guard over him to prevent his escape. Sam-Chung, however, was doomed to death, and the Demon, in revenge for the disgrace he had brought upon him, and in the hope of prolonging his own life by a thousand years, decided that on the morrow he would feast upon his flesh. But he made his plans without taking into consideration the fact that Sam-Chung was an especial favourite with the Goddess.

During the night a tremendous commotion occurred. The waters of the river fled in every direction as before the blast of a hurricane, and the caverns where the demons were assembled were illuminated with a light so brilliant that their eyes became dazzled, and for a time were blinded by the sudden blaze that flashed from every corner. Screaming with terror, they fled in all directions. Only one remained, and that was the fierce spirit who had wrought such sorrow amongst the people of the land near by. He too would have disappeared with the rest, had not some supernatural power chained him to the spot where he stood.

Soon the noble figure of the Goddess of Mercy appeared, accompanied by a splendid train of Fairies who hovered round her to do her bidding. Her first act was to release Sam-Chung, who lay bound ready for his death, which but for her interposition would have taken place within a few hours. He and his two companions were entrusted to the care of a chosen number of her followers, and conveyed with all speed across the river.

The Goddess then gave a command to some who stood near her person, and in a moment, as if by a flash of lightning, the cowering, terrified Demon had vanished, carried away to be confined in one of the dungeons where persistent haters of mankind are kept imprisoned, until their hearts are changed by some noble sentiment of compassion and the Goddess sees that they are once more fit for liberty.

And then the lights died out, and the sounds of fairy voices ceased. The waters of the river, which had been under a divine spell, returned to their course, and the Goddess with her magnificent train of beneficent spirits departed to her kingdom in the far-off Western Heaven.

The Spirit of the River

Pu Songling

In a small village along the river Tsz lived a fisherman named Siu. He started every night with his nets, and took very great care not to forget to bring with him a small jar of spirits. Before throwing his cast-net, he drank a small cup of the fragrant liquor and poured some drops into the slow current, praying aloud:

"O Spirit-of-the-river, please accept these offerings and favour your humble servant. I am poor and I must take some of the fishes that live in your cold kingdom. Don't be angry against me and don't prevent the eels and trouts coming to me!"

When every fisherman on the river brought back only one basket of fishes, he always proudly bore home a heavy charge of two or three baskets full to the brim.

Once, on a rosy dawn of early spring, when the sun, still below the horizon, began to eat with its golden teeth the vanishing darkness, he said aloud:

"O Spirit-of-the-river! For many years, every night I have drunk with you a good number of wine-cups; but I never saw your face; won't you favour me with your presence? We could sit together, and the pleasure of drinking would be much greater."

Hardly had he finished these words when, from the middle of the stream, emerged a beautiful young man clothed in pink, who slowly walked on the smooth surface of the limpid water, and sat on the boat's end, saying:

"Here I am."

The fisherman, being half-drunk, was not troubled in any way; he bowed to the young man, offered him, with his two hands, a cup of the strong wine, and said:

"Well! I long wished to receive your instructions, and I am very glad to see you. You must be mighty tired of living in that water; the few drops of wine I pour every night are quite lost in such a quantity of tasteless liquid. You had better come up every night; we will drink together and enjoy each other's company."

From this day, when darkness closed in, the Spirit waited for the fisherman and partook of his provisions. As soon as the sun rose above the horizon he suddenly disappeared. The fisherman did not find that very convenient; he asked his companion if he could not arrange to stay with him sometimes in the daytime.

"Impossible; we can't do such a thing, we spirits and ghosts. We belong to the kingdom of shadows. When the shadows, fighting the daylight, bring with them the Night, we are free to go and wander about. But as soon as the herald of the morn, the cock, has proclaimed the daily victory of the sun, we are powerless and must disappear."

On the same day the fisherman was sitting on the bank, smoking a pipe before going home with his baskets, when he saw a woman holding a child in her arms and hastening along the river towards a ford some hundred yards up stream. She was already in the water, when she missed her footing, fell into the river, and was rolled away by the stream. The child, by some happy chance, had fallen on the bank and lay there, crying.

The fisherman could easily have gone in his boat and saved the woman, who was still struggling to regain the bank, but he was a prudent man:

"This woman, whom I don't know, seems to be beautiful," thought he. "Maybe it is my friend The-Spirit-of-the-river who has arranged all this, and chosen the girl to be his wife. If I prevent her going down to his cold lodgings, he will be angry and ruin my fishing. All I could do is to adopt this boy until somebody comes and asks for him."

And he did not move, until the poor woman had disappeared in the yellow stream; then he took the child. Once back in the village, he inquired about the mother; nobody could tell who she was. The days passed and nobody asked for the boy. This was strange enough, but, stranger still, from this day the fisherman never saw The-Spirit-of-the-river again. He offered him many cups of wine, and his fishing was as good as ever, but though he prayed heartily, his companion of so many nights did not appear any more.

When the boy was three years old he insisted on accompanying his adopted father in his night fishing. Summer had come; the cold was no more to be feared. The man consented to take his adopted son with him; they started together in the twilight.

As soon as the darkness closed, the boy's voice changed; his appearance was different.

"What a silly man you are!" said he. "Don't you know me now? For more than two years I waited for an opportunity to tell you who I was. But you always went out at night and you never came back before the sun was high in the sky. You had never failed to present your offerings; so I could not resist your prayer when you asked me to stay with you in the daytime. Now, here I am, till your death; when the sun is up I shall only be your son, but when the night closes I shall be your companion, and we will enjoy together what longevity the Fate allows you."

The Ghost in Love

Pu Songling

On the 15th day of the First Moon, in the second year of the period of "Renewed Principles," the streets of the town of the Eastern Lake were thronged with people who were strolling about.

At the setting of the sun every shop was brightly lit up; processions of people moved hither and thither; strings of boys were carrying lanterns of every form and colour; whole families passed, every member of whom, young or old, small or big, was holding at the end of a thin bamboo the lighted image of a bird, an animal, or a flower.

Richer ones, several together, were carrying enormous dragons whose luminous wings waved at every motion and whose glaring eyes rolled from right to left. It was the Fête of the Lanterns.

A young man, clothed in a long pale green dress, allowed himself to be pushed about by the crowd; the passers-by bowed to him:

"How is my Lord Li The-peaceful?"

"The humble student thanks you; and you, how are you?"

"Very well, thanks to your happy influence."

"Does the precious student soon pass his second literary examination?"

"In two months; ignorant that I am. I am idling instead of working."

The fête was drawing to a close when The-peaceful quitted the main street, and went towards the East Gate, where the house was to be found in which he lived alone.

He went farther and farther: the moving lights were rarer; ere long he only saw before him the fire of a white lantern decorated with two red peonies. The paper globe was swinging to the steps of a tiny girl clothed in the blue linen that only slaves wore. The light, behind, showed the elegant silhouette of another woman, this one covered with a long jacket made in a rich pink silk edged with purple.

As the student drew nearer, the belated walker turned round, showing an oval face and big long eyes, wherein shone a bright speck, cruel and mysterious.

Li The-peaceful slackened his pace, following the two strangers, whose small feet glided silently on the shining flagstones of the street.

He was asking himself how he could begin a conversation, when the mistress turned round again, softly smiled, and in a low, rich voice, said to him:

"Is it not strange that in the advancing night we are following the same road?"

"I owe it to the favour of Heaven," he at once replied; "for I am returning to the East Gate; otherwise I should never have dared to follow you."

The conversation, once begun, continued as they walked side by side. The student learned that the pretty walker was called "Double-peony," that she was the daughter of Judge Siu, that she lived out of the city in a garden planted with big trees, on the road to the lake.

On arriving at his house The-peaceful insisted that his new friend should enter and take a cup of tea. She hesitated; then the two young people pushed the door, crossed the small yard bordered right and left with walls covered with tiles, and disappeared in the house....

The servant remained under the portal.

Daylight was breaking when the young girl came out again, calling the servant, who was asleep. The next evening she came again, always accompanied by the slave bearing the white lantern with two red peonies. It was the same each day following.

A neighbour who had watched these nocturnal visits was inquisitive enough to climb the wall which separated his yard from that of the lovers, and to wait, hidden in the shade of the house.

At the accustomed hour the street-door, left ajar, opened to let in the visitors.

Once in the courtyard, they were suddenly transformed, their eyes became flaming and red; their faces grew pale; their teeth seemed to lengthen; an icy mist escaped from their lips.

The neighbour did not see any more: terrified, he let himself slide to the ground and ran to his inner room.

The next morning he went to the student and told him what he had seen. The lover was paralysed with fear: in order to reassure himself he resolved to find out everything he could about his mistress.

He at once went outside the ramparts, on the road to the lake, hoping to find the house of Judge Siu. But at the place he had been told of there was no habitation; on the left, a fallow plain, sown with tombs, went up to the hills; on the right, cultivated fields extended as far as the lake.

However, a small temple was hidden there under big trees. The student had given up all hope; he entered, notwithstanding, into the sacred enclosure, knowing that travellers stayed there sometimes for several weeks.

In the first yard a bonze was passing in his red dress and shaven head; he stopped him.

"Do you know Judge Siu? He has a daughter——"

"Judge Siu's daughter?" asked the priest, astonished. "Well—yes—but wait, I will show her to you."

The-peaceful felt his heart overflowing with joy; his beloved one was living; he was going to see her by the light of day. He quickly followed his companion.

Passing the first court, they crossed a threshold and found themselves in a yard planted with high pine-trees and bordered by a low pavilion. The bonze, passing in first, pushed a door, and, turning round, said:

"Here is Judge Siu's daughter!"

The other stopped, terrified; on a trestle a heavy black lacquered coffin bore this inscription in golden letters: "Coffin of Double-peony, Judge Siu's daughter."

On the wall was an unfolded painting representing the little maid; a white lantern decorated with two red peonies was hung over it.

"Yes, she has been there for the last two years; her parents, according to the rite, are waiting for a favourable day to bury her."

The student silently turned on his heel and went back, not deigning to reply to the mocking bow of the priest.

Evening arrived; he locked himself in, and, covering his head with his blankets, he waited; sleep came to him only at daybreak.

But he could not cease to think of her whom he no longer saw; his heart beat as if to burst, when in the street he perceived the silhouette of a woman which reminded him of his friend.

At last he was incapable of containing himself any longer; one evening he stationed himself behind the door. After a few minutes there was a knock; he opened the door; it was only the little maid:

"My mistress is in tears; why do you never open the door? I come every evening. If you will follow me, perhaps she will forgive you."

The-peaceful, blinded by love, started at once, walking by the light of the white lantern.

The next day the neighbours, seeing that the student's door was open, and that his house was empty, made a declaration to the governor of the town.

The police made an inquest; they collected the evidence of several people who had been watching the nightly visitors the student had received. The bonze of the temple outside the city walls came to say what he knew. The chief of the police went to the road leading to the lake; he crossed the threshold of the little edifice, passed the first yard and at last opened the door of the pavilion.

Everything was in order, but under the lid of the heavy coffin one could see the corner of the long green dress of the student.

In order to do away with evil influences there was a solemn funeral.

Ever since this time, on light clear nights, the passers-by often meet the two lovers entwined together, slowly walking on the road which leads to the lake.

The Laughing Ghost

Pu Songling

Siu Long-mountain was one of the most celebrated students of the district of Perfect-flowers. Having mastered the mysterious theories of the ancient Classics, he took a fancy in the researches of the Taoist magicians, whose temples may be found in the smallest villages of the Empire. He soon discovered that, for the greater number, they were impostors; and, being proud of his newly acquired science, he concluded that none of them possessed any occult power.

When he came to this somewhat hasty conclusion, he was seated alone in his library; the night was already advancing; a small oil lamp hardly illuminated his books on the table he was sitting at.

"Yes, there is no doubt; nothing exists outside the material appearances. There is nothing occult in the world, and nothing can come out of nothingness."

As he was saying these words half aloud, he was startled by an unearthly laugh which seemed to come from behind his back. He turned quickly round; but nothing was to be seen.

His heart beating, he was listening intently; the laugh came from another part of the room.

Long-mountain was brave, but as people are brave who have only met the ordinary dangers of civilised life, such as barking dogs, insulting coolies, or angry dealers presenting a long-deferred bill. He tried in vain to believe it was only a joke imposed on him by some friend; nothing could prevail upon his growing terror.

Straining his eyes, he looked at the part of the room the laugh seemed to come from. At first he could not see anything, but by degrees he perceived a black shadow moving in a corner, then a strange form with a horse's head and a man's body, all covered with long black hair; the teeth were big and sharp as so many mountain-peaks. The eyes of this dreadful creature began shining so much that the whole room was illuminated. Then it began moving towards the man.

This was too much; the student screamed like a dying donkey, and, bursting the door open, he ran out into the courtyard.

From an open door in the western pavilion a ray of light crossed the darkness; four or five men were playing cards, drinking, and swearing. Long-mountain ran into their room, and, panting, explained his vision.

The men, being drunk, wanted to see the Thing; holding lanterns and lamps, they accompanied their visitor back to his studio. When they passed the doorway, Long-mountain screamed again; the Thing was still there. He would have run away had not the men, laughing and jesting, shown him what the Ghost in reality was—a long dress hung in a corner to a big hook, on which sat a black cat mewing desperately.

When the men closed the door and left him alone, the student was deeply ashamed of his terror; shaken by his emotion, he went to bed and tried to sleep. Sleep would not come; his nervousness seemed to increase. Starting at the smallest noise, he remained a long time wide awake; then he lost consciousness.

In the silence one only heard the cries of the night-birds and the buzzing of the autumn's insects; the lamp was out, but a brilliant moon began to pour its silver light through the window.

The door suddenly creaked; Long-mountain awoke and sat up on his bed; the door slowly opened, and the same Thing he had seen and heard entered the room and advanced towards the bed, while the same unearthly laugh came from the long and unshapely head; the flaming eyes were fixed on the student.

When the Thing was near the bed, Long-mountain fell heavily and did not move any more.

The Ghost stopped, put his hand on the breast of the man, remained in that position a moment, then went quickly and silently out of the room.

A man was standing outside.

"What did he say?" asked he.

"Be quiet!" said the Ghost, taking off his horse's head and discovering a man's very serious face. "The joke was good. But we have done it too well. I think he is dead of terror; we had better be as silent as a tomb about all this. The magistrate would never believe in a joke; we would be held responsible for this death and pay a heavy penalty."

Deceiving Shadows

Pu Songling

Night was falling when the horseshoes of the mules of my caravan resounded on the slippery flagstones of the village.

Tired by a long day of walking, I directed my steps towards the large hall of the inn, with the intention of resting a moment while my repast was being prepared.

In the darkened room the glimmer of a small opium-lamp lit up the pale and hollow face of an old man, occupied in holding over the flame a small ball of the black drug, which would soon be transformed into smoke, source of forgetfulness and dreams.

The old man returned my greeting, and invited me to lie down on the couch opposite to him. He handed me a pipe already prepared and we began talking together. As ordered by the laws of politeness, I remarked to my neighbour that he seemed robust for his age.

"My age? Do you, then, think I am so old?"

"But, as you are so wise, you must have seen sixty harvests?"

"Sixty! I am not yet thirty years old! But you must have come from a long way off, not to know who I am."

And while rolling the balls with dexterity in the palm of his hand, and making them puff out to the heat of the lamp, he told me his story.

His name was Liu Favour-of-heaven. Born and brought up in the capital, he had been promoted six years before to the post of sub-prefect in the town on which our refuge was dependent.

When coming to take his post, he stopped at the inn, the same one where we were. The house was full; but he had remarked, on entering, a long pavilion which seemed uninhabited. The landlord, being asked, looked perplexed; he ended by saying that the pavilion had been shut for the last two years; all the travellers had complained of noises and strange visions; probably mischievous spirits lived there.

Favour-of-heaven, having lived in the capital, but little believed in phantoms. He found the occasion excellent to establish his reputation in braving imaginary dangers.

His wife and his children implored him in vain; he persisted in his intention of remaining the night alone in the haunted house.

He had lights brought; installed himself in a big armchair, and placed across his knees a long and heavy sword.

Hours passed by; the sonorous noise of the gong struck by the watchman announced successively the hours, first of the Pig, then of the Rat. He grew drowsy. Suddenly, he was awakened by the gnashing of teeth. All the lights were out; the darkness, however, was not deep enough to prevent his being able to distinguish everything confusedly. Anguish seized him; his heart beat with violence; his staring eyes were fixed on the door.

By the half-opened door he perceived a round white mass, the deformed head of a monster, who, appearing little by little, stretched long hands with twisted fingers and claws.

Favour-of-heaven mechanically raised his weapon; his blood frozen in his veins, he tried to strike the head, whose indistinct features were certainly dreadful. Without doubt the blow had struck, for a frightful cry was heard; all the demons of the inferior regions seemed let loose with this yell; calls were heard from all sides. The trellised frames of the windows were shaken with violence. The monster gained the door. Favour-of-heaven pursued him and threw him down.

His terror was such that he felt he must strike and kill. Hardly had he finished than there entered, rolling from side to side, a little being, quite round, brandishing unknown weapons at the end of innumerable small hands. The prefect, with one blow, cut him in two like a watermelon.

However, the windows were shaken with growing rage; unknown beings entered by the door without interruption; the prefect threw them down one after another: a black shadow first, then a head balancing itself at the end of a huge neck, then the jaw of a crocodile, then a big bird with the chest and feet of a donkey.

Trembling all over, the man struck right and left, exhausted and panting; a cold perspiration overwhelmed him; he felt his strength gradually giving way, when the cock crowed at last the coming of the day.

Little by little, grey dawn designed the trellis of the windows, then the sun suddenly appeared above the horizon and darted its rays across the rents in the paper.

Favour-of-heaven felt his heart stand still; on the floor inundated with blood, the bodies lying there had human forms, forms that he knew: this one looked like his second wife, and this one, this little head that had rolled against the foot of the table, he would have sworn that it was his last son.

With a mad cry he threw away his weapon and ran to open the door, through which the sun poured in.

An armed crowd was moving in the yard.

"My family! my family! where is my family?"

"They are all with you in the pavilion!"

But as they were speaking they saw with stupor the hair of the young man becoming white, and the wrinkles of age cover his face, while he remained motionless as well as insensible.

They drew near; he rolled fainting on the ground. "And thus," ended the sub-prefect in the silence of the dark hall, where only the little light of the opium-lamp was shining, "I remained several days without knowledge of anything. When I came to myself, I had to bear the sorrow of having killed my whole family in these atrocious circumstances. I resigned my post: I had magnificent tombs built for all those who were killed this fatal night, and, since then, I smoke without ceasing the agreeable drug, in order to fly away from the remembrance, which will haunt me until my last day."

Magical Arts

Pu Songling

A certain Mr. Yü was a spirited young fellow, fond of boxing and trials of strength. He was able to take two kettles and swing them round about with the speed of the wind. Now, during the reign of Ch'ung Chêng,[67] when up for the final examination at the capital, his servant became seriously ill. Much troubled at this, he applied to a necromancer in the market-place[68] who was skilful at determining the various leases of life allotted to men. Before he had uttered a word, the necromancer asked him, saying, "Is it not about your servant, Sir, that you would consult me?" Mr. Yü was startled at this, and replied that it was. "The sick man," continued the necromancer, "will come to no harm; you, Sir, are the one in danger." Mr. Yü then begged him to cast his nativity, which he proceeded to do, finally saying to Mr. Yü, "You have but three days to live!" Dreadfully frightened, he remained some time in a state of stupefaction, when the necromancer quietly observed that he possessed the power of averting this calamity by magic, and would exert it for the sum of ten ounces of silver. But Mr. Yü reflected that Life and Death are already fixed,[69] and he didn't see how magic could save him. So he refused, and was just going away, whereupon the necromancer said, "You grudge this trifling outlay. I hope you will not repent it." Mr. Yü's friends also urged him to pay the money, advising him rather to empty his purse than not secure the necromancer's compassion. Mr. Yü, however, would not hear of it and the three days slipped quickly away. Then he sat down calmly in his inn to see what was going to happen. Nothing did happen all day, and at night he shut his door and trimmed the lamp; then, with a sword at his side, he awaited the approach of death.

By-and-by, the clepsydra[70] shewed that two hours had already gone without bringing him any nearer to dissolution; and he was thinking about lying down, when he heard a scratching at the window, and then saw a tiny little man creep through, carrying a spear on his shoulder, who, on reaching the ground, shot up to the ordinary height. Mr. Yü seized his sword and at once struck at it; but only succeeded in cutting the air. His visitor instantly shrunk down small again, and made an attempt to escape through the crevice of the window; but Yü redoubled his blows and at last brought him to the ground. Lighting the lamp, he found only a paper man,[71] cut right through the middle. This made him afraid to sleep, and he sat up watching, until in a little time he saw a horrid hobgoblin creep through the same place. No sooner did it touch the ground than he assailed it lustily with his sword, at length cutting it in half. Seeing, however, that both halves kept on wriggling about, and fearing that it might get up again, he went on hacking at it. Every blow told, giving forth a hard sound, and when he came to examine his work, he found a clay image all knocked to pieces. Upon this he moved his seat near to the window, and kept his eye fixed upon the crack. After some time, he heard a noise like a bull bellowing outside the window, and something pushed against the window-frame with such force as to make the whole house tremble and seem about to fall. Mr. Yü, fearing he should be buried under the ruins, thought he could not do better than fight outside; so he accordingly burst open the door with a crash and rushed out. There he found a huge devil, as tall as the house, and he saw by the dim light of the moon that its face was as black as coal. Its eyes shot forth yellow fire: it had nothing either upon its shoulders or feet; but held a bow in its hand and had some arrows at its waist. Mr. Yü was terrified; and the devil discharged an arrow at him which he struck to the ground with his sword. On Mr. Yü preparing to strike, the devil let off another arrow which the former avoided by jumping aside, the arrow quivering in the wall beyond with a smart crack. The devil here got very angry, and drawing his sword flourished it like a whirlwind, aiming a tremendous blow at Mr. Yü. Mr. Yü ducked, and the whole force of the blow fell upon the stone wall of the house, cutting it right in two. Mr. Yü then ran out from between the devil's legs, and began hacking at its back—whack!—whack! The devil now became furious, and roared like thunder, turning round to get another blow at his assailant. But Mr. Yü again ran between his legs, the devil's sword merely cutting off a piece of his coat. Once more he hacked away—whack!—whack!—and at length the devil came tumbling down flat. Mr. Yü cut at him right and left, each blow resounding like the watchman's wooden gong; and then, bringing a light, he found it was a wooden image about as tall as a man. The bow and arrows were still there, the latter attached to its waist. Its carved and painted features were most hideous to behold; and wherever Mr. Yü had struck it with his sword, there was blood. Mr. Yü sat with the light in his hand till morning, when he awaked to the fact that all these devils had been sent by the necromancer in order to kill him, and so evidence his own magical power. The next day, after having told the story far and wide, he went with some others to the place where the necromancer had his stall; but the latter, seeing them coming, vanished in the twinkling of an eye. Some one observed that the blood of a dog would reveal a person who had made himself invisible, and Mr. Yü immediately procured some and went back with it. The necromancer disappeared as before, but on the spot where he had been standing they quickly threw down the dog's blood. Thereupon they saw his head and face all smeared over with the blood, his eyes glaring like a devil's; and at once seizing him, they handed him over to the authorities, by whom he was put to death.

The Patch of Lamb's Skin

Pu Songling

In the twenty-fourth year K'ang-hsi lived in a remote district of the western provinces, a man who could remember his former lives. He was now a "tsin-shi," "entered-among-the-learned," renowned, and much considered by his friends.

When speaking of the existences he had gone through, he used to say:

"As far as I remember, I was first a soldier—it was in the last days of the Ming dynasty; my regiment was encamped at The-Divided-roads on the Ten-thousand-miles-great-wall. My remembrances are not very clear as to whom we fought with, but I remember the joy of striking the enemy, the hissing of the arrows, the yelling of the charging troops.

"I was still young when I was killed. After death, of course I was called before the tribunal of The-King-of-shadows. Closing my eyes, I can still see the big caldrons full of boiling oil for the trying of criminals; the Judge in embroidered dress seated behind a red table; the satellites everywhere, ready to act on the first word,—in fact, everything exactly the same as in the worldly tribunals, excepting that, in the eastern part of the hall, there were huge wooden stands from which hung skins of every description—horse-skins, lambs' skins, dogs' skins, and human skins of every age and condition; skins of old men, of fat and important people, of lean and shrivelled men, of boys and girls.

"The trial began; the souls, according to their deeds, were condemned to put on one of the skins and to come up again to the Lighted World in this new shape.

"When my turn came I was sentenced to put a dog's skin on; and in this low shape I was thrown again in the stream of life. But as I had not forgotten my former condition, I was so ashamed, that the first day I came on earth I threw myself under the wheels of a heavy carriage and died.

"The-King-of-shadows was extremely surprised to see me again so soon; the dogs, as a rule, having no conscience, he could not suppose I had killed myself, and did not hold me responsible for it.

"This time, I was born again as a pig. Pigs are valuable, and there are always people to look after them; so I could not kill myself. I tried to starve myself to death, but hunger was the strongest, and I had to endure such a life. Happily, the butcher soon put a speedy end to it.

"When my name was called to the tribunal of Darkness, the King-of-shadows looked over the pages of the Book and said:

"'He must be a lamb now.'

"The runners took a white lamb's skin, brought it, and began putting it over my body. While this was going on, the secretary, who was writing the sentence in the Book, started and said to the Judge:

"'Your Honour, there is a mistake. Please Your Honour read over again; this soul has to be a man now.'

"You know that, on the Big Book of Shadows, all our past deeds are recorded as well as our future destiny.

"The Judge looked at it over again and said:

"'True! Happily, you saw the mistake.'

"Then, turning to the runners, he ordered them to take off the skin, which already covered more than half my body. They had to exert all their strength, and even so, they tore it off into pieces. It hurt me so much that I thought I could not stand it and I should die; but I was dead, and I could not die more than that.

"At last they left me bleeding and panting, and I was born again in my present condition. But they had forgotten a piece of lamb's skin on my right shoulder, and I still have it now."

And he uncovered his arm and shoulder to show a piece of white woollen hair on his right shoulder.

The Corpse the Blood-Drinker

Pu Songling

Night was slowly falling in the narrow valley. On the winding path cut in the side of the hill about twenty mules were following each other, bending under their heavy load; the muleteers, being tired, did not cease to hurry forward their animals, abusing them with coarse voices.

Comfortably seated on mules with large pack-saddles, three men were going along at the same pace as the caravan of which they were the masters. Their thick dresses, their fur boots, and their red woollen hoods protected them from the cold wind of the mountain.

In the darkness, rendered thicker by a slight fog, the lights of a village were shining, and soon the mules, hurrying all together, jostling their loads, crowded before the only inn of the place.

The three travellers, happy to be able to rest, got down from their saddles when the innkeeper came out on the step of his door and excused himself, saying all his rooms were taken.

"I have still, it is true, a large hall the other side of the street, but it is only a barn, badly shut. I will show it to you."

The merchants, disappointed, consulted each other with a look; but it was too late to continue their way; they followed their landlord.

The hall that was shown to them was big enough and closed at the end by a curtain. Their luggage was brought; the bed-clothes rolled on the pack-saddles were spread out, as usual, on planks and trestles.

The meal was served in the general sitting-room, in the midst of noise, laughing, and movement – smoking rice, vegetables preserved in vinegar, and lukewarm wine served in small cups. Then every one went to bed; the lights were put out and profound silence prevailed in the sleeping village.

However, towards the hour of the Rat, a sensation of cold and uneasiness awoke one of the three travellers named Wang Fou, Happiness-of-the-kings. He turned in his bed, but the snoring of his two companions annoyed him; he could not get to sleep. Again, seeing that his rest was finished, he got up, relit the lamp which was out, took a book from his baggage, and stretched himself out again. But if he could not sleep, it was just as impossible to read. In spite of himself, his eyes quitted the columns of letters laid out in lines and searched into the darkness that the feeble light did not contrive to break through.

A growing terror froze him. He would have liked to awaken his companions, but the fear of being made fun of prevented him.

By dint of looking, he at last saw a slight movement shake the big curtain which closed the room. There came from behind a crackling of wood being broken. Then a long, painful threatening silence began again.

The merchant felt his flesh thrill; he was filled with horror, in spite of his efforts to be reasonable.

He had put aside his book, and, the coverlet drawn up to his nose, he fixed his enlarged eyes on the shadowy corners at the end of the room.

The side of the curtain was lifted; a pale hand held the folds. The stuff, thus raised, permitted a being to pass, whose form, hardly distinct, seemed penetrated by the shadow.

Happiness-of-kings would have liked to scream; his contracted throat allowed no sound to escape. Motionless and speechless, he followed with his horrified look the slow movement of the apparition which approached.

He, little by little, recognised the silhouette of a female, seen by her short quilted dress and her long narrow jacket. Behind the body he perceived the curtain again moving.

The spectre, in the meantime bending over the bed of one of the sleeping travellers, appeared to give him a long kiss.

Then it went towards the couch of the second merchant. Happiness-of-kings distinctly saw the pale figure, the eyes, from which a red flame was shining, and sharp teeth, half-exposed in a ferocious smile, which opened and shut by turns on the throat of the sleeper.

A start disturbed the body under the cover, then all stopped: the spectre was drinking in long draughts.

Happiness-of-kings, seeing that his turn was coming, had just strength enough to pull the coverlet over his head. He heard grumblings; a freezing breath penetrated through the wadded material.

The paroxysm of terror gave the merchant full possession of his strength; with a convulsive movement he threw his coverlet on the apparition, jumped out of his bed, and, yelling like a wild beast, he ran as far as the door and flew away in the night.

Still running, he felt the freezing breath in his back, he heard the furious growlings of the spectre.

The prolonged howling of the unhappy man filled the narrow street and awoke all the sleepers in their beds, but none of them moved; they hid themselves farther and farther under their coverlets. These inhuman cries meant nothing good for those who should have been bold enough to go outside.

The bewildered fugitive crossed the village, going faster and faster. Arriving at the last houses, he was only a few feet in advance and felt himself fainting.

The road at the extremity of the village was bordered with narrow fields shaded with big trees. The instinct of a hunted animal drove on the distracted merchant; he made a brisk turn to the right, then to the left, and threw himself behind the knotted trunk of a huge chestnut-tree. The freezing hand already touched his shoulder; he fell senseless.

* * *

In the morning, in broad daylight, two men who came to plough in this same field were surprised to perceive against the tree a white form, and, on the ground, a man stretched out. This fact coming after the howling in the night appeared strange to them; they turned back and went to find the Chief of the Elders. When they returned, the greater part of the inhabitants of the village followed them.

They approached and found that the form against the tree was the corpse of a young woman, her nails buried in the bark; from her mouth a stream of blood had flowed and stained her white silk jacket. A shudder of horror shook the lookers-on: the Chief of the Elders recognised his daughter dead for the last six months whose coffin was placed in a barn, waiting for the burial, a favourable day to be fixed by the astrologers.

The innkeeper recognised one of his guests in the man stretched on the ground, whom no care could revive.

They returned in haste to find out in what condition the coffin was: the door of the barn was still open. They went in; a coverlet was thrown on the ground near the entrance; on two beds the great sun lit up the hollow and greenish aspect of the corpses whose blood had been emptied.

Behind the drawn curtain the coffin was found open. The corpse of the young woman evidently had not lost its inferior soul, the vital breath. Like all beings deprived of conscience and reason, her ferocity was eager for blood.

The River of Sorrows

Pu Songling

Along the path leading to the city of All-virtues, in the obscure night, a poor coolie, grumbling under a heavy load of salt, was trudging on as fast as he could.

"I shall never get there before the hour of the Rat, and my wife will say again; 'Wang The-tenth has drunk too many cups of wine.' She does not know the weight of that stuff!"

As he was thus thinking, two men suddenly jumped from either side of the road and held him by the arms.

"What do you want?" cried the poor man. "I am only an unhappy carrier, and my load is only salt, very common salt."

"We don't want your salt, and you had better throw it down. We are sent from the Regions below and we want you to come down with us."

"Am I dead already?" asked The-tenth. "I did not know. I must tell my wife. Can't you come again tomorrow night?"

"Impossible to wait. You must come immediately. But I don't think you are dead. It is only to work for a few days down below."

"This is rather strange," replied The-tenth. "With all the people who have died since the world has been the world you still want living men? We don't go and ask you to do our work, do we?"

While thus arguing, he felt himself suffocated by a heavy smell and lost consciousness.

When he awoke, he was on the bank of a fairly large river. Hundreds of men were standing in the water; some of them carried baskets; others, with spades and different utensils, were dragging out what they could from the bottom. Soldiers with heavy sticks struck those who stopped even for a second.

On the bank several men were standing, and a number of others came from time to time. A magistrate was sitting behind a big red table, turning over the pages of a book. At last, he called "Wang The-tenth."

"Wang The-tenth!" repeated the soldiers. And they threw the poor man down in a kneeling position in front of the magistrate, who looked on the book and said:

"You have been an undutiful son; do you remember the day when you told your father he was a fool?"

Then speaking to the soldiers, he said:

"To the river!"

The guards pushed the man, gave him a basket, and ordered him to help in the cleaning of the river.

The water was red and thick; its stench was abominable; the bodies of the workmen were all red, and The-tenth discovered it was blood. He looked at the first basket he took to the bank; it was only putrid flesh and broken bones.

Thus he worked day by day without stopping. When he was not going fast enough, the guards struck him with their sticks, and their sticks were bones. In the deep places he had to put his head into the water and felt the filthy stuff fill his nostrils and mouth.

Among the workers he recognised many people he used to know. A great number died and were carried away by the stream.

At last two guards called his name, helped him to the bank, and suddenly he found himself again on the path leading to the city of All-virtues.

Now, on the night when The-tenth was taken away, his wife waited for him. Troubled not to see him, she started as soon as the sun beamed, and looked for him on the road. She soon found his body lying unconscious. Trying in vain to revive him, she thought him dead, and wept bitterly.

Not being strong enough to bring home his body, she came back to town in order to ask the help of her family. In the afternoon, clad in the white dress of mourning, and accompanied by her four brothers, she started again.

What was her astonishment and fear when, approaching the place where she had found the body, she saw her husband walking towards her. He was all covered with blood, and the stench was so strong that everybody pinched his nose.

When he had explained what had happened, they all returned to the village. The-tenth knelt reverently before his ancestors' tablet, offered butter and rice, and burnt incense.

This very day he asked a Taoist priest what was the river he had worked in. The priest explained to him it was called the River-of-sorrows. It took its source in the outer world in every tear that was shed. The people that killed themselves out of despair were floated down its stream to the kingdom of shadows.

Sometimes the sorrows on earth were so great that people killed themselves by thousands and did not shed any tears; the blood then was too thick to wash away the decayed remains, and the river-bed had to be cleaned lest it should overflow and drown the whole world. Living men alone were employed in this work, for only living men can cure living men's sorrows.

The Marble Arch

Pu Songling

When the troubles began to break out in Hankow, many families were alarmed. Those who were not ignorant of the powerful organisation of the revolutionists left the town as soon as possible, anticipating that it would soon be plundered and burnt.

The retired prefect, Kiun, was amongst the first to embark in order to go down the river. His house was situated at several lis from the river, on the confines of the suburbs, outside the fortified enclosure. He had only been married a short time, and was living with his father and mother.

When the baggage at last was ready, the bearers fixed it in the middle of their long bamboos and set off two by two, grumbling under the heavy load. The two old people followed; Kiun and his young wife, the charming Seaweed, helped them as well as they could.

In order to avoid crossing the centre of the town, they followed the crenellated wall by an almost deserted road. A young man and woman alone were sauntering in the same direction, carrying parcels on their shoulders.

"Where are you going to?" they asked, as it is the custom to do between travellers.

"As far as the river," replied Kiun. "And you?"

"We also," said the young man. "What is your precious name?"

"My contemptible name is Kiun. But you, deign to inform me about your family?"

"My name is Wang The-king. We are flying from the insurrection."

They thus talked while walking in company.

Seaweed took the advantage of a moment when the new-comers were a little in front to bend towards her husband.

"Do not let us get in the same junk with these strangers. The man has looked at me several times in a rude way; his eyes are unsteady and fickle; I am afraid of him."

Kiun made a sign of assent. But when they had arrived on the quay, Wang The-king gave himself so much trouble to find a junk and help to embark the luggage that the prefect, bound by the rites, could not avoid asking him to get on board the boat with him.

They unmoored; Wang The-king established himself on the prow with his wife, near the mariners; he spoke a long time with them while they were passing the last houses of the large city.

When night fell, they were in a part of the river where it got broader to such an extent that you could no longer distinguish the banks. The wind was blowing rather violently and the unfurling waves projected heavy showers on the mats which covered the quarter-deck.

Kiun, uneasy, went to the prow of the boat in order to question the master. The bright moon was rising, lighting the dark line of the bank. They approached in order to throw the anchor.

Wang The-king was on the narrow bridge; when Kiun came to his side, he coolly pushed the poor prefect overboard. Kiun's father was two paces behind; Wang ran to him and threw him also into the tumultuous waters of the rapid current. Kiun's mother, hearing a cry and a struggle, went to see what was happening, and she also was precipitated into the foaming river.

Seaweed, from the cabin, had seen all; but she took good care not to go outside; she moaned:

"Alas! my father-in-law and my mother-in-law are dead! My husband has been killed! I am going to die, too!"

While she was crying, Wang The-king entered the cabin.

"Fear nothing," said he; "forget those people who are no more and won't come back. I am going to take you home to the city of The-Golden-tombs. There I have fields and houses belonging to me; I will give them to you."

The young woman kept back her sobs and said nothing; she thought it wise not to provoke the murderer.

Wang The-king, very satisfied with his prospects, went back to the mariners, gave them the greater part of what his victims had brought in silver and luggage; then he quietly took his dinner and retired to his cabin with his wife. The woman had a strange look, but she did not say anything, and they went to sleep.

Towards the hour of the Rat, the woman began to groan; then she started out of her sleep and cried to her husband:

"Kill me, repudiate me! I can no longer stay with you! Thunder and lightning will strike you! I have dreamt it; I will no longer be the wife of a murderer and a thief!"

Wang, furious, struck her. But as she continued, he took her in his arms and threw her into the river.

On the second day the boat arrived at The-Golden-tombs. Wang took Seaweed to his family. When his old mother asked what he had done with his first wife, he replied:

"She fell in the river, and I will marry this one."

They were soon settled in the house. Wang wished to take liberties with Seaweed, who gently drove him back.

"We must not neglect the rites. Do not let us forget to empty first the marriage cup."

Wang joyously accepted; and soon, seated opposite each other, they began exchanging cups of wine in the ritual way.

Seaweed, however, pretended to drink, and tried to make her lover tipsy; she contrived this little by little.

Wang, rendered sleepy by the wine, undressed himself, got on the bed, and ordered the young woman to put out the lamps and come to him.

She carefully blew the lamps and said:

"I will come in a minute!"

Then she quickly went to her luggage, took out a sword she had hidden there, and came back. Feeling with her hands in the darkness, she found the throat of the man and struck him as hard as she could: the man screamed and tried to get up; she struck again and again: there was a moaning, a gurgle, and then silence.

However, Wang's mother, having heard some noise, came with a lantern. Seaweed killed her before the old woman could even say a word.

Then the young woman, having avenged her family, tried to cut her own throat, in order to join her husband. The sword was blunt and she was only able to scratch herself. She then remembered that, outside the house, there was a fairly big pond; she ran out and threw herself into the water.

Some neighbours saw her and ran to her help; other people came; lanterns were brought forth; the poor girl at last was taken out of the pond, and brought back to her house. But, when the new-comers entered the room, they saw the bodies and the blood.

"Murder! Murder!" cried they.

And they immediately sent a boy to call the police. The constables came and looked all over the room; they soon found in Seaweed's luggage a note prepared by the unfortunate woman and stating the truth about her family's death. The assistants were loud in their praise of her act:

"She avenged her husband; she has been witty enough to beguile the murderer; and now she has killed herself! Such an act of courage and virtue has not been heard of for centuries. We must ask the authorities to build her a marble arch to commemorate her history, and be an example to future generations."

While all this was going on, they tried to revive the woman; everything was done, but in vain. A coffin was then brought in, and the girl transferred to it, covered with her best garments and jewels. The lid was screwed on, and everybody left the house.

We must now come back to the evening when Wang pushed into the water Seaweed's husband. Kiun was a strong man and a very good swimmer; surprised by this sudden attack, all he could do at first was to keep his head out of the tumultuous water. He then thought to go back to the boat, but, on the foaming expanse nothing was to be seen; the rapid current had driven him too far. At last the water brought him to a curving beach, where he was able to land.

Walking disconsolately on the sand, he saw a human body rolled by the surge; he approached, and recognised his father; farther on he saw his mother; both he dragged out of the water. Most uneasy about his wife, he walked on the river's edge, straining his eyes; the moon was shining; he saw at last a human being holding a big piece of wood. He swam to her, pushed her to the beach, and took her he thought was his wife to the dry sand. He undid the upper garment in order to rub her members; when he saw she was not so cold, he wiped her hair out of her face. His stupor was immense in recognising Wang's wife.

The sun rose at last and warmed them. The young woman sighed, opened her eyes, and, completely herself again, told Kiun what she had seen:

"My husband is a murderer. In a dream I saw the King-of-Shadows himself sitting behind his tribunal and writing his name on the death-list. Besides, he is in love with your wife. If you wish it, we will go together straight to The Golden-tombs and do what we can to avenge ourselves."

Kiun, seeing a man coming to work in a field not far from there, went to him and told him in a few words what had happened; the man led them to his landlord, a rich man, who gave them food and warm dresses, sent men to bring the drowned bodies to a side house and have them properly buried. Then he advanced a certain sum of money to Kiun, who agreed to send it back when he should get to a place where he could find a correspondent of his bankers.

Then Kiun and his companion engaged a small boat and went down the river. When they got to The Golden-tombs, they questioned the people in the street about Wang. A month had elapsed since the events we have told of; the first man they questioned looked at them in wonder:

"How is it you don't know what happened? Wang is dead; he has been killed by a virtuous woman whose family he had murdered and who killed herself afterwards. You have only to go on; in the first street to your right you will see a new marble arch which has just been erected to commemorate virtuous Seaweed's courageous death."

Kiun thought his heart would burst; he dragged his companion to the marble arch and read the inscription. Then he bought a bundle of those imitations of gold and silver ingots made with paper which people burn on the tombs in order to send some money to the dead; he went to the tomb in the place indicated by the inscription.

There he reverently knelt, and, after having knocked the ground with his forehead, he burnt the paper-ingots, rose, and went away with Wang's wife.

When they were back in their boat, they discussed their plans and resolved to go down the river to Shanghai.

They were leaving the harbour, when a small boat crossed their way; two women sat on the bench. One of them reminded Kiun strangely of his late wife. The woman had looked up at him and seemed surprised. The retired prefect, moved by a mysterious strength, pronounced aloud a sentence which used to make his wife laugh when they were together happy in Hankow:

"I see wild geese flying high in the sky."

Seaweed, when she was alive, used to answer by a phrase which had nothing to do with the first sentence, and had made them laugh very often by its stupidity. The woman in the boat said it too:

"The dog wants the cat's biscuit; you quickly shut it in the house."

Kiun, wondering whether it was Seaweed's ghost, asked the mariners to go alongside the other boat; he jumped in it; the woman threw her arms round his neck, and they wept together.

"Are you alive? or is it only your ghost I hold in my arms?" asked he.

"I am alive!"

Then she told him her adventures; when she was put into the coffin, she had some jewels on. One of the assistants resolved to steal them; he waited till everybody was gone and the house empty; then he deliberately unscrewed the coffin's lid and rifled what he could. He was trying to take a ring off her hand, when the supposed corpse rose and screamed.

The poor man thought his last hour had come and did not move. Seaweed, seeing her jewels in his hands, and seeing the coffin she was in, grasped the situation at a glance.

"You want my jewels! Have them if you like; you saved my life, and without you I would have been stifled in this gruesome box."

The man at first dared not accept; then he said:

"In exchange for your kindness, I will tell you something. In the third house in the first street lives a rich widow; she is alone and would like to adopt a girl; go to her and tell her everything. She will be happy to give you a home."

Then he helped her to get out of the coffin, screwed the lid again, and disappeared. Seaweed went straight to the house. The widow received her with the greatest kindness, and asked of her to let everybody believe she was dead; if not, there would have been a lawsuit.

Both women, now united by the closest affection, had been out on the river for pleasure's sake when they saw Kiun's bark. The widow, when the explanations were finished, opened her arms to Kiun; she called him her son-in-law. Seaweed asked Wang's wife to be the second wife of her husband. And they all lived long and happy.

The Marriage of the Fox's Daughter

Pu Songling

A president of the Board of Civil Office, named Yin, and a native of Li-ch'êng, when a young man, was very badly off, but was endowed with considerable physical courage. Now in his part of the country there was a large establishment, covering several acres, with an unbroken succession of pavilions and verandahs, and belonging to one of the old county families; but because ghosts and apparitions were frequently seen there, the place had for a long time remained untenanted, and was overgrown with grass and weeds, no one venturing to enter in even in broad daylight. One evening when Yin was carousing with some fellow-students, one of them jokingly said, "If anybody will pass a night in the haunted house, the rest of us will stand him a dinner." Mr. Yin jumped up at this, and cried out, "What is there difficult in that?" So, taking with him a sleeping-mat, he proceeded thither, escorted by all his companions as far as the door, where they laughed and said, "We will wait here a little while. In case you see anything, shout out to us at once." "If there are any goblins or foxes," replied Yin, "I'll catch them for you." He then went in, and found the paths obliterated by long grass, which had sprung up, mingled with weeds of various kinds. It was just the time of the new moon, and by its feeble light he was able to make out the door of the house. Feeling his way, he walked on until he reached the back pavilion, and then went up on to the Moon Terrace, which was such a pleasant spot that he determined to stop there. Gazing westwards, he sat for a long time looking at the moon – a single thread of light embracing in its horns the peak of a hill – without hearing anything at all unusual; so, laughing to himself at the nonsense people talked, he spread his mat upon the floor, put a stone under his head for a pillow, and lay down to sleep. He had watched the Cow-herd and the Lady until they were just disappearing, and was on the point of dropping off, when suddenly he heard footsteps down below coming up the stairs. Pretending to be asleep, he saw a servant enter, carrying in his hand a lotus-shaped lantern, who, on observing Mr. Yin, rushed back in a fright, and said to someone behind, "There is a stranger here!" The person spoken to asked who it was, but the servant did not know; and then up came an old gentleman, who, after examining Mr. Yin closely, said, "It's the future President: he's as drunk as can be. We needn't mind him; besides, he's a good fellow, and won't give us any trouble." So they walked in and opened all the doors; and by-and-by there were a great many other people moving about, and quantities of lamps were lighted, till the place was as light as day. About this time Mr. Yin slightly changed his position, and sneezed; upon which the old man, perceiving that he was awake, came forward and fell down on his knees, saying, "Sir, I have a daughter who is to be married this very night. It was not anticipated that Your Honour would be here. I pray, therefore, that we may be excused." Mr. Yin got up and raised the old man, regretting that, in his ignorance of the festive occasion, he had brought with him no present. "Ah, Sir," replied the old man, "your very presence here will ward off all noxious influences; and that is quite enough for us." He then begged Mr. Yin to assist in doing the honours, and thus double the obligation already conferred. Mr. Yin readily assented, and went inside to look at the gorgeous arrangements they had made. He was here met by a lady, apparently about forty years of age, whom the old gentleman introduced as his wife; and he had hardly made his bow when he heard the sound of flageolets, and someone came hurrying in, saying, "He has come!" The old gentleman flew out to meet this personage, and Mr. Yin also stood up, awaiting his arrival. In no long time, a bevy of people with gauze lanterns ushered in the bridegroom himself, who seemed to be about seventeen or eighteen years old, and of a most refined and prepossessing appearance. The old gentleman bade him pay his respects first to their worthy guest; and upon his looking towards Mr. Yin, that gentleman came forward to welcome him on behalf of the host. Then followed ceremonies between the old man and his son-in-law; and when these were over, they all sat down to supper. Hosts of waiting-maids brought in profuse quantities of wine and meats, with bowls and cups of jade or gold, till the table glittered again. And when the wine had gone round several times, the old gentleman told one of the maids to summon the bride. This she did, but some time passed and no bride came. So the old man rose and drew aside the curtain, pressing the young lady to come forth; whereupon a number of women escorted out the bride, whose ornaments went *tinkle tinkle* as she walked along, sweet perfumes being all the time diffused around. Her father told her to make the proper salutation, after which she went and sat by her mother. Mr. Yin took a glance at her, and saw that she wore on her head beautiful ornaments made of kingfisher's feathers, her beauty quite surpassing anything he had ever seen. All this time they had been drinking their wine out of golden goblets big enough to hold several pints, when it flashed across him that one of these goblets would be a capital thing to carry back to his companions in evidence of what he had seen. So he secreted it in his sleeve, and, pretending to be tipsy, leaned forward with his head upon the table as if going off to sleep. "The gentleman is drunk," said the guests; and by-and-by Mr. Yin heard the bridegroom take his leave, and there was a general trooping downstairs to the tune of a wedding march. When they were all gone the old gentleman collected the goblets, one of which was missing, though they hunted high and low to find it. Someone mentioned the sleeping guest; but the old gentleman stopped him at once for fear Mr. Yin should hear, and before long silence reigned throughout. Mr. Yin then arose. It was dark, and he had no light; but he could detect the lingering smell of the food, and the place was filled with the fumes of wine. Faint streaks of light now appearing in the east, he began quietly to make a move, having first satisfied himself that the goblet was still in his sleeve. Arriving at the door, he found his friends already there; for they had been afraid he might come out after they left, and go in again early in the morning. When he produced the goblet they were all lost in astonishment; and on hearing his story, they were fain to believe it, well knowing that a poor student like Yin was not likely to have such a valuable piece of plate in his possession.

Later on Mr. Yin took his doctor's degree, and was appointed magistrate over the district of Fei-ch'iu, where there was an old-established family of the name of Chu. The head of the family asked him to a banquet in honour of his arrival, and ordered the servants to bring in the large goblets. After some delay a slave-girl came and whispered something to her master which seemed to make him very angry. Then the goblets were brought in, and Mr. Yin was invited to drink. He now found that these goblets were of precisely the same shape and pattern as the one he had at home, and at once begged his host to tell him where he had had these made. "Well," said Mr. Chu, "there should be eight of them. An ancestor of mine had them made, when he was a minister at the capital, by an experienced artificer. They have been handed down in our family from generation to generation, and have now been carefully laid by for some time; but I thought we would have them out today as a compliment to your Honour. However, there are only seven to be found. None of the servants can have touched them, for the old seals of ten years ago are still upon the box, unbroken. I don't know what to make of it." Mr. Yin laughed, and said, "It must have flown away! Still, it is a pity to lose an heirloom of that kind; and as I have a very similar one at home, I shall take upon myself to send it to you." When the banquet was over, Mr. Yin went home, and taking out his own goblet, sent it off to Mr. Chu. The latter was somewhat surprised to find that it was identical with his own, and hurried away to thank the magistrate for his gift, asking him at the same time how it had come into his possession. Mr. Yin told him the whole story, which proves conclusively that although a fox may obtain possession of a thing, even at a distance of many hundred miles, he will not venture to keep it altogether.

Miss Lien-Hsiang

Pu Songling

There was a young man named Sang Tzŭ-ming, a native of I-chou, who had been left an orphan when quite young. He lived near the Saffron market, and kept himself very much to himself, only going out twice a day for his meals to a neighbour's close by, and sitting quietly at home all the rest of his time. One day the said neighbour called, and asked him in joke if he wasn't afraid of devil-foxes, so much alone as he was. "Oh," replied Sang, laughing, "what has the superior man to fear from devil-foxes. If they come as men, I have here a sharp sword for them; and if as women, why, I shall open the door and ask them to walk in." The neighbour went away, and having arranged with a friend of his, they got a young lady of their acquaintance to climb over Sang's wall with the help of a ladder, and knock at the door. Sang peeped through, and called out, "Who's there?" to which the girl answered, "A devil!" and frightened Sang so dreadfully that his teeth chattered in his head. The girl then ran away, and next morning when his neighbour came to see him, Sang told him what had happened, and said he meant to go back to his native place. The neighbour then clapped his hands, and said to Sang, "Why didn't you ask her in?" Whereupon Sang perceived that he had been tricked, and went on quietly again as before.

Some six months afterwards, a young lady knocked at his door; and Sang, thinking his friends were at their old tricks, opened it at once, and asked her to walk in. She did so; and he beheld to his astonishment a perfect Helen for beauty. Asking her whence she came, she replied that her name was Lien-hsiang, and that she lived not very far off, adding that she had long been anxious to make his acquaintance. After that she used to drop in every now and again for a chat; but one evening when Sang was sitting alone expecting her, another young lady suddenly walked in. Thinking it was Lien-hsiang, Sang got up to meet her, but found that the new-comer was somebody else. She was about fifteen or sixteen years of age, wore very full sleeves, and dressed her hair after the fashion of unmarried girls, being otherwise very stylish-looking and refined, and apparently hesitating whether to go on or go back. Sang, in a great state of alarm, took her for a fox; but the young lady said, "My name is Li, and I am of a respectable family. Hearing of your virtue and talent, I hope to be accorded the honour of your acquaintance." Sang laughed, and took her by the hand, which he found was as cold as ice; and when he asked the reason, she told him that she had always been delicate, and that it was very chilly outside. She then remarked that she intended to visit him pretty frequently, and hoped it would not inconvenience him; so he explained that no one came to see him except another young lady, and that not very often. "When she comes, I'll go," replied the young lady, "and only drop in when she's not here." She then gave him an embroidered slipper, saying that she had worn it, and that whenever he shook it she would know that he wanted to see her, cautioning him at the same time never to shake it before strangers. Taking it in his hand he beheld a very tiny little shoe almost as fine pointed as an awl, with which he was much pleased; and next evening, when nobody was present, he produced the shoe and shook it, whereupon the young lady immediately walked in. Henceforth, whenever he brought it out, the young lady responded to his wishes and appeared before him. This seemed so strange that at last he asked her to give him some explanation; but she only laughed, and said it was mere coincidence. One evening after this Lien-hsiang came, and said in alarm to Sang, "Whatever has made you look so melancholy?" Sang replied that he did not know, and by-and-by she took her leave, saying, they would not meet again for some ten days. During this period Miss Li visited Sang every day, and on one occasion asked him where his other friend was. Sang told her; and then she laughed and said, "What is your opinion of me as compared with Lien-hsiang?" "You are both of you perfection," replied he, "but you are a little colder of the two." Miss Li didn't much like this, and cried out, "Both of us perfection is what you say to me. Then she must be a downright Cynthia, and I am no match for her." Somewhat out of temper, she reckoned that Lien-hsiang's ten days had expired, and said she would have a peep at her, making Sang promise to keep it all secret. The next evening Lien-hsiang came, and while they were talking she suddenly exclaimed, "Oh, dear! how much worse you seem to have become in the last ten days. You must have encountered something bad." Sang asked her why so; to which she answered, "First of all your appearance; and then your pulse is very thready. You've got the devil-disease."

The following evening when Miss Li came, Sang asked her what she thought of Lien-hsiang. "Oh," said she, "there's no question about her beauty; but she's a fox. When she went away I followed her to her hole on the hill side." Sang, however, attributed this remark to jealousy, and took no notice of it; but the next evening when Lien-hsiang came, he observed, "I don't believe it myself, but some one has told me you are a fox." Lien-hsiang asked who had said so, to which Sang replied that he was only joking; and then she begged him to explain what difference there was between a fox and an ordinary person. "Well," answered Sang, "foxes frighten people to death, and, therefore, they are very much dreaded." "Don't you believe that!" cried Lien-hsiang; "and now tell me who has been saying this of me." Sang declared at first that it was only a joke of his, but by-and-by yielded to her instances, and let out the whole story. "Of course I saw how changed you were," said Lien-hsiang; "she is surely not a human being to be able to cause such a rapid alteration in you. Say nothing, tomorrow I'll watch her as she watched me." The following evening Miss Li came in; and they had hardly interchanged half-a-dozen sentences when a cough was heard outside the window, and Miss Li ran away. Lien-hsiang then entered and said to Sang, "You are lost! She is a devil, and if you do not at once forbid her coming here, you will soon be on the road to the other world." "All jealousy," thought Sang, saying nothing, as Lien-hsiang continued, "I know that you don't like to be rude to her; but I, for my part, cannot see you sacrificed, and tomorrow I will bring you some medicine to expel the poison from your system. Happily, the disease has not yet taken firm hold of you, and in ten days you will be well again." The next evening she produced a knife and chopped up some medicine for Sang, which made him feel much better; but, although he was very grateful to her, he still persisted in disbelieving that he had the devil-disease. After some days he recovered and Lien-hsiang left him, warning him to have no more to do with Miss Li. Sang pretended that he would follow her advice, and closed the door and trimmed his lamp. He then took out the slipper, and on shaking it Miss Li appeared, somewhat cross at having been kept away for several days. "She merely attended on me these few nights while I was ill," said Sang; "don't be angry." At this Miss Li brightened up a little; but by-and-by Sang told her that people said she was a devil. "It's that nasty fox," cried Miss Li, after a pause, "putting these things into your head. If you don't break with her, I won't come here again." She then began to sob and cry, and Sang had some trouble in pacifying her. Next evening Lien-hsiang came and found out that Miss Li had been there again; whereupon she was very angry with Sang, and told him he would certainly die. "Why need you be so jealous?" said Sang, laughing; at which she only got more enraged, and replied, "When you were nearly dying the other day and I saved you, if I had not been jealous, where would you have been now?" Sang pretended he was only joking, and said that Miss Li had told him his recent illness was entirely owing to the machinations of a fox; to which she replied, "It's true enough what you say, only you don't see whose machinations. However, if any thing happens to you, I should never clear myself even had I a hundred mouths; we will, therefore, part. A hundred days hence I shall see you on your bed." Sang could not persuade her to stay, and away she went; and from that time Miss Li became a regular visitor.

Two months passed away, and Sang began to experience a feeling of great lassitude, which he tried at first to shake off, but by-and-by he became very thin, and could only take thick gruel. He then thought about going back to his native place; however, he could not bear to leave Miss Li, and in a few more days he was so weak that he was unable to get up. His friend next door, seeing how ill he was, daily sent in his boy with food and drink; and now Sang began for the first time to suspect Miss Li. So he said to her, "I am sorry I didn't listen to Lien-hsiang before I got as bad as this." He then closed his eyes and kept them shut for some time; and when he opened them again Miss Li had disappeared. Their acquaintanceship was thus at an end, and Sang lay all emaciated as he was upon his bed in his solitary room longing for the return of Lien-hsiang. One day, while he was still thinking about her, some one drew aside the screen and walked in. It was Lien-hsiang; and approaching the bed she said with a smile, "Was I then talking such nonsense?" Sang struggled a long time to speak; and, at length, confessing he had been wrong, implored her to save him. "When the disease has reached such a pitch as this," replied Lien-hsiang, "there is very little to be done. I merely came to bid you farewell, and to clear up your doubts about my jealousy." In great tribulation, Sang asked her to take something she would find under his pillow and destroy it; and she accordingly drew forth the slipper, which she proceeded to examine by the light of the lamp, turning it over and over. All at once Miss Li walked in, but when she saw Lien-hsiang she turned back as though she would run away, which Lien-hsiang instantly prevented by placing herself in the doorway. Sang then began to reproach her, and Miss Li could make no reply; whereupon Lien-hsiang said, "At last we meet. Formerly you attributed this gentleman's illness to me; what have you to say now?" Miss Li bent her head in acknowledgment of her guilt, and Lien-hsiang continued, "How is it that a nice girl like you can thus turn love into hate?" Here Miss Li threw herself on the ground in a flood of tears and begged for mercy; and Lien-hsiang, raising her up, inquired of her as to her past life. "I am a daughter of a petty official named Li, and I died young, leaving the web of my destiny incomplete, like the silkworm that perishes in the spring. To be the partner of this gentleman was my ardent wish; but I had never any intention of causing his death." "I have heard," remarked Lien-hsiang, "that the advantage devils obtain by killing people is that their victims are ever with them after death. Is this so?" "It is not," replied Miss Li; "the companionship of two devils gives no pleasure to either. Were it otherwise, I should not have wanted for friends in the realms below. But tell me, how do foxes manage not to kill people?" "You allude to such foxes as suck the breath out of people?" replied Lien-hsiang; "I am not of that class. Some foxes are harmless; no devils are, because of the dominance of the yin in their compositions." Sang now knew that these two girls were really a fox and a devil; however, from being long accustomed to their society, he was not in the least alarmed. His breathing had dwindled to a mere thread, and at length he uttered a cry of pain. Lien-hsiang looked round and said, "How shall we cure him?" upon which Miss Li blushed deeply and drew back; and then Lien-hsiang added, "If he does get well, I'm afraid you will be dreadfully jealous." Miss Li drew herself up, and replied, "Could a physician be found to wipe away the wrong I have done to this gentleman, I would bury my head in the ground. How should I look the world in the face?" Lien-hsiang here opened a bag and drew forth some drugs, saying, "I have been looking forward to this day. When I left this gentleman I proceeded to gather my simples, as it would take three months for the medicine to be got ready; but then, should the poison have brought anyone even to death's door, this medicine is able to call him back. The only condition is that it be administered by the very hand which wrought the ill." Miss Li did as she was told and put the pills Lien-hsiang gave her one after another into Sang's mouth. They burnt his inside like fire; but soon vitality began to return, and Lien-hsiang cried out, "He is cured!" Just at this moment Miss Li heard the cock crow and vanished, Lien-hsiang remaining behind in attendance on the invalid, who was unable to feed himself. She bolted the outside door and pretended that Sang had returned to his native place, so as to prevent visitors from calling. Day and night she took care of him, and every evening Miss Li came in to render assistance, regarding Lien-hsiang as an elder sister, and being treated by her with great consideration and kindness. Three months afterwards Sang was as strong and well as ever he had been, and then for several evenings Miss Li ceased to visit them, only staying a few moments when she did come, and seeming very uneasy in her mind. One evening Sang ran after her and carried her back in his arms, finding her no heavier than so much straw; and then, being obliged to stay, she curled herself up and lay down, to all appearance in a state of unconsciousness, and by-and-by she was gone. For many days they heard nothing of her, and Sang was so anxious that she should come back that he often took out her slipper and shook it. "I don't wonder at your missing her," said Lien-hsiang, "I do myself very much indeed." "Formerly," observed Sang, "when I shook the slipper she invariably came. I thought it very strange, but I never suspected her of being a devil. And now, alas! all I can do is to sit and think about her with this slipper in my hand." He then burst into a flood of tears.

Now a young lady named Yen-êrh, belonging to the wealthy Chang family, and about fifteen years of age, had died suddenly, without any apparent cause, and had come to life again in the night, when she got up and wished to go out. They barred the door and would not hear of her doing so; upon which she said, "I am the spirit daughter of a petty magistrate. A Mr. Sang has been very kind to me, and I have left my slipper at his house. I am really a spirit; what is the use of keeping me in?" There being some reason for what she said, they asked her why she had come there; but she only looked up and down without being able to give any explanation. Some one here observed, that Mr. Sang had already gone home, but the young lady utterly refused to believe them. The family was much disturbed at all this; and when Sang's neighbour heard the story, he jumped over the wall, and peeping through beheld Sang sitting there chatting with a pretty-looking girl. As he went in, there was some commotion, during which Sang's visitor had disappeared, and when his neighbour asked the meaning of it all, Sang replied, laughing, "Why, I told you if any ladies came I should ask them in." His friend then repeated what Miss Yen-êrh had said; and Sang, unbolting his door, was about to go and have a peep at her, but unfortunately had no means of so doing. Meanwhile Mrs. Chang, hearing that he had not gone away, was more lost in astonishment than ever, and sent an old woman-servant to get back the slipper. Sang immediately gave it to her, and Miss Yen-êrh was delighted to recover it, though when she came to try it on it was too small for her by a good inch. In considerable alarm, she seized a mirror to look at herself; and suddenly became aware that she had come to life again in some one else's body. She therefore told all to her mother, and finally succeeded in convincing her, crying all the time because she was so changed for the worse as regarded personal appearance from what she had been before. And whenever she happened to see Lien-hsiang, she was very much disconcerted, declaring that she had been much better off as a devil than now as a human being. She would sit and weep over the slipper, no one being able to comfort her; and finally, covering herself up with bed-clothes, she lay all stark and stiff, positively refusing to take any nourishment. Her body swelled up, and for seven days she refused all food, but did not die; and then the swelling began to subside, and an intense hunger to come upon her which made her once more think about eating. Then she was troubled with a severe irritation, and her skin peeled entirely away; and when she got up in the morning, she found that the shoes had fallen off. On trying to put them on again, she discovered that they did not fit her any longer; and then she went back to her former pair which were now exactly of the right size and shape. In an ecstasy of joy, she grasped her mirror, and saw that her features had also changed back to what they had formerly been; so she washed and dressed herself and went in to visit her mother. Every one who met her was much astonished; and when Lien-hsiang heard the strange story, she tried to persuade Mr. Sang to make her an offer of marriage. But the young lady was rich and Sang was poor, and he did not see his way clearly. However, on Mrs. Chang's birthday, when she completed her cycle of sixty-one years, Sang went along with the others to wish her many happy returns of the day; and when the old lady knew who was coming, she bade Yen-êrh take a peep at him from behind the curtain. Sang arrived last of all; and immediately out rushed Miss Yen-êrh and seized his sleeve, and said she would go back with him. Her mother scolded her well for this, and she ran in abashed; but Sang, who had looked at her closely, began to weep, and threw himself at the feet of Mrs. Chang who raised him up without saying anything unkind. Sang then took his leave, and got his uncle to act as medium between them; the result being that an auspicious day was fixed upon for the wedding. At the appointed time Sang proceeded to the house to fetch her; and when he returned he found that, instead of his former poor-looking furniture, beautiful carpets were laid down from the very door, and thousands of coloured lanterns were hung about in elegant designs. Lien-hsiang assisted the bride to enter, and took off her veil, finding her the same bright girl as ever. She also joined them while drinking the wedding cup,and inquired of her friend as to her recent transmigration; and Yen-êrh related as follows: – "Overwhelmed with grief, I began to shrink from myself as some unclean thing; and, after separating from you that day, I would not return any more to my grave. So I wandered about at random, and whenever I saw a living being, I envied its happy state. By day I remained among trees and shrubs, but at night I used to roam about anywhere. And once I came to the house of the Chang family, where, seeing a young girl lying upon the bed, I took possession of her mortal coil, unknowing that she would be restored to life again." When Lien-hsiang heard this she was for some time lost in thought; and a month or two afterwards became very ill. She refused all medical aid and gradually got worse and worse, to the great grief of Mr. Sang and his wife, who stood weeping at her bedside. Suddenly she opened her eyes, and said, "You wish to live; I am willing to die. If fate so ordains it, we shall meet again ten years hence." As she uttered these words, her spirit passed away, and all that remained was the dead body of a fox. Sang, however, insisted on burying it with all the proper ceremonies.

Now his wife had no children; but one day a servant came in and said, "There is an old woman outside who has got a little girl for sale." Sang's wife gave orders that she should be shown in; and no sooner had she set eyes on the girl than she cried out, "Why, she's the image of Lien-hsiang!" Sang then looked at her, and found to his astonishment that she was really very like his old friend. The old woman said she was fourteen years old; and when asked what her price was, declared that her only wish was to get the girl comfortably settled, and enough to keep herself alive, and ensure not being thrown out into the kennel at death. So Sang gave a good price for her; and his wife, taking the girl's hand, led her into a room by themselves. Then, chucking her under the chin, she asked her, smiling, "Do you know me?" The girl said she did not; after which she told Mrs. Sang that her name was Wei, and that her father, who had been a pickle-merchant at Hsü-ch'êng, had died three years before. Mrs. Sang then calculated that Lien-hsiang had been dead just ten years; and, looking at the girl, who resembled her so exactly in every trait, at length patted her on the head, saying, "Ah, my sister, you promised to visit us again in ten years, and you have not played us false." The girl here seemed to wake up as if from a dream, and, uttering an exclamation of surprise, fixed a steady gaze upon Sang's wife. Sang himself laughed, and said, "Just like the return of an old familiar swallow." "Now I understand," cried the girl, in tears; "I recollect my mother saying that when I was born I was able to speak; and that, thinking it an inauspicious manifestation, they gave me dog's blood to drink, so that I should forget all about my previous state of existence. Is it all a dream, or are you not the Miss Li who was so ashamed of being a devil?" Thus they chatted of their existence in a former life, with alternate tears and smiles; but when it came to the day for worshipping at the tombs, Yen-êrh explained that she and her husband were in the habit of annually visiting and mourning over her grave. The girl replied that she would accompany them; and when they got there they found the whole place in disorder, and the coffin wood all warped. "Lien-hsiang and I," said Yen-êrh to her husband, "have been attached to each other in two states of existence. Let us not be separated, but bury my bones here with hers." Sang consented, and opening Miss Li's tomb, took out the bones and buried them with those of Lien-hsiang, while friends and relatives, who had heard the strange story, gathered round the grave in gala dress to the number of many hundreds.

I learnt the above when travelling through I-chou, where I was detained at an inn by rain, and read a biography of Mr. Sang written by a comrade of his named Wang Tzŭ-chang. It was lent me by a Mr. Liu Tzŭ-ching, a relative of Sang's, and was quite a long account. This is merely an outline of it.

The Magic Sword

Pu Songling

Ning Lai-ch'ên was a Chekiang man, and a good-natured, honourable fellow, fond of telling people that he had only loved once. Happening to go to Chinhua, he took shelter in a temple to the north of the city; very nice as far as ornamentation went, but overgrown with grass taller than a man's head, and evidently not much frequented. On either side were the priest's apartments, the doors of which were ajar, with the exception of a small room on the south side, where the lock had a new appearance. In the east corner he espied a group of bamboos, growing over a large pool of water-lilies in flower; and, being much pleased with the quiet of the place, determined to remain; more especially as, the Grand Examiner being in the town, all lodgings had gone up in price. So he roamed about waiting till the priests should return; and in the evening, a gentleman came and opened the door on the south side. Ning quickly made up to him, and with a bow informed him of his design. "There is no one here whose permission you need ask," replied the stranger; "I am only lodging here, and if you don't object to the loneliness, I shall be very pleased to have the benefit of your society." Ning was delighted, and made himself a straw bed, and put up a board for a table, as if he intended to remain some time; and that night, by the beams of the clear bright moon, they sat together in the verandah and talked. The stranger's name was Yen Ch'ih-hsia, and Ning thought he was a student up for the provincial examination, only his dialect was not that of a Chekiang man. On being asked, he said he came from Shensi; and there was an air of straightforwardness about all his remarks. By-and-by, when their conversation was exhausted, they bade each other good night and went to bed; but Ning, being in a strange place, was quite unable to sleep; and soon he heard sounds of voices from the room on the north side. Getting up, he peeped through a window, and saw, in a small court-yard the other side of a low wall, a woman of about forty with an old maid-servant in a long faded gown, humped-backed and feeble-looking. They were chatting by the light of the moon; and the mistress said, "Why doesn't Hsiao-ch'ien come?" "She ought to be here by now," replied the other. "She isn't offended with you; is she?" asked the lady. "Not that I know of," answered the old servant; "but she seems to want to give trouble." "Such people don't deserve to be treated well," said the other; and she had hardly uttered these words when up came a young girl of seventeen or eighteen, and very nice looking. The old servant laughed, and said, "Don't talk of people behind their backs. We were just mentioning you as you came without our hearing you; but fortunately we were saying nothing bad about you. And, as far as that goes," added she, "if I were a young fellow why I should certainly fall in love with you." "If you don't praise me," replied the girl, "I'm sure I don't know who will;" and then the lady and the girl said something together, and Mr. Ning, thinking they were the family next door, turned round to sleep without paying further attention to them. In a little while no sound was to be heard; but, as he was dropping off to sleep, he perceived that somebody was in the room.

Jumping up in great haste, he found it was the young lady he had just seen; and detecting at once that she was going to attempt to bewitch him, sternly bade her begone. She then produced a lump of gold which he threw away, and told her to go after it or he would call his friend. So she had no alternative but to go, muttering something about his heart being like iron or stone. Next day, a young candidate for the examination came and lodged in the east room with his servant. He, however, was killed that very night, and his servant the night after; the corpses of both shewing a small hole in the sole of the foot as if bored by an awl, and from which a little blood came. No one knew who had committed these murders, and when Mr. Yen came home, Ning asked him what he thought about it. Yen replied that it was the work of devils, but Ning was a brave fellow, and that didn't frighten him much. In the middle of the night Hsiao-ch'ien appeared to him again, and said, "I have seen many men, but none with a steel cold heart like yours. You are an upright man, and I will not attempt to deceive you. I, Hsiao-ch'ien, whose family name is Nieh, died when only eighteen, and was buried alongside of this temple. A devil then took possession of me, and employed me to bewitch people by my beauty, contrary to my inclination. There is now nothing left in this temple to slay, and I fear that imps will be employed to kill you." Ning was very frightened at this, and asked her what he should do. "Sleep in the same room with Mr. Yen," replied she. "What!" asked he, "cannot the spirits trouble Yen?" "He is a strange man," she answered, "and they don't like going near him." Ning then inquired how the spirits worked. "I bewitch people," said Hsiao-ch'ien, "and then they bore a hole in the foot which renders the victim senseless, and proceed to draw off the blood, which the devils drink. Another method is to tempt people by false gold, the bones of some horrid demon; and if they receive it, their hearts and livers will be torn out. Either method is used according to circumstances." Ning thanked her, and asked when he ought to be prepared; to which she replied, "Tomorrow night." At parting she wept, and said, "I am about to sink into the great sea, with no friendly shore at hand. But your sense of duty is boundless, and you can save me. If you will collect my bones and bury them in some quiet spot, I shall not again be subject to these misfortunes." Ning said he would do so, and asked where she lay buried. "At the foot of the aspen-tree on which there is a bird's nest," replied she; and passing out of the door, disappeared. The next day Ning was afraid that Yen might be going away somewhere, and went over early to invite him across. Wine and food were produced towards noon; and Ning, who took care not to lose sight of Yen, then asked him to remain there for the night. Yen declined, on the ground that he liked being by himself; but Ning wouldn't hear any excuses, and carried all Yen's things to his own room, so that he had no alternative but to consent. However, he warned Ning, saying, "I know you are a gentleman and a man of honour. If you see anything you don't quite understand, I pray you not to be too inquisitive; don't pry into my boxes, or it may be the worse for both of us." Ning promised to attend to what he said, and by-and-by they both lay down to sleep; and Yen, having placed his boxes on the window-sill, was soon snoring loudly. Ning himself could not sleep; and after some time he saw a figure moving stealthily outside, at length approaching the window to peep through. It's eyes flashed like lightning, and Ning in a terrible fright was just upon the point of calling Yen, when something flew out of one of the boxes like a strip of white silk, and dashing against the window-sill returned at once to the box, disappearing very much like lightning. Yen heard the noise and got up, Ning all the time pretending to be asleep in order to watch what happened. The former then opened the box, and took out something which he smelt and examined by the light of the moon. It was dazzlingly white like crystal, and about two inches in length by the width of an onion leaf in breadth. He then wrapped it up carefully and put it back in the broken box, saying, "A bold-faced devil that, to come so near my box;" upon which he went back to bed; but Ning, who was lost in astonishment, arose and asked him what it all meant, telling at the same time what he himself had seen. "As you and I are good friends," replied Yen, "I won't make any secret of it. The fact is I am a Taoist priest. But for the window-sill the devil would have been killed; as it is, he is badly wounded." Ning asked him what it was he had there wrapped up, and he told him it was his sword, on which he had smelt the presence of the devil. At Ning's request he produced the weapon, a bright little miniature of a sword; and from that time Ning held his friend in higher esteem than ever.

Next day he found traces of blood outside the window which led round to the north of the temple; and there among a number of graves he discovered the aspen-tree with the bird's nest at its summit. He then fulfilled his promise and prepared to go home, Yen giving him a farewell banquet, and presenting him with an old leather case which he said contained a sword, and would keep at a distance from him all devils and bogies. Ning then wished to learn a little of Yen's art; but the latter replied that although he might accomplish this easily enough, being as he was an upright man, yet he was well off in life, and not in a condition where it would be of any advantage to him. Ning then pretending he had to go and bury his sister, collected Hsiao-ch'ien's bones, and, having wrapped them up in grave-clothes, hired a boat, and set off on his way home. On his arrival, as his library looked towards the open country, he made a grave hard by and buried the bones there, sacrificing, and invoking Hsiao-ch'ien as follows: – "In pity for your lonely ghost, I have placed your remains near my humble cottage, where we shall be near each other, and no devil will dare annoy you. I pray you reject not my sacrifice, poor though it be." After this, he was proceeding home when he suddenly heard himself addressed from behind, the voice asking him not to hurry; and turning round he beheld Hsiao-ch'ien, who thanked him, saying, "Were I to die ten times for you I could not discharge my debt. Let me go home with you and wait upon your father and mother; you will not repent it." Looking closely at her, he observed that she had a beautiful complexion, and feet as small as bamboo shoots, being altogether much prettier now that he came to see her by daylight. So they went together to his home, and bidding her wait awhile, Ning ran in to tell his mother, to the very great surprise of the old lady. Now Ning's wife had been ill for a long time, and his mother advised him not to say a word about it to her for fear of frightening her; in the middle of which in rushed Hsiao-ch'ien, and threw herself on the ground before them. "This is the young lady," said Ning; whereupon his mother in some alarm turned her attention to Hsiao-ch'ien, who cried out, "A lonely orphan, without brother or sister, the object of your son's kindness and compassion, begs to be allowed to give her poor services as some return for favours shewn." Ning's mother, seeing that she was a nice pleasant-looking girl, began to lose fear of her, and replied, "Madam, the preference you shew for my son is highly pleasing to an old body like myself; but this is the only hope of our family, and I hardly dare agree to his taking a devil-wife." "I have but one motive in what I ask," answered Hsiao-ch'ien, "and if you have no faith in disembodied people, then let me regard him as my brother, and live under your protection, serving you like a daughter." Ning's mother could not resist her straightforward manner, and Hsiao-ch'ien asked to be allowed to see Ning's wife, but this was denied on the plea that the lady was ill. Hsiao-ch'ien then went into the kitchen and got ready the dinner, running about the place as if she had lived there all her life. Ning's mother was, however, much afraid of her, and would not let her sleep in the house; so Hsiao-ch'ien went to the library, and was just entering when suddenly she fell back a few steps, and began walking hurriedly backwards and forwards in front of the door. Ning seeing this, called out and asked her what it meant; to which she replied, "The presence of that sword frightens me, and that is why I could not accompany you on your way home." Ning at once understood her, and hung up the sword-case in another place; whereupon she entered, lighted a candle, and sat down. For some time she did not speak: at length asking Ning if he studied at night or not – "For," said she, "when I was little I used to repeat the Lêng-yen sutra; but now I have forgotten more than half, and, therefore, I should like to borrow a copy, and when you are at leisure in the evening you might hear me." Ning said he would, and they sat silently there for some time, after which Hsiao-ch'ien went away and took up her quarters elsewhere. Morning and night she waited on Ning's mother, bringing water for her to wash in, occupying herself with household matters, and endeavouring to please her in every way. In the evening before she went to bed, she would always go in and repeat a little of the sutra, and leave as soon as she thought Ning was getting sleepy. Now the illness of Ning's wife had given his mother a great deal of extra trouble – more, in fact, than she was equal to; but ever since Hsiao-ch'ien's arrival all this was changed, and Ning's mother felt kindly disposed to the girl in consequence, gradually growing to regard her almost as her own child, and forgetting quite that she was a spirit. Accordingly, she didn't make her leave the house at night; and Hsiao-ch'ien, who being a devil had not tasted meat or drink since her arrival, now began at the end of six months to take a little thin gruel. Mother and son alike became very fond of her, and henceforth never mentioned what she really was; neither were strangers able to detect the fact. By-and-by, Ning's wife died, and his mother secretly wished him to espouse Hsiao-ch'ien, though she rather dreaded any unfortunate consequences that might arise. This Hsiao-ch'ien perceived, and seizing an opportunity said to Ning's mother, "I have been with you now more than a year, and you ought to know something of my disposition. Because I was unwilling to injure travellers I followed your son hither. There was no other motive; and, as your son has shewn himself one of the best of men, I would now remain with him for three years in order that he may obtain for me some mark of Imperial approbation which will do me honour in the realms below." Ning's mother knew that she meant no evil, but hesitated to put the family hopes of a posterity into jeopardy. Hsiao-ch'ien, however, reassured her by saying that Ning would have three sons, and that the line would not be interrupted by his marrying her. On the strength of this the marriage was arranged to the great joy of Ning, a feast prepared, and friends and relatives invited; and when in response to a call the bride herself came forth in her gay wedding-dress, the beholders took her rather for a fairy than for a devil. After this, numbers of congratulatory presents were given by the various female members of the family, who vied with one another in making her acquaintance; and these Hsiao-ch'ien returned by gifts of paintings of flowers, done by herself, in which she was very skilful, the receivers being extremely proud of such marks of her friendship. One day she was leaning at the window in a despondent mood, when suddenly she asked where the sword-case was. "Oh," replied Ning, "as you seemed afraid of it, I moved it elsewhere." "I have now been so long under the influence of surrounding life," said Hsiao-ch'ien, "that I shan't be afraid of it any more. Let us hang it on the bed." "Why so?" asked Ning. "For the last three days," explained she, "I have been much agitated in mind; and I fear that the devil at the temple, angry at my escape, may come suddenly and carry me off." So Ning brought the sword-case, and Hsiao-ch'ien, after examining it closely, remarked, "This is where the magician puts people. I wonder how many were slain before it got old and worn out as it is now. Even now when I look at it my flesh creeps." The case was then hung up, and next day removed to over the door. At night they sat up and watched, Hsiao-ch'ien warning Ning not to go to sleep; and suddenly something fell down flop like a bird. Hsiao-ch'ien in a fright got behind the curtain; but Ning looked at the thing, and found it was an imp of darkness, with glaring eyes and a bloody mouth, coming straight to the door. Stealthily creeping up it made a grab at the sword-case, and seemed about to tear it in pieces, when bang! – the sword-case became as big as a wardrobe, and from it a devil protruded part of his body and dragged the imp in. Nothing more was heard, and the sword-case resumed its original size. Ning was greatly alarmed, but Hsiao-ch'ien came out rejoicing, and said, "There's an end of my troubles." In the sword-case they found only a few quarts of clear water; nothing else.

After these events Ning took his doctor's degree and Hsiao-ch'ien bore him a son. He then took a concubine, and had one more son by each, all of whom became in time distinguished men.

The Painted Skin

Pu Songling

At T'ai-yUan there lived a man named Wang. One morning he was out walking when he met a young lady carrying a bundle and hurrying along by herself. As she moved along with some difficulty, Wang quickened his pace and caught her up, and found she was a pretty girl of about sixteen. Much smitten he inquired whither she was going so early, and no one with her. "A traveller like you," replied the girl, "cannot alleviate my distress; why trouble yourself to ask?" "What distress is it?" said Wang; "I'm sure I'll do anything I can for you." "My parents," answered she, "loved money, and they sold me as concubine into a rich family, where the wife was very jealous, and beat and abused me morning and night. It was more than I could stand, so I have run away."

Wang asked her where she was going; to which she replied that a runaway had no fixed place of abode. "My house," said Wang, "is at no great distance; what do you say to coming there?" She joyfully acquiesced; and Wang, taking up her bundle, led the way to his house. Finding no one there, she asked Wang where his family were; to which he replied that that was only the library. "And a very nice place, too," said she; "but if you are kind enough to wish to save my life, you mustn't let it be known that I am here." Wang promised he would not divulge her secret, and so she remained there for some days without anyone knowing anything about it. He then told his wife, and she, fearing the girl might belong to some influential family, advised him to send her away. This, however, he would not consent to do; when one day, going into the town, he met a Taoist priest, who looked at him in astonishment, and asked him what he had met. "I have met nothing," replied Wang. "Why," said the priest, "you are bewitched; what do you mean by not having met anything?" But Wang insisted that it was so, and the priest walked away, saying, "The fool! Some people don't seem to know when death is at hand." This startled Wang, who at first thought of the girl; but then he reflected that a pretty young thing as she was couldn't well be a witch, and began to suspect that the priest merely wanted to do a stroke of business. When he returned, the library door was shut, and he couldn't get in, which made him suspect that something was wrong; and so he climbed over the wall, where he found the door of the inner room shut too. Softly creeping up, he looked through the window and saw a hideous devil, with a green face and jagged teeth like a saw, spreading a human skin upon the bed and painting it with a paint-brush. The devil then threw aside the brush, and giving the skin a shake out, just as you would a coat, threw it over its shoulders, when, lo! it was the girl. Terrified at this, Wang hurried away with his head down in search of the priest who had gone he knew not whither; subsequently finding him in the fields, where he threw himself on his knees and begged the priest to save him. "As to driving her away," said the priest, "the creature must be in great distress to be seeking a substitute for herself; besides, I could hardly endure to injure a living thing." However, he gave Wang a fly-brush, and bade him hang it at the door of the bedroom, agreeing to meet again at the Ch'ing-ti temple. Wang went home, but did not dare enter the library; so he hung up the brush at the bedroom door, and before long heard a sound of footsteps outside. Not daring to move, he made his wife peep out; and she saw the girl standing looking at the brush, afraid to pass it. She then ground her teeth and went away; but in a little while came back, and began cursing, saying, "You priest, you won't frighten me. Do you think I am going to give up what is already in my grasp?" Thereupon, she tore the brush to pieces, and bursting open the door, walked straight up to the bed, where she ripped open Wang and tore out his heart, with which she went away. Wang's wife screamed out, and the servant came in with a light; but Wang was already dead and presented a most miserable spectacle. His wife, who was in an agony of fright, hardly dared cry for fear of making a noise; and next day she sent Wang's brother to see the priest. The latter got into a great rage, and cried out, "Was it for this that I had compassion on you, devil that you are?" proceeding at once with Wang's brother to the house, from which the girl had disappeared without anyone knowing whither she had gone. But the priest, raising his head, looked all round, and said, "Luckily she's not far off." He then asked who lived in the apartments on the south side, to which Wang's brother replied that he did; whereupon the priest declared that there she would be found. Wang's brother was horribly frightened and said he did not think so; and then the priest asked him if any stranger had been to the house. To this he answered that he had been out to the Ch'ing-ti temple and couldn't possibly say; but he went off to inquire, and in a little while came back and reported that an old woman had sought service with them as a maid-of-all-work, and had been engaged by his wife. "That is she," said the priest, as Wang's brother added she was still there; and they all set out to go to the house together. Then the priest took his wooden sword, and standing in the middle of the court-yard, shouted out, "Base-born fiend, give me back my fly-brush!" Meanwhile the new maid-of-all-work was in a great state of alarm, and tried to get away by the door; but the priest struck her and down she fell flat, the human skin dropped off, and she became a hideous devil. There she lay grunting like a pig, until the priest grasped his wooden sword and struck off her head. She then became a dense column of smoke curling up from the ground, when the priest took an uncorked gourd and threw it right into the midst of the smoke. A sucking noise was heard, and the whole column was drawn into the gourd; after which the priest corked it up closely and put it in his pouch. The skin, too, which was complete even to the eyebrows, eyes, hands, and feet, he also rolled up as if it had been a scroll, and was on the point of leaving with it, when Wang's wife stopped him, and with tears entreated him to bring her husband to life. The priest said he was unable to do that; but Wang's wife flung herself at his feet, and with loud lamentations implored his assistance. For some time he remained immersed in thought, and then replied, "My power is not equal to what you ask. I myself cannot raise the dead; but I will direct you to someone who can, and if you apply to him properly you will succeed." Wang's wife asked the priest who it was; to which he replied, "There is a maniac in the town who passes his time grovelling in the dirt. Go, prostrate yourself before him, and beg him to help you. If he insults you, shew no sign of anger." Wang's brother knew the man to whom he alluded, and accordingly bade the priest adieu, and proceeded thither with his sister-in-law.

They found the destitute creature raving away by the road side, so filthy that it was all they could do to go near him. Wang's wife approached him on her knees; at which the maniac leered at her, and cried out, "Do you love me, my beauty?" Wang's wife told him what she had come for, but he only laughed and said, "You can get plenty of other husbands. Why raise the dead one to life?" But Wang's wife entreated him to help her; whereupon he observed, "It's very strange: people apply to me to raise their dead as if I was king of the infernal regions." He then gave Wang's wife a thrashing with his staff, which she bore without a murmur, and before a gradually increasing crowd of spectators. After this he produced a loathsome pill which he told her she must swallow, but here she broke down and was quite unable to do so. However, she did manage it at last, and then the maniac crying out, "How you do love me!" got up and went away without taking any more notice of her. They followed him into a temple with loud supplications, but he had disappeared, and every effort to find him was unsuccessful. Overcome with rage and shame, Wang's wife went home, where she mourned bitterly over her dead husband, grievously repenting the steps she had taken, and wishing only to die. She then bethought herself of preparing the corpse, near which none of the servants would venture; and set to work to close up the frightful wound of which he died.

While thus employed, interrupted from time to time by her sobs, she felt a rising lump in her throat, which by-and-by came out with a pop and fell straight into the dead man's wound. Looking closely at it, she saw it was a human heart; and then it began as it were to throb, emitting a warm vapour like smoke. Much excited, she at once closed the flesh over it, and held the sides of the wound together with all her might. Very soon, however, she got tired, and finding the vapour escaping from the crevices, she tore up a piece of silk and bound it round, at the same time bringing back circulation by rubbing the body and covering it up with clothes. In the night, she removed the coverings, and found that breath was coming from the nose; and by next morning her husband was alive again, though disturbed in mind as if awaking from a dream and feeling a pain in his heart. Where he had been wounded, there was a cicatrix about as big as a cash, which soon after disappeared.

The Punishment of Greed

Dr R. Wilhelm

Once upon a time there lived a man south of the Yangtze-kiang. He had taken a position as a teacher in Sutschoufu, on the border of Shantung. But when he got there he found that the schoolhouse had not yet been completed. Yet a two-story building in the neighborhood had been rented, in which the teacher was to live and hold school in the meantime. This house stood outside the village, not far from the river bank. A broad plain, overgrown with tangled brush, stretched out from it on every side. The teacher was pleased with the view.

Well, one evening he was standing in the door of his house watching the sun go down. The smoke that rose from the village chimneys gradually merged with the twilight shadows. All the noises of the day had died away. Suddenly, off in the distance, along the river bank, he beheld a fiery gleam. He hurried away at once in order to see what it might be. And there, on the bank, he found a wooden coffin, from which came the radiance he had noticed. Thought the teacher to himself: "The jewels with which they adorn the dead on their journey shine by night. Perhaps there are gems in the coffin!" And greed awoke in his heart, and he forgot that a coffin is a resting-place of the dead and should be respected. He took up a large stone, broke the cover of the coffin, and bent over to look more closely. And there in the coffin lay a youth. His face was as white as paper, he wore a mourning turban on his head, his body was wrapped in hempen garments, and he wore straw sandals on his feet. The teacher was greatly frightened and turned to go away. But the corpse had already raised itself to a sitting posture. Then the teacher's fear got the better of him, and he began to run. And the corpse climbed out of its coffin and ran after him. Fortunately the house was not far away. The teacher ran as fast as he could, flew up the steps and locked the door after him. Gradually he caught his breath again. Outside there was not a sound to be heard. So he thought that perhaps the corpse had not followed him all the way. He opened the window and peered down. The corpse was leaning against the wall of the house. Suddenly it saw that the window had been opened, and with one leap it bounded up and in through it. Overcome by terror, the teacher fell down the stairs of the house, and rolled unconscious to the bottom of the flight. And when he did so the corpse fell down on the floor of the room above.

At the time the school children had all long since gone home. And the owner of the house lived in another dwelling, so that no one knew anything about what had happened. On the following morning the children came to school as usual. They found the door locked, and when they called no one answered. Then they broke down the door and found their teacher lying unconscious on the ground. They sprinkled him with ginger, but it took a long time before he woke from his coma. When they asked he told them all that had occurred. Then they all went upstairs and took away the corpse. It was taken outside the village limits and burned, and the bones which remained were once more laid in the coffin. But the teacher said, with a sigh: "Because of a moment's greed, I nearly lost my life!" He resigned his position, returned home and never, through all the days of his life, did he speak of gain again.

Note: The corpse wears a mourning turban and is dressed in mourning. According to local tradition, young people who die before their parents, are laid in their coffins clad in mourning, so that even in death they may do their duty and be able to mourn their parents when the latter shall have died. The tale is taken from the Su Tsi Hia.

The Constable

Dr R. Wilhelm

In a city in the neighborhood of Kaiutschou there once lived a constable by the name of Dung. One day when he returned from a hunt after thieves the twilight had already begun to fall. So before he waded through the stream that flowed through the city he sat down on the bank, lit a pipe and took off his shoes. When he looked up, he suddenly saw a man in a red hat dressed as a constable crouching beside him.

Astonished, he inquired: "Who are you? Your clothes indicate that you are a member of our profession, but I have never yet seen you among the men of our local force. Tell me, pray, whence you come?"

The other answered: "I am weary, having come a long journey, and would like to enjoy a pipeful of tobacco in your company. I am sure you will not object to that."

Dung handed him a pipe and tobacco.

But the other constable said: "I do not need them. Just you keep on smoking. It is enough for me to enjoy the odor."

So they chatted awhile together, and together waded through the stream. And gradually they became quite confidential and the stranger said: "I will be quite frank with you. I am the head constable of the Nether World, and am subject to the Lord of the Great Mountain. You yourself are a constable of reputation here in the upper world. And, because of my skill, I have standing in the world below. Since we are so well suited to each other, I should like to enter into a bond of brotherhood with you."

Dung was agreeable and asked: "But what really brings you here?"

Said the other: "In your district there lives a certain Wang, who was formerly superintendent of the granaries, and at that time caused the death of an officer. This man has now accused him in the Nether World. The King of the Nether World cannot come to a decision in the case, and therefore has asked the Lord of the Great Mountain to settle it. The Lord of the Great Mountain has ordered that Wang's property and life be shortened. First his property is to be sequestered here in the upper world, and then his soul is to be dragged to the nether one. I have been sent out by the Judge of the Dead to fetch him. Yet the established custom is, when some one is sent for, that the constable has first to report to the god of the city. The god of the city then issues a summons, and sends one of his own spirit constables to seize the soul and deliver it over to me. Only then may I take it away with me."

Dung asked him further particulars; but the other merely said: "Later on you will see it all for yourself."

When they reached the city Dung invited his colleague to stay at his home, and entertained him with wine and food. But the other only talked and touched neither the goblet nor the chop-sticks.

Said Dung: "In my haste I could not find any better meal for you. I am afraid it is not good enough."

But his guest replied: "Oh no, I am already surfeited and satisfied! We spirits feed only on odors; in which respect we differ from men."

It was late at night before he set out to visit the temple of the city god.

No sooner did morning dawn than he reappeared to take farewell and said: "Now all is in order: I am off! In two years' time you will go to Taianfu, the city near the Great Mountain, and there we will meet again."

Dung began to feel ill at ease. A few days later, in fact, came the news that Wang had died. The district mandarin journeyed to the dead man's natal village in order to express his sympathy. Among his followers was Dung. The inn-keeper there was a tenant of Wang's.

Dung asked him: "Did anything out of the ordinary happen when Sir Wang died?"

"It was all very strange," answered the inn-keeper, "and my mother who had been very busy in his house, came home and fell into a violent fever. She was unconscious for a day and a night, and could hardly breathe. She came to on the very day when the news of Sir Wang's death was made public, and said: 'I have been to the Nether World and I met him there. He had chains about his neck and several devils were dragging him along. I asked him what he had done, but he said: "I have no time to tell you now. When you return ask my wife and she will tell you all!"' And yesterday my mother went there and asked her. And Wang's wife told her with tears: 'My master was an official, but for a long time he did not make any head-way. He was superintendent of the granaries in Nanking, and in the same city was a high officer, with whom my master became very intimate. He always came to visit at our house and he and my master would talk and drink together. One day my master said to him: "We administrative mandarins have a large salary and a good income besides. You are an officer, and have even reached the second step in rank, yet your salary is so small that you cannot possibly make it do. Have you any other income aside from it?" The officer replied: "We are such good friends that I know I can speak openly to you. We officers are compelled to find some additional sources of revenue in order that our pockets may not be altogether empty. When we pay our men we make a small percentage of gains on the exchange; and we also carry more soldiers on our rosters than there actually are present. If we had to live on our salaries we would die of hunger!"

"'When my husband heard him say this he could not rid himself of the idea that by disclosing these criminal proceedings the State would be indebted to him, and that it would surely aid his plans for advancement. On the other hand, he reflected that it would not be right to abuse his friend's confidence. With these ideas in his mind he retired to his inner rooms. In the courtyard stood a round pavilion. Lost in heavy thought, he crossed his hands behind his back, and for a long time walked round and round the pavilion. Finally he said with a sigh: "Charity begins at home; I will sacrifice my friend!" Then he drew up his report, in which the officer was indicted. An imperial order was issued, the matter was investigated, and the officer was condemned to death. My husband, however, was at once increased in rank, and from that time on advanced rapidly. And with the exception of myself no one ever knew anything of the matter.' When my mother told them of her encounter with Wang in the Nether World, the whole family burst into loud weeping. Four tents full of Buddhist and Taoist priests were sent for, who fasted and read masses for thirty-five days in order that Wang might be delivered. Whole mountains of paper money, silk and straw figures were burned, and the ceremonies have not as yet come to an end."

When Dung heard this he was very much frightened.

Two years later he received an order to journey to Taianfu in order to arrest some robbers there. He thought to himself: "My friend, the spirit, must be very powerful indeed, to have known about this trip so far in advance. I must inquire for him. Perhaps I will see him again."

When he reached Taianfu he sought out an inn.

The inn-keeper received him with the words: "Are you Master Dung, and have you come from the bay of Kaiutschou?"

"I am the man," answered Dung, alarmed, "how do you happen to know me?"

The inn-keeper replied: "The constable of the temple of the Great Mountain appeared to me last night and said: 'Tomorrow a man by the name of Dung who is a good friend of mine is coming from the bay of Kaiutschou!' And then he described your appearance and your clothes to me exactly, and told me to make careful note of them, and when you came to treat you with the greatest consideration, and to take no pay from you, since he would repay me lavishly. So when I saw you coming everything was exactly as my dreams had foretold, and I knew you at once. I have already prepared a quiet room for you, and beg that you will condescend to make yourself at ease."

Joyfully Dung followed him, and the inn-keeper waited on him with the greatest consideration, and saw that he had great plenty to eat and to drink.

At midnight the spirit arrived. Without having opened the door, he stood by Dung's bedside, gave him his hand, and asked how things had gone with him since he had last seen him.

Dung answered all his questions and thanked him into the bargain for appearing to the inn-keeper in a dream.

He continued to live for some days at the inn. During the day he went walking on the Great Mountain and at night his friend came to visit him and talked with him, and at the same time asked him what had happened to Sir Wang.

"His sentence has already been spoken," answered the other. "This man pretended to be conscientious, and traitorously brought about the death of his friend. Of all sins there is no greater sin than this. As a punishment he will be sent forth again into the world as an animal." Then he added: "When you reach home you must take constant care of your health. Fate has allowed you seventy-eight years of mortal life. When your time is up I will come to fetch you myself. Then I will see that you obtain a place as constable in the Nether World, where we can always be together."

When he had said this, he disappeared.

Note: "The Constable" is a tale of modern origin. The Lord of the Great Mountain (Taischan) is even greater than Yan Wang, the God of Death. His Temple of the Easterly Holy Mountain (Dung Yuo Miau), is to be found in every district capital. These temples play an important part in the care of the dead before interment.

The Dangerous Reward

Dr R. Wilhelm

Once upon a time a man named Hu-Wu-Bau, who lived near the Great Mountain, went walking there one day. And there, under a tree, he met a messenger in a red robe who called out to him: "The Lord of the Great Mountain would like to see you!" The man was much frightened, but dared offer no objection. The messenger bade him shut his eyes, and when he was allowed to open them again after a short time, he found himself standing before a lofty palace. He entered it to see the god. The latter had a meal prepared for him and said: "I only sent for you today because I had heard you intended traveling to the West. And in that case I should like to give you a letter to take to my daughter."

"But where is your daughter?" asked the man.

"She is married to the river-god," was the reply. "All you need to do is to take along the letter lying there. When you reach the middle of the Yellow River, beat against the side of the ship and call out: 'Greencoat!' Then some one will appear and take the letter from you."

And with these words he handed Hu-Wu-Bau the letter, and he was taken back again to the upper world.

When he came to the Yellow River on his journey, he did what the Lord of the Great Mountain had told him, and cried: "Greencoat!" And sure enough, a girl in green garments rose from the water, took him by the hand and told him to close his eyes. Then she led him into the palace of the river-god and he delivered the letter. The river-god entertained him splendidly, and thanked him as best he knew how. At parting he said: "I am grateful that you have made this long journey to see me. I have nothing to give you, however, save this pair of green silk shoes. While you are wearing them you can keep on walking as long as you like and never grow weary. And they will give you the second sight, so that you will be able to see the spirits and gods."

The man thanked him for the gift and returned to his ship. He continued on his journey to the West, and after a year had passed, came back again. When he reached the Great Mountain, he thought it would be fit and proper to report to the god. So he once more knocked against the tree and gave his name. In a moment the red-clad messenger appeared and led him to the Lord of the Mountain. So he reported that he had delivered the letter to the river-god, and how all things were there, and the Lord of the Mountain thanked him. During the meal which the god had prepared for him, he withdrew for a few moments to a quiet spot. Suddenly he saw his deceased father, bound and loaded with chains, who together with several hundred other criminals, was doing menial labor.

Moved to tears, he asked: "O my father, why are you here?"

His father replied: "During my life on earth I happened to tread on bread, hence I was condemned to hard labor at this spot. I have passed two years in this manner, yet their bitterness has been unspeakable. Since you are acquainted with the Lord of the Mountain, you might plead for me, and beg him to excuse me from this task and make me the field-god in our village."

His son promised to do so, and went back and pleaded with the Lord of the Mountain as he had agreed. The latter seemed inclined to listen to his prayer, yet said warningly: "The quick and the dead tread different paths. It is not well for the dead and the living to abide near one another permanently."

The man returned home. Yet, in about a year's time nearly all his children had died. In the terror of his heart he turned to the Lord of the Great Mountain. He beat on the tree; the red-coat came and led him into the palace. There he told of his misfortune and begged the god to protect him. The Lord of the Mountain smiled: "Did I not tell you in the start that the quick and the dead tread different paths, and that it is not well if they abide near each other permanently? Now you see what has happened!" Yet he sent his messenger to fetch the man's father. The father came and the god spake to him as follows: "I forgave you your offense and sent you back to your home as a field-god. It was your duty to bring happiness to your family. Instead, nearly all of your grand-children have died off. Why is this?"

And the father said: "I had been away from home so long that I was overjoyed to return. Besides I had meat and drink in overflowing measure. So I thought of my little grand-children and called them to me."

Then the Lord of the Great Mountain appointed another field-god for that village, and also gave the father another place. And from that time no further misfortune happened to the family of Hu-Wu-Bau.

Note: The Lord of the Great Mountain was originally Huang Fe-Hu, a faithful servant of the tyrant Dschou-Sin. Because of an insult offered him, he joined King Wu, and when the latter overcame the tyrant, was made Lord of the Mountain, and overlord of the ten princes of the nether world.

[illegible]

Biographies & Sources

Herbert A. Giles

Translator, *Strange Stories from a Chinese Studio* (1880)

Herbert Allen Giles (1845–1935) was a British diplomat and sinologist, working in Mawei, Shanghai, Tamsui and finally as British Consul at Ningpo. In 1897 he became professor of Chinese language at Cambridge University, a post that lasted for 35 years. He published many writings on Chinese language, as well as on literature and religion, such as his *Chinese-English Dictionary* (1891), and several translations of classic Chinese tales, including Pu Songling's *Strange Stories from a Chinese Studio* (1880).

Lafcadio Hearn

The Soul of the Great Bell, The Legend Of Tchi-Niu, The Tale Of The Porcelain-God

(Originally published in *Some Chinese Ghosts*, 1886)

Patrick Lafcadio Hearn (1850–1904, also known as Koizumi Yakumo) was a journalist and writer whose wandering life led him eventually to find a home in Japan, which would prove to be his true inspiration. He wrote about the country and, especially, its legends and ghost stories. His books about Japan include *Japanese Fairy Tales* (1898) and *In Ghostly Japan* (1899). His intriguing *Some Chinese Ghosts* (1887) retells Chinese ghost stories through a Japanese lens, aided by his writer's artistry.

Rev. J. Macgowan

The God of the City, The Tragedy of the Yin Family, Kwang-Jui and the God of the River, The Beautiful Daughter of Liu-Kung, The Vengeance of the Goddess, The Wonderful Man, Sam-Chung and the Water-Demon

(Originally published in *Chinese Folk-Lore Tales*, 1910)
John Macgowan (1835–1922) was born in Belfast and became a missionary to China with the London Missionary Society, where he helped to found the anti-footbinding Natural Foot Society. He was author of many books about Chinese culture and history. As well as *Chinese Folk-Lore Tales* (1910), his works include *English and Chinese Dictionary of the Amoy Dialect* (1883) and *Men and Manners of Modern China* (1912).

Frederick H. Martens
Translator, *The Chinese Fairy Book* (1921)
Frederick Herman Martens (1874–1932) was an author, lyricist and translator, whose work includes a translation of Pietro Yon's 1917 Christmas carol 'Gesu Bambino', a biography of the musician A.E. Uhe (1922), *A Thousand and One Nights of Opera* (1926), *Violin Mastery (Talks with Master Violinists and Teachers)* (1919), and fairy-tale translations in *The Chinese Fairy Book* (ed. Dr. R. Wilhelm).

Xueting C. Ni
Introduction
Xueting C. Ni has written extensively on Chinese culture, translated China's literary as well as other output in arts and entertainment, for over a decade, working with companies, institutions, and festivals, to help improve understanding of China's heritage, culture and innovation. She is the author of *From Kuan Yin to Chairman Mao: An Essential Guide to Chinese Deities* (Weiser Books) and *Chinese Myths* (Amber Books). Her curated anthology of Chinese science fiction *Sinopticon* (Solaris),

won Best Anthology at the BFS Awards, 2022. *Sinophagia*, her new collection of contemporary Chinese horror fiction (Solaris), will be published in September 2024. She is currently working on a cultural history of Xia storytelling.

Pu Songling

The Spirit of the River, The Ghost in Love, The Laughing Ghost, Deceiving Shadows, Magical Arts, The Patch of Lamb's Skin, The Corpse the Blood Drinker, The River of Sorrows, The Marble Arch (Oringally published in *Strange Stories from the Lodge of Leisures*, 1913)

The Marriage of the Fox's Daughter, Miss Lien-Hsiang, The Magic Sword, The Painted Skin

(Originally published in *Strange Stories from a Chinese Studio*, 1880)

Pu Songling (1640–1715) was a private tutor and writer in Qing Dynasty China, best known as the author of *Strange Stories from a Chinese Studio* (*Liaozhai Zhiyi*), a collection of classical Chinese stories often of a fantastical or supernatural character which implicitly criticise contemporary societal issues.

George Soulié

Translator, *Strange Stories from the Lodge of Leisures* (1913)

Diplomat and scholar George Soulié de Morant (1878–1955) was taught Chinese by a Jesuit priest when he was only eight years old. As an adult, he joined the French diplomatic corps, and worked as French consul in numerous Chinese cities, including Shanghai. He translated many Chinese texts, particularly on acupuncture, and is in fact best-known for introducing acupuncture to the West.

Dr R. Wilhelm

The Punishment of Greed, The Constable, The Dangerous Reward
(Originally published in *The Chinese Fairy Book*, 1921)
Richard Wilhelm (1873–1930) was a German theologian, missionary and sinologist. He is best known for his works of translations of philosophical works from Chinese into German, including his translation of the *I Ching* and *The Secret of the Golden Flower*. He also edited The Chinese Fairy Book (1921).

A Selection of Fantastic Reads

A range of Gothic novels, horror, crime,
mystery, fantasy, adventure, dystopia, utopia,
science fiction, myth, folklore and more:
available and forthcoming from Flame Tree 451

Categories: Bio = Biographical, BL = Black Literature, C = Crime, F = Fantasy, FL = Feminist Literature, G = Gothic, H = Horror, L = Literary, M = Mystery, MF = Myth & Folklore, P = Political, SF = Science Fiction, TH = Thriller. Organized by year of first publication.

1764	*The Castle of Otranto*, Horace Walpole	G
1786	*The History of the Caliph Vathek*, William Beckford	G
1768	*Barford Abbey*, Susannah Minifie Gunning	G
1783	*The Recess Or, a Tale of Other Times*, Sophia Lee	G
1791	*Tancred: A Tale of Ancient Times*, Joseph Fox	G
1872	*In a Glass Darkly*, Sheridan Le Fanu	C, M
1794	*Caleb Williams*, William Godwin	C, M
1794	*The Banished Man*, Charlotte Smith	G
1794	*The Mysteries of Udolpho*, Ann Radcliffe	G
1795	*The Abbey of Clugny*, Mary Meeke	G
1796	*The Monk*, Matthew Lewis	G
1798	*Wieland*, Charles Brockden Brown	G
1799	*St. Leon*, William Godwin	H, M
1799	*Ormond, or The Secret Witness*, Charles Brockden Brown	H, M
1801	*The Magus,* Francis Barrett	H, M
1807	*The Demon of Sicily*, Edward Montague	G
1811	*Undine*, Friedrich de la Motte Fouqué	G
1814	*Sintram and His Companions*, Friedrich de la Motte Fouqué	G
1818	*Northanger Abbey*, Jane Austen	G
1818	*Frankenstein*, Mary Shelley	H, G
1820	*Melmoth the Wanderer*, Charles Maturin	G
1826	*The Last Man*, Mary Shelley	SF

1828	*Pelham*, Edward Bulwer-Lytton	C, M
1831	*Short Stories & Poetry*, Edgar Allan Poe (to 1949)	C, M
1838	*The Amber Witch*, Wilhelm Meinhold	H, M
1842	*Zanoni*, Edward Bulwer-Lytton	H, M
1845	*Varney the Vampyre*, Thomas Preskett Prest	H, M
1846	*Wagner, the Wehr-wolf*, George W.M. Reynolds	H, M
1847	*Wuthering Heights*, Emily Brontë	G
1850	*The Scarlet Letter*, Nathaniel Hawthorne	H, M
1851	*The House of the Seven Gables*, Nathaniel Hawthorne	H, M
1852	*Bleak House*, Charles Dickens	C, M
1853	*Twelve Years a Slave*, Solomon Northup	Bio, BL
1859	*The Woman in White*, Wilkie Collins	C, M
1859	*Blake, or the Huts of America*, Martin R. Delany	BL
1860	*The Marble Faun*, Nathaniel Hawthorne	H, M
1861	*East Lynne*, Ellen Wood	C, M
1861	*Elsie Venner*, Oliver Wendell Holmes	H, M
1862	*A Strange Story*, Edward Bulwer-Lytton	H, M
1862	*Lady Audley's Secret*, Mary Elizabeth Braddon	C, M
1864	*Journey to the Centre of the Earth*, Jules Verne	SF
1868	*The Huge Hunter*, Edward Sylvester Ellis	SF
1868	*The Moonstone*, Wilkie Collins	C, M
1870	*Twenty Thousand Leagues Under the Sea*, Jules Verne	SF
1872	*Erewhon*, Samuel Butler	SF
1874	*The Temptation of St. Anthony*, Gustave Flaubert	H, M
1874	*The Expressman and the Detective*, Allan Pinkerton	C, M

1876	*The Man-Wolf and Other Tales*, Erckmann-Chatrian	H, M
1878	*The Haunted Hotel*, Wilkie Collins	C, M
1878	*The Leavenworth Case*, Anna Katharine Green	C, M
1886	*The Mystery of a Hansom Cab*, Fergus Hume	C, M
1886	*Robur the Conqueror*, Jules Verne	SF
1886	*The Strange Case of Dr Jekyll & Mr Hyde*, R.L. Stevenson	SF
1887	*She*, H. Rider Haggard	F
1887	*A Study in Scarlet*, Arthur Conan Doyle	C, M
1890	*The Sign of Four*, Arthur Conan Doyle	C, M
1891	*The Picture of Dorian Gray*, Oscar Wilde	G
1892	*The Big Bow Mystery*, Israel Zangwill	C, M
1894	*Martin Hewitt, Investigator*, Arthur Morrison	C, M
1895	*The Time Machine*, H.G. Wells	SF
1895	*The Three Imposters*, Arthur Machen	H, M
1897	*The Beetle*, Richard Marsh	G
1897	*The Invisible Man*, H.G. Wells	SF
1897	*Dracula*, Bram Stoker	H
1898	*The War of the Worlds*, H.G. Wells	SF
1898	*The Turn of the Screw*, Henry James	H, M
1899	*Imperium in Imperio*, Sutton E. Griggs	BL, SF
1899	*The Awakening*, Kate Chopin	FL
1899	*The Conjure Woman*, Charles W. Chesnutt	H
1902	*The Hound of the Baskervilles*, Arthur Conan Doyle	C, M
1902	*Of One Blood: Or, The Hidden Self*, Pauline Hopkins	FL, BL
1903	*The Jewel of Seven Stars*, Bram Stoker	H, M

1904	*Master of the World*, Jules Verne	SF
1905	*A Thief in the Night*, E.W. Hornung	C, M
1906	*The Empty House & Other Ghost Stories*, Algernon Blackwood	G
1906	*The House of Souls*, Arthur Machen	H, M
1907	*Lord of the World*, R.H. Benson	SF
1907	*The Red Thumb Mark*, R. Austin Freeman	C, M
1907	*The Boats of the 'Glen Carrig'*, William Hope Hodgson	H, M
1907	*The Exploits of Arsène Lupin*, Maurice Leblanc	C, M
1907	*The Mystery of the Yellow Room*, Gaston Leroux	C, M
1908	*The Mystery of the Four Fingers*, Fred M. White	SF
1908	*The Ghost Kings*, H. Rider Haggard	F
1908	*The Circular Staircase*, Mary Roberts Rinehart	C, M
1908	*The House on the Borderland*, William Hope Hodgson	H, M
1909	*The Ghost Pirates*, William Hope Hodgson	H, M
1909	*Jimbo: A Fantasy*, Algernon Blackwood	G
1909	*The Necromancers*, R.H. Benson	SF
1909	*Black Magic*, Marjorie Bowen	H, M
1910	*The Return*, Walter de la Mare	H, M
1911	*The Lair of the White Worm*, Bram Stoker	H
1911	*The Innocence of Father Brown*, G.K. Chesterton	C, M
1911	*The Centaur*, Algernon Blackwood	G
1912	*Tarzan of the Apes*, Edgar Rice Burroughs	F
1912	*The Lost World*, Arthur Conan Doyle	SF
1913	*The Return of Tarzan*, Edgar Rice Burroughs	F
1913	*Trent's Last Case*, E.C. Bentley	C, M

1913	*The Poison Belt*, Arthur Conan Doyle	SF
1915	*The Valley of Fear*, Arthur Conan Doyle	C, M
1915	*Herland*, Charlotte Perkins Gilman	SF, FL
1915	*The Thirty-Nine Steps*, John Buchan	TH
1917	*John Carter: A Princess of Mars*, Edgar Rice Burroughs	F
1917	*The Terror*, Arthur Machen	H, M
1917	*The Job*, Sinclair Lewis	L
1917	*The Sturdy Oak*, Ed. Elizabeth Jordan	FL
1918	*When I Was a Witch & Other Stories,* Charlotte Perkins Gilman	FL
1918	*Brood of the Witch-Queen*, Sax Rohmer	H, M
1918	*The Land That Time Forgot*, Edgar Rice Burroughs	F
1918	*The Citadel of Fear*, Gertrude Barrows Bennett (as Francis Stevens)	FL, TH
1919	*John Carter: A Warlord of Mars*, Edgar Rice Burroughs	F
1919	*The Door of the Unreal*, Gerald Biss	H
1919	*The Moon Pool*, Abraham Merritt	SF
1919	*The Three Eyes*, Maurice Leblanc	SF
1920	*A Voyage to Arcturus*, David Lindsay	SF
1920	*The Metal Monster*, Abraham Merritt	SF
1920	*Darkwater*, W.E.B. Du Bois	BL
1922	*The Undying Monster*, Jessie Douglas Kerruish	H
1925	*The Avenger*, Edgar Wallace	C
1925	*The Red Hawk*, Edgar Rice Burroughs	SF
1926	*The Moon Maid*, Edgar Rice Burroughs	SF
1927	*Witch Wood,* John Buchan	H, M
1927	*The Colour Out of Space*, H.P. Lovecraft	SF

1927	*The Dark Chamber*, Leonard Lanson Cline	H, M
1928	*When the World Screamed*, Arthur Conan Doyle	F
1928	*The Skylark of Space*, E.E. Smith	SF
1930	*Last and First Men*, Olaf Stapledon	SF
1930	*Belshazzar*, H. Rider Haggard	F
1934	*The Murder Monster*, Brant House (Emile C. Tepperman)	H
1934	*The People of the Black Circle*, Robert E. Howard	F
1935	*Odd John*, Olaf Stapledon	SF
1935	*The Hour of the Dragon*, Robert E. Howard	F
1935	*Short Stories Selection 1*, Robert E. Howard	F
1935	*Short Stories Selection 2*, Robert E. Howard	F
1936	*The War-Makers*, Nick Carter	C, M
1937	*Star Maker*, Olaf Stapledon	SF
1936	*Red Nails*, Robert E. Howard	F
1936	*The Shadow Out of Time*, H.P. Lovecraft	SF
1936	*At the Mountains of Madness*, H.P. Lovecraft	SF
1938	*Power*, C.K.M. Scanlon writing in *G-Men*	C, M
1939	*Almuric*, Robert E. Howard	SF
1940	*The Ghost Strikes Back*, George Chance	SF
1937	*The Road to Wigan Pier*, George Orwell	P, Bio
1938	*Homage to Catalonia*, George Orwell	P, Bio
1945	*Animal Farm*, George Orwell	P, F
1949	*Nineteen Eighty-Four*, George Orwell	P, F
1953	*The Black Star Passes*, John W. Campbell	SF
1959	*The Galaxy Primes*, E.E. Smith	SF

New Collections of Ancient Myths, Folklore and Early Literature

2014	*Celtic Myths*, J.K. Jackson (ed.)	MF
2014	*Greek & Roman Myths*, J.K. Jackson (ed.)	MF
2014	*Native American Myths*, J.K. Jackson (ed.)	MF
2014	*Norse Myths*, J.K. Jackson (ed.)	MF
2018	*Chinese Myths*, J.K. Jackson (ed.)	MF
2018	*Egyptian Myths*, J.K. Jackson (ed.)	MF
2018	*Indian Myths*, J.K. Jackson (ed.)	MF
2018	*Myths of Babylon*, J.K. Jackson (ed.)	MF
2019	*African Myths*, J.K. Jackson (ed.)	MF
2019	*Aztec Myths*, J.K. Jackson (ed.)	MF
2019	*Japanese Myths*, J.K. Jackson (ed.)	MF
2020	*Arthurian Myths*, J.K. Jackson (ed.)	MF
2020	*Irish Fairy Tales*, J.K. Jackson (ed.)	MF
2020	*Polynesian Myths*, J.K. Jackson (ed.)	MF
2020	*Scottish Myths*, J.K. Jackson (ed.)	MF
2021	*Viking Folktales*, J.K. Jackson (ed.)	MF
2021	*West African Folktales*, J.K. Jackson (ed.)	MF
2022	*East African Folktales*, J.K. Jackson (ed.)	MF
2022	*Persian Myths*, J.K. Jackson (ed.)	MF
2022	*The Tale of Beowulf*, Dr Victoria Symons (Intro.)	MF
2022	*The Four Branches of the Mabinogi*, Shân Morgain (Intro.)	MF
2023	*Slavic Myths*, Ema Lakinska (Intro.)	MF
2023	*Turkish Folktales*, Nathan Young (Intro.)	MF
2023	*Gawain and the Green Knight*, Alan Lupack (Intro.)	MF

2023	*Hungarian Folktales*, Boglárka Klitsie-Szabad (Intro.)	MF
2023	*Korean Folktales*, Dr Perry Miller (Intro.)	MF
2023	*Southern African Folktales*, Prof. Enongene Mirabeau Sone (Intro.)	MF
2024	*Central African Folktales*, Prof. Enongene Mirabeau Sone (Intro.)	MF
2024	*Serbian Folktales*, Dr. Margaret H. Beissinger (Intro.)	MF
2024	*Czech Folktales*, Rajendra Chitnis (Intro.)	MF
2024	*Chinese Folktales*, Xiulu Wang & Chuanju Hu (Intro.)	MF

New Collections of Ancient, Folkloric and Classic Ghost Stories

2022	*American Ghost Stories*, Brett Riley (Intro.)	H, G
2022	*Irish Ghost Stories*, Maura McHugh (Intro.)	H, G
2022	*Scottish Ghost Stories*, Helen McClory (Intro.)	H, G
2022	*Victorian Ghost Stories*, Reggie Oliver (Intro.)	H, G
2023	*Ancient Ghost Stories*, Camilla Grudova (Intro.)	H, G
2023	*Haunted House Stories*, Hester Fox (Intro.)	H, G
2023	*Indian Ghost Stories*, Dr Mithuraaj Dusiya (Intro.)	H, G
2023	*Japanese Ghost Stories*, Hiroko Yoda (Intro.)	H, G
2024	*Chinese Ghost Stories*, Xueting C. Ni (Intro.)	H, G
2024	*Classic Ghost Stories*, Lisa Tuttle (Intro.)	H, G